The Long Ride

Learning About Life From an Outlaw Biker

Francis Hicks

Black Rose Writing | Texas

ISBN: 978-1-68433-254-0
PUBLISHED BY BLACK ROSE WRITING
www.blackrosewriting.com

Printed in the United States of America
Suggested Retail Price (SRP) $18.95

The Long Ride is printed in Garamond

Dedication

To my friends in The San Antonio Writer's Guild who put up with my early drafts and lack of polish. To Marci, sorry you missed this. To Tim, thanks for being a wonderful son.

Acknowledgments

Thanks to Black Rose Writing for publishing this story. I have been helped along the way by many, many people. Marjorie, thanks for telling me over and over again that I am a good writer. Dan, thanks for letting me know stories need tension. April, thanks for taking me seriously. To my beta readers and the many others who have encouraged me, thank you.

The Long Ride

Chapter 1

A guy pulled into the toll plaza in an old rusty Rambler with the windows rolled down. He stopped in front of me and leaned across the front seat. "Where you headed?"

I squatted next to the passenger window. The sides of the driver's head were shaved boot-camp short. He wore a boonie hat with the chin strap hanging down. My long hair reflected in the lenses of his mirrored sunglasses.

The tension in his jaw creeped me out. I assumed he was just back from Nam. The National Guard had recently shot those four kids in Ohio, so anything even remotely military made me nervous.

I tried to swallow, but my throat was too dry. "West. To Milwaukee."

"Well, I'm goin' quite a ways in that direction and would be happy ta help you out, but I had a boy in the car a while back that pulled a knife and cut me pretty bad. I'll give you a ride, but you hafta wear handcuffs while you're in the car. Whaddya think?"

My eyes played over the four lanes that lead to the toll booths. Not another car in sight. No place to get out of the sun. My heart sank at the thought of being stuck here another four hours. I stood and backed away from the car. "I'll wait it out."

"Huh. Didn't figure you for such a pussy." The man settled back into the driver's seat. Tires squealed as he peeled off, leaving a cloud of exhaust smoke.

I slumped down on my pack again, still pissed that my so-called friend Jim bailed on me and took off with that girl. Jesus! "C'mon, Nate," he'd said back in Milwaukee. "I know people. I'll make sure we get back safe."

Lying asshole. All he wanted was the $50.00 he knew I had. But, I desperately wanted to be liked so, even knowing his crappy motives, I had agreed to go. Now I was on my own, dealing with crazy people like the handcuff guy. So much for making friends. Why can't everybody be like me? If I ran the world, everyone would get along.

I was hungry, hot, smelly, exhausted from nights half-awake watching my backpack, worrying over my last three dollars, afraid of what might happen the next time I got into a car. I'd been stuck at this New York Thruway toll plaza all morning, and it was driving me crazy. Hitchhiking had seemed so exciting when Jim suggested it, but after two weeks of bored misery, interrupted by an adrenaline rush every time a car slowed down, followed by anxiety at what might happen if I got in, hitchhiking sucked. I had no relief from sun, rain, or fear. I just wanted to get back home, even though home was not a happy place.

It wasn't the destination I longed for, but an end to the journey. My Catholic mother, with her pointed verbal warnings and intermittent silent stares, regularly reminded me of the dangers of hell. It wore on me because the priests reinforced this belief. I believed her and them. I feared God and feared her.

Dad was an "America, love it or leave it" type, always bragging about my brother's two tours in Vietnam. Pete made it home safe, even said he liked it over there. But, I hated the war, mostly because I was scared of getting my ass shot off. They hadn't drafted me yet, and I told dad I wasn't going to go if they did. He called me a coward. Maybe I was, but at least I would have a better chance at a long life.

Fatigue weighed on my eyelids until I drifted off. A blaring horn shot me awake. Three guys in a convertible flew past. The driver yelled, "Get a job, you fucking hippie."

I threw my hands up and extended my middle fingers, partly from anger, but mostly from surprise. Brake lights lit up. The car skidded to a stop and sat idling. The driver looked in the mirror.

Oh shit. I stood and picked up my backpack, eyes locked on the guys in the convertible. An ass whipping seemed headed my way. I looked around the plaza for a place to disappear, but it was just a wide spot in the road before the toll booth.

The car backed up. It was a shiny, new Cutlass 442. The driver wore sunglasses and was about my age, maybe a little older.

"Hey," he said. "Where you headed?"

I stared at him, trying to figure out how to answer. He didn't *look* hostile. He smiled with white, straight teeth. The guy next to him was tuning the radio. The rider in the back seat had his head down like he was asleep. All I could see of him was a mass of matted, black curly hair. He seemed different from the other two, out of it, like he was in a different time zone. Just like in junior high, it was three against me.

"West," I said.

"Well, jump on in. We've got room." He raised his eyebrows and pursed his lips, then said, "We're going all the way to Cleveland."

Sweat dripped into my eyes, and my head itched. I desperately wanted a ride, but the guys in front were slightly older versions of the kids that used beat me up. "Cleveland? That's quite a ways, but you guys just called me a fucking hippie." I pushed my hair out of my face. "I mean, I am a hippie, proud of it. But, you don't seem to dig it."

The driver looked at me sideways. "Look, let's start over. This is Sean." He pointed to the passenger. "And I'm Brian. We were just messing with you. What do you say? Jump on in."

I wanted to believe him. At least he hadn't asked me to wear handcuffs. Still, something didn't seem right. Who was the third guy?

My need to get off the toll plaza made me decide to take a chance. I threw my pack into the rear seat and vaulted into the open car.

As I settled in, the driver put the top up on the car and pulled toward the toll booth. After we passed the toll collector, Sean turned around and held up a can of beer.

"How about a cold one?"

The guy to my left jerked upright. "Beer? Sure."

"Yeah, man," I said. "It's hot out there."

Sean turned back to the front. I heard a can hiss open and then a second one. It took a few seconds before the man handed the beer over his shoulder, first to the curly-headed guy then to me.

The beer was cold, and we both downed it fast. "Bridge Over Troubled Waters" wafted from the radio. The driver said something I couldn't make out. Suddenly, I was drowsy and felt like puking.

·   ·   ·   ·   ·

I woke up in a perfectly still, stifling-hot car. The sun was low in the west. The curly headed guy was passed out in the seat next to me. My pack was nowhere in sight.

I poked him. "Hey, wake up."

Nothing.

I poked him harder. "Wake up!"

His head shot up, and he waved his arms. "What? What? What?" He looked at me, then toward the front seat. "Where the fuck are we?"

"I don't know. Where are your friends?"

"I dunno." The man rubbed his face. "They picked me up just before you."

"You didn't know them? Where's my pack?"

"Beats me." He shook his head as if to clear it, then turned to look out the rear window. The trunk lid stood open. "Aw, no. My pack was in the trunk. They got my shit. Aw, man. They got my shit."

He lurched forward, grabbing for the door handle, shoved against the back side of the front seat and fell out the door, tumbling onto gravel. He scrambled up and peered into the open trunk, picked up a backpack, turned it upside down and shook it. Empty. He threw it on the ground and paced back and forth behind the car.

I slid over and climbed out.

Curly-headed guy was about 5'7". His dirty jeans covered scuffed engineer boots with rusty buckles. A gray t-shirt stretched over a beer belly, and his fingernails were black with grease.

The Cutlass was parked at the edge of a large gravel lot bordered by tall weeds growing up through the carcasses of rusty pickups and school buses. Gas pumps stood fifty yards off. A rusty sign read, "Mel's Super Service." The breeze had died. A swarm of gnats floated in the waning sunlight.

My head hurt, my hands trembled. I spied my pack in the front seat, my clothes a heap on the floor. I opened the passenger side door. "At least they left my stuff." I crammed my dirty clothes back into the pack. "They need to come back for the car."

My fellow passenger leaned on the left rear quarter panel. "prob'ly not. It's stolen."

"Why do you say that?" I asked.

"Look, dumbass." He pointed.

A tangle of wires hung below the dash under the steering wheel. Bile burned my throat. I had been kidnapped in a hot-wired car and left at a no-name gas station in a remote place with a population of two. Guessing by the sun, we'd been passed out for at least five hours. I didn't know what town I was in, or even what state.

I was dizzy and leaned against the car to regain my balance. What do I do now? I stuck my hand into my pocket and felt crumpled dollar bills. Three bucks. On a dead, two-lane blacktop. And the sun was going down.

I slid down the car and landed heavily on the gravel.

"What's your name?" the guy asked.

"Nate."

"I'm Spider."

Spider slid down next to me. The stink of stale sweat drifted from him. He pulled a pack of Camels out of his jeans. "Man, this is some bad spot." His head sagged. "Well, let that be a lesson," he mumbled. He lit up a smoke and took a drag.

"What?" I asked.

"My friend Norma used to say that when I was little, whenever I did stupid stuff and got hurt like jumpin' off a porch roof or riding a bike with no brakes."

That sounded like something my mother would have said, as if I was supposed to know how life worked. Just how was I supposed to know? No one ever told me anything until it was too late. "What'd they steal from you?"

He raised his head and stared at me, then sighed. "They stole $2,000 worth of top-shelf bennies."

I knew what bennies were because several of my friends used them. I had long hair and tried to act all cool, but I never used the drugs that were always around, except for weed. A lot of my friends used speed. They used downers, too. A couple of them had tried heroin. One died within six months, the other was just gone. I lumped all "hard" drugs together. Bennies included.

I stood. "I gotta get going."

Spider lifted his head and squinted as he looked at me. "Where to?"

I looked left, then right. My eyes settled on the two-lane blacktop that ran in front of the gas station. "I dunno. Can't stay here. What if they catch us with that stolen car?"

Spider tossed the butt of his cigarette and pulled off his right boot. A clear baggie fell onto the gravel. "Sons a bitches didn't get my cash." A stack of bills showed through the bag. "I got about four hunnert. How much you got?"

I looked around again, then back to Spider. "Some."

Spider put his boot back on and got up. He grinned, revealing a missing tooth. "Aw, it's all right if you're broke." He held a ten dollar bill out. "I'll spot ya ten."

I wanted that money, but this guy was a drug dealer. Who knew what his motives were. And I'd ridden here in a stolen car. I could wind up in jail; all things my mother warned me about. I kept looking at the ten-dollar bill and thought about the three bucks in my pocket. But I didn't move.

"You'll take it soon enough." He pocketed the money.

The metallic rumble of an overhead door sounded across the empty lot. A man walked towards us, wiping his hands on a red shop towel. I reached into the front seat of the Cutlass and grabbed my pack, intending to walk away.

"Too late now, brother," Spider said. He walked to the trunk and started stuffing what remained of his things into his backpack.

"You guys still here?" the man asked as he approached. A patch on his coveralls read "Charlie."

I looked at Spider.

He shrugged. "Oh, yeah. We're still here."

"Your two pals used my phone a couple of hours ago. Somebody came and picked 'em up. Said you was gonna stay with the car. You need repairs, or gas or somethin'?"

"That's okay, Charlie. No, we're not in need of anything. We just, ah, needed to rest a little before we took off."

"Well, you fellas take care then. I need to get going." Charlie headed back toward the garage.

"Hey buddy," Spider said. "What town is this?"

"Warren, Pennsylvania."

"Is there a diner here?"

Charlie nodded.

"Them guys took the keys, so we're sorta stuck. Could we catch a ride with you?"

The mechanic pulled a watch out of his pocket. "If you hurry up and get your stuff, I just got time to drop you."

Spider grabbed his pack and slammed the trunk closed. "Let's go," he said and walked after the man.

Not a single car passed since Spider, and I had come to. I felt tired and a little sick. As iffy as he was, Spider seemed like my best bet at the moment, so I followed him to Charlie's old pickup and climbed in.

Charlie let us out on the main street of Warren in front of the only place that was lit up. The sign on the door read, "Open 'til midnight seven days a week." The Finer Diner was long and narrow with a few tables and a lunch counter. The place was empty except for a gray-haired man wearing a stained white apron, standing behind the counter scraping the grill.

We took a table and ordered coffee. The clock on the back wall read 8:30.

The man in the apron set down two steaming mugs. "You gonna eat?"

"No, just coffee for me," I said.

"You *are* broke, aren't you?" Spider said.

"I have a few bucks."

Spider looked at me and then at the cook. "Bring me three eggs over easy with bacon and American fries. And toast. With lots of butter." He looked back at me and grunted. "And bring this sad sack the same thing."

I hadn't eaten since the night before. I didn't protest.

We sat sipping coffee, the restaurant quiet except for the clanging of the cook's spatula on the iron grill. The aroma of bacon and potatoes frying made my stomach burn with hunger.

Spider's forearms rested on the tabletop. His eyelids sagged. I was tired, too, but couldn't relax. My mother's voice ran around in my head, gaining momentum with every lap. *"How do you get into these messes? Why don't you think first? Can't you stay away from trouble? Now you're stuck with this criminal and you don't even know where you are."*

"Shut *up!*" I hollered and slammed my hand on the tabletop.

The grill man spun around and stared. Spider jerked back in his chair and almost fell over. "What the hell?"

Heat rose in my face. I hunched over and stared at the table's scarred surface. "I'm not crazy," I mumbled even though I felt like I was.

The spatula clanked and scraped for another minute, then the man appeared at our table and set down full plates.

Spider shoveled a pile of potatoes into his mouth, ignoring me.

I dug in, too.

After he finished his food, he leaned back and lit a cigarette.

"Man, you are some changeable son of a bitch. I don't know whether to feel sorry for you or be afraid."

"Why would you be scared of me? I've been getting my ass kicked since I was in grade school. I get overwhelmed sometimes, and stuff leaks out. But you're a drug dealer, and who knows what else. I should be afraid of you."

"You need to keep your voice down." Spider leaned his elbows on the table and whispered, "Hmph. Drug dealer. That's a laugh. I don't have any drugs for sale at the moment. But, I see what you're sayin', with them assholes stealing the bennies from me and all. I guess that makes me seem like a drug dealer."

Leaning back, I studied the miles on Spider's face. He appeared about thirty, but it was hard to tell. There were scars and gouges that said he'd been around a while.

"Sold everythin' I had, even my Harley. I didn't wanna borrow money, and for sure I didn't want any partners. I had $2500 and a plan. But that's all done with now."

"So, you're not a drug dealer?"

"Not hardly." He mashed the end of his cigarette into the ashtray and leaned back. "I feel like a repeat dumbass. I get great ideas, then hold on to them until they explode all over me. It's a wonder I'm still alive."

Spider's lament made sense. I'd run off on a hitch-hiking trip with a guy I knew was a flake. We split up a week ago, and now I was broke and stranded in a town 100 miles from nowhere.

"See, I had this great idea," Spider said. "I grew up in Cleveland. I know a lotta people. Cleveland's not exactly New York or LA, so I figured if I could get a supply of good drugs I could open up a market. That $2000 worth of pills? I could've gotten $10,000 on the street. Enough for a new bike, a nice place to live and a lot of leisure time. So, I asked around and found a guy that had the stuff. That's why I was in New York. He would only meet me upstate in the boonies. I think he was maybe in some trouble with the mob. He may have ripped those pills off from them. Oh well. His problem."

Spider opened his mouth as if to speak, then closed it again. He sat up straight, his brow furrowed, his lips pressed together. After a moment he said,"Hmph. I guess Norma was right about that, too." He slouched back in his chair.

"About what?" I asked, sitting up straight.

He rubbed his chin for a minute and leaned onto the table again. "When she wasn't telling me 'let that be a lesson' she was sayin', 'what goes around comes around'. See, I bought them pills from a guy who stole 'em from somebody else, who had probably stole 'em, too. So then, I get ripped off. The bad juju just keeps rolling. I almost feel sorry for them poor sons-a-bitches that ripped me off. The bad luck them pills have built up might be enough to wipe them out altogether."

"Sorry for the guys that drugged us and left us in the middle of nowhere? Why?"

Spider shrugged. "Personal philosophy, I guess."

"Why didn't you just buy a bus ticket back? You had $400.00."

"Yeah well, I was gonna do just that, but I got to feelin' like everyone would know what I was doin'. I bought a backpack to put the box of pills in. Somehow, stickin' my thumb out made me feel less conspicuous."

"Really?"

He shrugged again. "What can I tell ya?" Then he leaned back in his chair and stared at his lap.

The diner door banged open. Three men in greasy coveralls walked in and took a table. By the time they were seated, the door had opened again, and a stream of workmen filled the place. The noise level rose as the diner filled up.

I drained the last of my coffee and looked around the tight space that was the Finer Diner. The other tables and most of the counter were filled with men who looked like they were on a break from a ditch-digging project, their clothes and boots covered in mud and grease.

"...So I told Carlin," one of the men at the next table said, "you can't do it like that, but he did it anyway, and the chain whipped around and slapped the back of his legs. Lucky it didn't break 'em. Dumb SOB." The other three men at the table shook their heads and kept sipping coffee and smoking cigarettes.

Spider sat up and appeared to come out of the fog he had been lost in. He leaned toward the table next to ours. "You guys workin' a drilling rig?"

The man's chair scraped the floor as he turned toward Spider and looked at him from behind half-lowered eyelids like he was assessing his worthiness to be answered. "Proud members of Oil, Chemical and Atomic workers, local number 8 out of Philly. Who're you?"

Spider's jaw flexed and his face took on a menacing, hard-edged stare. "Spider Kowalski, proud member of the Cleveland, Ohio branch of the Hells Angels."

He shifted his weight to the front of the chair and the balls of his feet, ready to swing at the roughneck.

The worker sat back and glanced at the other three men at his table. "Them Angels. They're pro-union." He looked back at Spider, stuck out his hand and said, "Jack Yoder. Nice to meet you."

Spider shook the man's hand. "Our president is an ironworker. Yeah, we stand with the workin' man. Nate and me are kind of in a shitty spot, though."

He told Jack and the others a slightly fictional version of getting ripped off and stranded. The way he spun the story, it sounded like we'd been picked up by the CEO of Ma Bell who had left us by the side of the road because we were poor working stiffs. By the end of Spider's tale, Jack and his friends were more than happy to give us a ride to a truck stop on the main highway.

On the way, Spider told stories of riding with the Hells Angels, stories of three-day booze and bennie binges, of bare-breasted girls leaning into his back as he motored the roads around Cleveland. His stories made the insanity attractive, especially when compared to the colorless path I had taken for fear of burning in hell.

But, Milwaukee was a long way from Bum-Fuck, Pennsylvania, and I still only had three dollars. Spider was rolling on the river. I was drowning.

Chapter 2

The roughnecks dropped us at a huge truck stop on the interstate. I sat across from Spider on one of the green vinyl couches that filled the trucker's lounge. The walls were cheap wood paneling covered with Kenworth and Peterbilt logos. Some of the truckers stared at my long hair.

My eyelids felt like sandpaper on my eyeballs, and my throat burned from the cigarette smoke that filled the place. I wished I were somewhere else, even the basement of my parent's house. At least there I could hide away from the uncertainty.

"How the hell did you end up here?" Spider asked. "Somethin' must have happened. You didn't just walk out your momma's door and stick out your thumb."

"I don't know, man. My friend said 'let's go', and we went. I didn't think too much about it. At the time it felt right."

"You 'didn't think too much' is right. You left a house with a bed and Mom's home cookin'. You musta thought you were like that Easy Rider dude, only you don't have a motorcycle." Spider chuckled. "How's it feel now?"

"Pretty stupid, man. Pretty stupid. When I woke up at that gas station, I was scared."

Spider's face drooped and his eyelids were half closed. He looked placid, like he was sitting on his own couch at home. "Oh, you're all right," he mumbled without seeming to move a muscle. "Life's about ninety percent how you take it and ten percent how you make it."

In the quiet that followed, I thought about what those assholes had done to us. Fear turned to anger. Anger at being broke, at not knowing what to do next. Spider being so relaxed made me even madder.

"I don't want to feel like this. Like anyone can do anything to me and I can't stop them."

Spider sat up straight, yawned and opened his eyes wider. "It's over. What you gonna do about it?"

"If I saw them guys I'd—"

"You'd do what?" Spider leaned in. "Shoot 'em? Knife 'em? Beat 'em with a ball bat? Ha. Them guys'd knock you on your ass faster than a cat on a rat. You can be as mad as you want, but the only ass that'll get kicked is yours."

"But—"

"Calm down, man. It's over." Spider sat upright. "They knocked us out with Mickey Finns and stole my drugs. You didn't even lose nothin'. Why are you so fired up over a done deal?"

"Mickey Finns? What's that?"

"What made us pass out. My guess is those guys only picked us up 'cause they figured we had drugs."

"Why do you say that?"

"Look at us, man. Those straight guys figure all us longer hair types are holdin'. That's the stupid thing about drinkin'. I didn't care if my life savings was in their trunk, I couldn't turn down that beer."

"You cared when you woke up. You were hollering 'They got my shit. They got my shit'. Now you make it sound like I'm an idiot for being mad, like I should just take it."

Spider's eyes flashed with anger, and his jaw tensed. "Let me tell you how it is, you pissant." He sat up and jabbed his finger at me. "My mother was a junkie. My father walked out on us when I was pretty young. Food was scarce, love was non-existent. Mama had men comin' and goin' all hours of the day and night from the shithole we lived in. Them assholes screwing her weren't fussy. Some of them looked at me like I was there for them to fuck too." Spider closed his eyes and ground his teeth, then inhaled and went on. "Sometimes mama'd be gone for hours, sometimes a day or two. I learned how to beg food from neighbors and steal it when that didn't work. I've been beaten until I passed out. I've beaten guys 'til they passed out. There was never enough man, never enough. Sit back on that couch and take a big fuckin' breath. You're out here as a volunteer on some adventure 'cause you're too dumb to see how good you had it. Get over it."

He sat back. "I'm tired. I don't have the energy to make you feel better right now. So do us both a favor and sit quiet." His jaw was still tense, but his eyes had softened, his lids at half-mast again. He settled into the chair, bowed his head and closed his eyes.

Heaviness in my chest made it hard to breathe. My stomach burned from coffee and greasy food and lack of sleep. I felt bad for getting pissy with Spider.

He'd done nothing except help me, yet I had jumped at the chance to blame him for how bad I felt. The frustration pressing on my insides, not finding a target outside myself, took a u-turn and aimed at me.

When I was fourteen, I got a job at a gas station. I only worked a few nights a week, but told my parents I worked Monday through Friday. On the off nights, I hung with my friends. I avoided my parents as much as I could, but my mother's voice, warning me of hellfire, played non-stop in my mind.

My friends were kids who broke into stores and stole beer and ripped radios out of parked cars. They weren't poor. Stealing was a game to them. I never went along when they committed crimes. I liked the idea of being a bad guy, but feared going to jail or worse yet, going to hell. I was afraid of my mother, my teachers, God, and half the people on the street. I was sure all of that would stop when I got out of high school, but here I was again, bewildered and hanging with a guy who was living on the edge.

My mom was a basket case. She was okay some of the time, then her mood would shift and no one could do anything right. She told me once, in a rare moment of confused sadness, that she had been prescribed Librium, "Because the doctor thinks I'm hyper-nervous." She shook her head as she said it, seemingly bewildered at the diagnosis.

I remember being bewildered by her bewilderment.

She had embedded fear in my every waking moment. I could see freedom past this wall of fear, but I couldn't seem to find the way over it. Hitchhiking was the gutsiest thing I had ever done. I was proud of being out here on my own and yet terrified because every day I saw more and more that I had no idea how things worked. I was like a baby that fell off the back of a wagon and was left behind in the wilderness. I had to figure out how to survive.

The Shell Rotella clock read 2 A.M. Spider was right, I hadn't thought about the privileges I had growing up in a middle-class family. Sitting across from him I felt embarrassed I had gotten angry. Fatigue took over. My eyelids sagged. My arm slipped off the arm of the couch, causing me to jerk awake long enough to adjust my body's position and fall into a deep sleep.

•   •   •   •   •

Slamming doors and a spatula clanging on a steel grill woke me. The smell of fresh coffee, cinnamon rolls and frying bacon overpowered the stink of stale cigarettes. Large men with several days' worth of stubble stumbled through the lounge toward the showers.

Spider's chair was empty. A young-looking guy wearing a cowboy hat sat at the other end of the couch. He looked my way as I straightened up and stretched, trying to finish waking up.

"Long trip?" he asked.

"Too long, man." I wanted was more sleep, but there was no chance of that happening.

"You with that curly-headed guy?" the cowboy asked.

"Yeah."

"I figured, what with you being a long-hair and all. Anyway, he asked me about getting a ride towards Cleveland. I can't take riders, but I met a guy in the coffee shop that might give you a lift. He's hauling cattle and has to get them to the slaughterhouse. But he's been up too long. Says he needs a talker, someone to make sure he stays awake."

I looked up to see Spider coming from the front of the store where the restaurant was.

"C'mon, man," he said, waving his arm. "We got us a ride."

Spider followed a tall man with leathery skin toward a cattle-hauling truck. I was a city kid, and had heard people talk about cows lowing. The cattle in this trailer were bellowing in long, desperate-sounding cries. Some were stomping the floor and kicking. Dung ran through the slats that made up the sides of the trailer. The smell made me want to puke.

"Man, the cattle seem restless," I said to no one in particular.

The driver half-turned and said, "That's why we got to get going. Them cows've been on this trailer too long. I had a dually go flat and only had one spare. Took forever to get the damn thing fixed." He scrambled into the cab of the truck.

Spider opened the door, then said to me, "You get in the sleeper."

I climbed onto the bed, pushed my backpack to the far end of the space and stretched out on the mattress.

"The sign on your door says Hildebrandt Meats," Spider asked the driver. "That the one on the east side of Cleveland?"

"Yeah."

"What're the odds?" he said. "I had a friend who used to work there."

Then I fell asleep.

•   •   •   •   •

The cab's lurching, and the sounds of whistles and steel bars banging the side of the trailer woke me. The two front seats were empty. I swung my legs over the side of the bunk and stumbled out of the truck.

Spider was leaning on the back corner of the cab. He turned around when I slammed the door.

"Sleeping Beauty rises," he said with a grin. "You sure didn't help keep that old man awake. Though I don't know why he thought he needed us to talk to him. He popped three little white pills and never shut up the whole way."

I stretched and yawned, feeling as rested as I had for a week. I realized Spider could have walked out of that truck stop while I slept. But he came and got me instead. That felt good, like everything was right with the world. "Thanks, man," I said.

Spider twisted his head halfway around and said, "For what?" then went back to watching the cattle stumble off the trailer.

The animals were covered in shit. Some of them slipped on the ramp as they were herded into the chute that led to the kill floor. I knew they were heading to their death, that these living, breathing, stinking animals would come out the front door of the slaughterhouse as steaks, roasts and hamburger. I'd never thought about it before, but now, watching them, their lives seemed pathetic. No one would step in for them. Their fate had been sealed before their mothers had birthed them onto the grass of the pasture.

When I first stuck out my thumb and left Milwaukee, I broke out of my own cattle trailer. There was no one here to feed and shelter me, but there was no chute leading to a certain end either. I was on my own for the first time and hoped for a better fate than the cattle.

"You boys still here?" a voice called out. "Get your stuff and get the hell out." The driver of the cattle truck walked around the front of his rig carrying a steel bar. "You got your ride. What're you waiting for?"

Spider said, "Sure. Okay. We're leavin'," and stepped toward the cab.

The driver raised the metal bar above his head. "You back off." He grimaced, his eyes showing only the black of his dilated pupils.

Spider froze, his eyes never leaving the driver's. "Get our stuff, Nate," he said. "You," he said to the driver, "take it easy."

I climbed into the cab and threw our packs to the ground. As I lowered myself out of the truck, the driver swung the metal bar at Spider's head. Spider ducked to his right. I pushed the door of the cab hard into the driver, knocking him off balance. Spider lunged at the falling man, yanked the bar from him and wound up like a batter about to swing for the fences.

"Spider! Don't!" I yelled.

He froze. His jaw worked side to side. He raised the bar a few inches, then let it hang loose. "Fuckin' hophead," Spider said to the driver.

The man shifted onto his side and started to get up.

Spider lifted the bar again. "Stay where you are 'til we're gone."

The man rolled onto his back, then raised himself up on his elbows and glared at us. His eyes were wide. "All I did was help you out." Spit shot from his mouth as he spoke. His chest heaved, his fists clenched.

Spider feinted toward the driver as if he was about to hit him with the bar. The man recoiled and covered his head.

"Stay put, big man," Spider said. "Don't move again until we're gone. Then you can get back in your truck. Try not to kill anybody, you sorry sack of shit."

We scooped up our packs and headed toward the gate. Spider looked back to make sure the driver was still on the ground. He threw down the bar and we walked toward the road.

The front of the packing house stood in sharp contrast to the smelly, muddy rear. A broad swath of mown grass lined the road in front of the business. A paved parking lot sat in front of freshly painted offices. As we crossed the lot, a beat-up Chevy Nova pulled into one of the parking spaces. Spider turned away to light a cigarette as a young woman with thick auburn hair climbed out of the clunker. She wore a sleeveless denim dress with buttons down the front. Freckles dotted her cheeks, accenting her emerald eyes. She reached back into the front seat and pulled out an enormous, crocheted purse, slung it over her shoulder, then slammed the car door just as Spider turned back.

"Spider? Oh my god," she said. Her eyebrows shot up and a smile took over her face. "It *is* you." She threw her arms around his neck and kissed him on the cheek. "What are you doing here?" Looking at the pack on his shoulder, she said, "You in the Boy Scouts now?" then laughed.

Spider's arms hung by his sides. Smoke drifted from his cigarette. He didn't push her away, but didn't hug her back, either. "Evelyn," he said without emotion.

She let go of Spider and dropped her arms. The ring of keys in her hand jingled. "I haven't seen you since Wendell's memorial. You been all right? You don't seem too good."

I drifted a few steps away, wondering who this girl was, what the odds were of meeting someone you knew in the middle of nowhere. Then I remembered we were in Cleveland, and what Spider said about a friend working at this packing house.

"Oh, I've been just peachy, Evvie," he answered, studying the ground at his feet. He took a long drag on his smoke and flicked the butt into the grass. Looking up he said, "How 'bout you?"

"Oh, you know me. I'm gettin' along all right. But I gotta go. I was runnin' errands and the boss is waitin' on me." Evvie dug in her purse, pulled out a scrap of paper and a pen and wrote on it. "Mom and me moved. Here's our new address." She stuffed the paper into Spider's pocket. "Come and see us. Please." She opened the office door, turned and said, "Please?" Then she went in.

"Old friend?" I asked.

"Painful memory," he replied.

"That girl is beautiful, man. How can you have any painful memories associated with that?"

Spider shook his head and took off toward the road.

I followed, still jacked up from having escaped the speed-freak trucker. Spider could be a moody SOB. Maybe I could cheer him up for once.

"You should be happy you even know a girl like that."

Spider kept walking until he reached the grass at the edge of the road. He slipped his pack off and threw it a couple of feet. He walked into the road and looked both ways. Traffic was nonexistent.

I dropped my pack to the grass and punched Spider's arm. "C'mon, man. Tell me about that babe. Maybe I could get her to go out with me."

He turned away from the road. "Leave it be."

"Aw, c'mon. Let me in on that little honey."

Spider took a step towards me. "I said, leave it."

In high school, I'd been beaten up several times by the angry boyfriends of girls I had made comments about. But, I never understood why they got upset. And the sun was shining on this beautiful day. And we had whipped that crazy trucker. I was on a roll.

"She is so fine. I'd like to take her to the prom and keep her out all night, if you know what I me—unhh."

Spider drove his fist into my solar plexus.

I doubled over, fell to the ground and rolled to my side trying to find my breath.

Spider stood over me with fists clenched. "Don't you ever say anything about Evvie. Anything. Got it?"

I nodded several times. "Hyess," I gasped.

"I like you okay, Hester, but your goddam mouth runs entirely too free of whatever brain you have. I'm glad we're in Cleveland. I'm sick of saving your sorry ass."

I wanted to be done with the whole hitchhiking thing, too. I was tired of the uncertainty, the discomfort. But Milwaukee was still a couple of days away at best. It would be dark in just a few hours, and I had no idea where the Interstate was. The high I had felt a few moments ago evaporated. So, I looked for someone to blame.

"You're home," I said. "Well, hooray for you. I'm sick of you acting like you're so wise and all. By the way, I saved *your* ass an hour ago. That trucker was aiming to clock you, man. If I hadn't slammed him with the door, you'd a been hurtin'."

"Yeah. Nice door action, Superman," he replied. "You're my fuckin' hero. You'd still be in Warren, Pennsylvania, washin' dishes in the Finer Diner if I hadn't been there. Hell, you'd still be leanin' on that stolen—"

The blast of a semi's horn shattered the air. The speedfreak's truck idled at the exit to the property. Air hissed as the brakes set. The passenger window rolled down, and the driver stuck his head out. "I'm going to kill you," he shouted, pointing at us. "Watch your backside, assholes." He disappeared back into the cab, and black smoke poured from the exhaust stacks as he motored away.

My irritation with Spider faded as fast as my fear reemerged. "You think that nutjob will come after us?" I asked.

"Hell no. He's all screwed up from the speed. That shit makes you paranoid. He's liable to whale on somebody else if they get in his way. Best thing he could do would be to drink a gallon of water and run around the block. Most likely, though, he'll drive to the nearest truck stop and crash. Or maybe he'll crash before he gets there, but I hope not."

Spider slumped. He'd stayed awake listening to the trucker chatter while I slept. The girl he'd run into seemed to have worn him out even more. But instead of being pissed, he was already hoping the damn trucker would be okay.

"Don't you ever stay mad at anyone besides me?" I asked. "Back in the diner, you said you felt sorry for the pricks that robbed us. That dickhead trucker tried to bash your head in, and now you sound like you sympathize with him, too. How are you okay with all that?"

He straightened his back, then turned his head to spit. As he turned back, his lips formed a thin line and the skin around his eyes wrinkled. His face became motionless, frozen, as he fixed me with a stare.

I held his gaze, afraid he might hit me again, then turned away. "Do you know where we are?" I asked, meaning, did he know how to get back to the highway.

"I'm home," Spider said. "That much I know. If you don't know where you are, maybe you should start paying attention."

"Pay attention to what?"

Spider grabbed his pack and started walking along the road toward the nearest intersection.

"Where're you going?" I asked.

He kept walking.

Chapter 3

"Goddamit," I said to the empty air. "Goddamit." I threw my hands up. "What is he talking about, pay attention? Does he think he's The Maharishi or something?" Then, louder, "You think you're The Maharishi or something?" I kept staring after Spider, thinking he'd look back. "Well kiss my ass, you sorry burn-out." He didn't turn around.

I sank to the ground and leaned against my pack. "Just fucking great," I said, still talking to thin air. The breeze died, intensifying the odor of scorched cowhide and steam-cleaned cattle dung. The only sound was a muffled whoosh from the blowers in the meat factory. Not even a bird whistled.

Spider's company meant a lot to me. Now that he was gone loneliness rushed in. I had no money, no food, no place to stay. "Shit."

A few old pickups and beat up cars rolled out from behind the metal wall that surrounded the rear of the processing plant. First shift must be over. Soon a line of vehicles pulled onto the road and turned left. I jumped up, lugged my pack to the exit and stuck out my thumb. No one even slowed to look my way. Five minutes later all that remained was the dust they had stirred up. My stomach growled. My mouth felt dry as sawdust. "Shit," I said again.

The red Nova was still here. I dragged my pack into the company's office hoping for a cold drink. The place was cool and quiet and smelled like burnt coffee. Spider's friend, Evvie, sat at a desk behind a counter. "Can I help you?" she said, without looking up.

"Do you have a bubbler?" I asked.

"A what?" she said, looking up. "Oh, it's you." She tilted her head and laughed. "What's a bubbler?"

"You know, where you get a drink.""You mean a water fountain? Yeah," she said, pointing to her left. "There's one in that hall, next to the restroom."

The water was cool going down, but cramped my empty belly. In the men's room, I took off my shirt, scrubbed my chest and armpits, then washed my face. My last shower had been days ago. I didn't want to smell bad, especially because of Evvie.

I eyed her as I walked back to the counter smoothing my dirty t-shirt.

"Find it okay?" Evvie asked.

"Yeah. Thanks." My pack was heavy as I swung it onto my shoulder, reminding me I didn't want to miss a chance to get a ride to the interstate. "Has everybody left for the day?"

Evvie straightened in her chair and looked around at the empty desks behind her. "Obviously not," she said. "I'm here. You're here. Oh, and Mr. Hildebrandt is in his office. Why? You thinking of robbing the place? You'll have to go through me, so you'll need Spider's help."

She plopped her elbows onto her desk and grinned. "Where *is* Spider?"

Her silly joke warmed me. "He took off a while ago."

Evvie's grin faded. "He left without saying goodbye to me?" Her brow wrinkled, and she frowned. "That boy has problems." She smiled again. "Who are you, and how did you ever meet *him*?"

Friendly girls, especially pretty ones, made me self-conscious. I wanted to be friendly back, and maybe impress her, but on the inside, I was trembling. "I'm Nate. Hester. Umm, I met Spider on the road a couple days ago. We were hitchhiking together." I didn't know what else to say. "And just so you know, I don't want to rob the place."

Evvie laughed. "Yeah, I knew that." She put her elbows on the desk and cupped her chin with her hands. "You hung with Spider for a couple of days? Either you're tougher than you look or Spider's changed. He eats you hippie-types for lunch. He didn't try to con you out of your granola, or something?"

My shoulders slumped, and I looked at the floor. This girl hadn't known me for five minutes, and she'd seen right through me. I felt stupid and turned to go. "Yeah, well, thanks for the water. I better head out."

"Aw, c'mon, Nate. I didn't mean to hurt your feelings. I was just surprised at how nice you are. Most of Spider's friends are pricks. Look, you need a ride to the highway, right?"

I nodded.

"It's almost five o'clock. Wait for me outside. I'll drop you off someplace."

"Sure. Thanks." Evvie was going to give me a ride! All was well again.

Outside, traffic noise drifted in from the main road. The sun was still up, but I knew nightfall was coming. Damn Spider for walking away on me. Him with his platitudes and homey advice. Who did he think he was, trying to tell me how to live my life? He was the one who'd sold all of his stuff to start a drug empire then ended up broke in the middle of nowhere. As usual, fear and anger duked it out in my mind. I didn't even notice Evvie walking out of the office.

"You ready?" She asked.

I jumped. "Uh, yeah."

Evvie led the way to the old Nova. The paint was faded, but the car was clean. Her door groaned as she pulled it open. "You can put your stuff in the back seat."

I tossed the pack in the back and climbed in. The cracked dash pad matched the split in the vinyl seat, but everything gleamed. Old parking tickets didn't stick out of the glove compartment. Trash didn't cover the floor. Usually, when I got a ride in a crappy car, it was a pig sty. Not this one.

Evvie turned the ignition key. Click-click-click. She turned it again. Click-click-click.

"Oh, no. Not this," she said.

"Sounds like a low battery."

"How do you know?"

"I worked at a garage until a few months ago. Let me take a look." I climbed out and opened the hood. Even the engine compartment was clean. I wiggled the battery cables, one of which was loose. "Got a screwdriver?" I asked.

Evvie stood on the driver's side, looking into the engine compartment. "I don't have any tools."

"Got a nail file?"

She pulled her purse onto her lap and rummaged through it. "There's gotta be one in here somewhere. I need to clean this thing out." After another second she held up her hand. "Bingo!"

I tightened the connector as tight as I could, then stuck the nail file into the top of the battery terminal and twisted, gouging the metal of both the terminal and the connector.

"Try it now."

Evvie turned the key, and the motor started, sending a cloud of blue smoke out of the tailpipe. I lowered the hood and got back into the car.

"How'd you do that?" she asked. "I've been having trouble for a few days now."

"It's not fixed. I just made the connection good enough to get it started. You need new battery connectors."

"Yeah, that's what Mr. Hildebrandt said too. He bought me some parts he said would fix it, but I just stuck 'em away. I'm no good with fixin' cars." Evvie reached over and pulled a couple of replacement connectors out of the glove compartment. "Do you know how to put these on?"

"It's pretty easy. I could put 'em on if I had a pair of pliers and a screwdriver."

Evvie ignored me and pulled into the street. "You're probably in a hurry to get going. Where can I take you?"

"I'm not in a hurry," I said. "This time of day it gets harder to get a ride, except from truckers, 'cause a lot of them drive at night. But I don't even know where we are. Can you drop me at a truck stop on the Interstate?"

Again, Evvie didn't answer. I had no plan at all, so her silence didn't bother me. She focused on the road, making a left onto a busy street and driving a few blocks in silence. Her jaw was set, and she squinted a couple of times, then smiled and glanced my way. "So you and Spider are friends."

"Well, we met up a couple days ago, but on the road, you kinda get to know people fast."

"I guess. I can't even imagine being on the road, not knowing where you'll be and all. How old are you, anyway?"

"Eighteen."

"Wow, eighteen. And out on the road. I'm nineteen, and I'd never do anything like that. I mean, stuff isn't always great around here, but at least I have a roof to sleep under. What's that like? Not knowing where you'll stay at night?"

"Oh, it's not too bad." Some nights I was scared to death, but I wasn't going to tell her that. "Most nights I've either been in a truck or sleeping at a truck stop. But I'm ready to be home. I'm sorry I pissed off Spider. He's helped me out a lot."

"Oh, Spider gets moody sometimes. He'd a probably walked away sooner or later. I haven't seen him for a quite a while before today. I wish he'd said goodbye before he wandered off. We were like family, you know? In fact, my mom sort of adopted him, 'cause his mom wasn't doing too well. But he hasn't come around since Wendell..." Evvie drew in a breath and eased it out. "My brother was killed in Vietnam two years ago."

I'd known a few people who had lost brothers or sons in the war, and their loss made me feel a little guilty. They'd gone to the war I refused to go to. "I'm sorry. That must be hard."

"It is. After all this time it still kills me. Wendell was the greatest guy." She looked unfocused for a minute, then looked back at me. "Seeing Spider made me miss Wendell even more. I'd of liked to have talked to Spider about it. He was like a brother to me, but after the funeral, he quit coming around. So, I lost him, too."

We stopped at a red light. "You seem like a nice person. If you're not in a hurry would you come with me to my mom's house and put those battery thingies on? And, I could use someone to hang out with besides my mom."

I was speechless.

"And I'm not a serial killer," she added, smiling. "I swear."

"I'd be happy to fix your car." I grinned. "And I'd love to hang out with you."

Evvie leaned across and kissed my cheek, then settled back into the driver's seat.

The afternoon heat hit me through the open car window as we pulled away from the light. I relaxed, resisting the urge to rub the spot on my cheek where Evvie had placed her lips. Life was good again. I didn't care if I ever made it back to Milwaukee now.

As she drove, Evvie started talking fast. "I don't live too far from here. Mom and me moved there a month ago. We finally got out of Southtown. Parma's a lot nicer. I'm pretty sure we still have tools and stuff at the house. Wendell had all that. The tools are there, but I might need to find them. You can work on the car in the driveway. By the way, my mom hasn't been the same since Wendell died. I mean, she's harmless, but she acts odd sometimes."

At last, Evvie stopped and drew a breath, then turned to look at me. "So, you still want to come to my house?"

"Uh, sure," I said. "Why wouldn't I?"

"Well, my mom. She'll act all normal for a while, then won't speak at all. I never know how she'll be." Evvie bit her fingernail and stared ahead at the road. "I don't want you to think we're weird because my mom's so sad about Wendell." She kept both hands on the wheel and stared straight ahead. "And I love my mom. I don't want people to hurt her."

I had experience with weird mothers. I hated bringing people to my house. My mother was a fanatical Catholic. Human faults were her favorite topic of discussion, and I never knew when she might try to make my friends and me kneel and recite the rosary.

"Don't worry about it. My mom is a whack-job, so nothing your mother could do would surprise me. If you want, I'll fix your car and leave. But you said you needed someone to hang out with. I'd sure like to hang out with you."

Evvie smiled. "Well, okay. But don't say I didn't warn ya."

It didn't take long to reach her neighborhood. The houses were small, with driveways that led to garages set back from the road. Kids playing ball in the street stopped their game and moved to the curb so we could pass. "Nice clunker," one of them said as we drove by.

"But it's my clunker, asshole," Evvie mumbled. She pulled into the driveway next to a small house with white aluminum siding.

"Kids here give you a lot of hassle?" I asked as we pulled up to the garage.

"No, they're just young."

Evvie got out of the car. "Let me get you the tools so you can put on them thingamajigs and I'll let mom know you're here." A minute later she came out with a small kit. "Here ya go. I'll be right back."

I opened the hood of the Nova and went to work. Replacing the first one was easy, but the other connector stuck on the battery post and wouldn't budge. I tapped on it with the handle of the screwdriver, then pried, tapped some more then pried again, harder. When it came loose, I scraped my knuckles on the edge of the fender.

"Shit," I said. I threw the screwdriver into the engine compartment and straightened up, slamming the back of my head against the raised hood. "Shit," I said again. "Piece of shit car."

I glanced toward the house. The heat in my face turned from anger to embarrassment. I hoped no one had seen me blow up. I wanted to make a good impression and not to look like I was a raving lunatic.

The screen door slammed. "How's it going?" Evvie asked.

"About normal," I replied. "I'm not an ace auto mechanic."

"Well, you're better at it than I am. I appreciate you doin' this for me. And by the way, I told Mom about you meeting Spider and you're staying for supper."

Evvie watched me search for the screwdriver underneath the car and then work on the second terminal. "Wendell woulda done this for me," she said. "I sure do miss him."

After a moment she looked toward the back door. Her lips curved up, but her eyes didn't smile. "Let's go eat," she said, and walked past me toward the house.

Chapter 4

The stove and fridge looked ancient, the kitchen walls a soft yellow. The aroma of roast chicken made my stomach groan from hunger.

"Mom, this is Nate, the guy who fixed my car," Evvie said.

A woman of about forty sat at the table, trim, dressed in slacks and a blouse. Her short brown hair was neatly brushed. "He's the one who knows where Spider is?"

"No, Mom. He came to town with Spider." Evvie looked at me and rolled her eyes. "This here's my mom. You can call her Norma."

"Hello Norma," I said.

She gave me a slight smile, but said nothing.

I smiled back, not knowing what else to say. The ticking of a clock made the air thick with Norma's silence.

"Mom, can you say something to Nate? He's gonna eat supper with us." Evvie glanced toward me. "Have a seat. I'll get the chicken."

I sat across from Norma. "So, are you from Cleveland?"

She still smiled, but didn't say anything.

"Yeah, she's from Cleveland." Evvie took the chicken out of the roasting pan and put it on a platter. "Sometimes Mom doesn't say much. Isn't that right, Mom? And sometimes she doesn't shut up. Don't let that throw you. She's a sweetheart, really." Evvie elbowed my shoulder as she slipped by with the platter. "Tell her about how you met Spider. I want to hear more about that myself."

"I was in Rochester, New York, on the turnpike and some guys picked me up. Spider was already in the car." I didn't want to tell them about Spider's plan to sell drugs, or how we were left, passed out in a stolen car. "Those guys gave us a ride for a ways, then Spider and I stayed together 'til today."

Evvie put the last of the food on the table and sat down. "That's all? Why'd Spider stay with you? He's not exactly a fan of company."

I shrugged. I didn't know why Spider stayed, but now that he was gone, I missed him.

"This boy's hungry, Evvie," Norma said. "Leave him alone for a minute. Let's eat." Her body had relaxed. She appeared present and engaged as she stabbed a chicken thigh and put it on her plate. "So you and Spider are friends. I'll bet he brought you to Cleveland so you could meet Evvie."

"Mo-ther," Evvie said, "where do you get these ideas?"

She turned toward me. "Mom thinks I need to find a man, preferably today." Looking back at her mom she said, "Jesus, Mom, I'm only nineteen."

Norma had gone back to being distant. Her knife and fork rested on her plate, hands in her lap.

"Mom?" Evvie said. "Oh well." She looked my way and shrugged. "Easy come, easy go."

Silence hung thick in the air again. Norma sat immobile while Evvie and I dug into the chicken and rice. As I ate, I wondered why Evvie had let me into her house. I wondered why her mom was worried about Evvie "finding a man," and why her mom faded out like that. Evvie warned me it was odd. It sure was uncomfortable.

"Evvie's a good cook," Norma said. "She made this chicken. It's good, isn't it?"

"It *is* good," I said. "She can cook *way* better than she can fix her car." I looked at Evvie and winked.

Evvie laughed. "Yeah, well. That's not sayin' much. Of course, I have my own mechanic, now. I cook chicken, and he cooks up fixes under the hood."

"Who's that, Evvie?" Norma asked. "Who's your mechanic? I'll bet this young man would fix your car if you asked. Isn't that right, Nate?"

Evvie rolled her eyes. "Jesus, Mom. I told you. Nate *did* fix my car."

"See? That proves I'm right." Norma took a bite of chicken. "Nate, ask Evvie to go out with you. She needs someone reliable in her life. Someone like you."

I almost choked. No one ever called me reliable. I was hitchhiking with no means of support and no plans for the future. But I didn't want to laugh. Despite how impossible it was, I liked Norma's idea.

Evvie got up from the table and started clearing dishes. I carried my plate and glass to the sink.

"See, Evvie. Don't let this one get away," Norma said.

Evvie ignored her as she cleared dishes and put away leftovers. She filled the sink with sudsy water, not saying a word.

Norma got up from the table and walked out of the kitchen. A door slammed.

Evvie shook her head. No words, just water and suds and dishes piling up in the drainer.

In my house, we often ate in silence and left without saying goodbye because we had nothing to say to each other. But this was different. Norma was clearly warmhearted, so her lapses and silent departure seemed extra odd.

I leaned on a wall watching Evvie. She was friendly and warm and welcoming. And quiet, and moody, and unpredictable. It was great to have a meal and the prospect of a place to stay, but I felt like an intruder. I was a guest in a silent house and didn't know the rules, but then, I never knew the rules. Not knowing what to say, I wiped the table and straightened the chairs hoping to make a good impression.

The dishes done, Evvie dried her hands. "Sorry about Mom. Like I told you, she's not been the same since Wendell died." She drew in a deep breath. "Let's sit in the living room."

Evvie sat on the couch and folded her legs under her. I sat in the only chair.

"Have you ever lost anyone close to you?" Evvie asked.

"My grandpa died eight years ago, but he'd been sick for a while."

Evvie nodded. "Wendell and me were real close, and I miss him every day. It tore me up. But after the funeral, Mom didn't know what to do, didn't understand how God, who she always paid attention to, always tried to please..." She stopped and drew a breath. Her voice dropped to a whisper. "...could just shit on her that way. Now, she acts nutty. I swear she knows what she's doin'. All that crap about Spider bringing you to meet me and all. She knows better. She's just obsessed with me getting a boyfriend. I guess she wants me to hurry up and make her grandkids to replace Wendell."

With her talking so openly about babies and the idea of me being with her, my body reacted. I shifted in the chair to hide my growing affection. "Aw, I dunno. Losing her son has to be tough. And she's got to be proud of you. I mean, you've got a job and make the meals and keep the house. And you're beautiful." I looked away. "She can't be worried about you finding a boyfriend. Boys must be chasing you all the time." I hoped she would say no, but knew better.

"Well, no. A lot of boys ask me out, but all they want is sex. I have plans for my life and having babies right now doesn't fit 'em."

I thought about sex all the time, too, but my mother's interpretation of the Ten Commandments was always background noise, screwing up the moment. "Sex is a sacred act between married people," she'd said, over and over. I guess I knew sex caused babies, but only in an abstract way, like the way I knew milk came from cows. Sex was a goal, something that one day I would experience. And I imagined it would be the best thing that ever happened to me. But, I hadn't thought about the consequences.

"What are your plans?" I asked.

"Go to school, get ahead. Me and Mom just got this house a month ago. Been in tough neighborhoods since I was born. We've never had a place this nice, and I don't intend to screw it up." Evvie unfolded her legs from under her. "Have you ever been poor?"

"Well, we were never rich. I grew up in neighborhoods like this. I never went hungry."

"Hmph," Evvie said. "I guess I'm just whinin', but damn, we always seemed to live where people were gettin' shot and stabbed and left in alleys to die. Bein' here is like livin' at the Ritz for Mom and me. Those boys makin' fun of my car? That was a joke to me. Them little bastards grew up here. They don't know anything except having nice stuff. They eat what they want. They don't ride the bus. They don't have to walk when there's no bus fare. They see my old car and think it's a clunker. It's the only car I've ever had. It may be old, but it's *mine*. Can you understand that?"

"Yeah, I guess."

"A stupid car isn't the main thing I'm thankful for, but it's something I always thought only rich people had. I don't even know why having stuff matters to me. Wendell's memory is more important than a car. But I was tired of people looking down at me and Mom. We deserved a good life, too. Just because we were from the poor side of town shouldn't mean we stay in a slum and live afraid of what might happen next. I was so sick of that." Evvie took a breath and sat back, stretching her legs.

"Wendell shouldn't even have been in Nam. His eyes were bad, but the draft board didn't care. All the boys from our neighborhood had eyesight good enough to go, and feet that weren't flat, and hearts that didn't beat funny. It's only Senators' sons who seem to have bad feet or crooked teeth or some other lame reason to not go get shot at. Why is that Nate? Why is life so unfair?"

Evvie balled her fists and pounded the tops of her thighs. "Dammit. Wendell came home in a box! He was the kindest, most giving, full-of-life person, you ever met. They sent him home in a fucking *box!*" Tears streamed from her eyes. She pulled her feet onto the couch, hugged her knees into her chest and sobbed.

I edged forward in my chair wanting to comfort her. Then I froze, afraid she would think I was hitting on her. I sat stiffly, with my hands on my legs.

After a moment she sat up and wiped her eyes. Her mascara ran, her nose dripped, her hair hung limp, but she didn't seem to be aware of any of that. She drew a deep breath and said, "Will you do me a favor?"

I nodded like a little boy. Her swollen eyes and splotchy face weren't pretty, but I would've done anything for her.

"Hold me." She put her feet back on the floor and patted the sofa next to her.

I moved to the sofa and hugged her. Heat came off her head as she leaned into me. Her hair smelled of flowers. Her body felt good resting in my arms. She pressed even closer to me. Sweat and warm girl aroma drifted from her. My body ached with anticipation. I wanted to hold her forever.

She stroked my chest and said, "Thank you."

I had no idea what to do next, but was determined not to do anything to end the moment.

After a while she said, "You probably have a girlfriend."

Truth was, I'd never had any encounter like this before. "Naw."

Evvie raised her head and looked at me. "Really?"

"Well, yeah. I mean, no." I didn't want her to know how inexperienced I was. "I don't have a girlfriend right now."

"Well, damn. Why not?" She laughed. "You afraid of having babies, too?"

I shrugged and looked at the floor.

"Aw, I've embarrassed you again. Is it me, or are you this shy with all the girls?"

My face felt hot. She was so close, and I felt so insecure. "I don't know. I guess I never thought girls would want to go with me."

Evvie laid her head back on my shoulder and leaned into me again. "I liked you from the moment you said you weren't going to rob the office. You came home with me and fixed my car and never tried to stand too close. I didn't feel like I had to guard myself. You held me when I asked you to. You listened like a friend. *I'd* like to go with you."

Now, I was burning all over. "Really?"

She sat up and pulled back from my embrace. Evvie bit her bottom lip and looked into my eyes. She took my face in both of her hands and pulled my lips into hers. The tip of her tongue flicked my lip, then she pulled back for a beat and smiled. Her arms pulled me back to her. We were no longer she and me. We were just lips and tongues and slippery heat. I had never felt so lost and so found. I wanted Evvie, all of Evvie, and was beginning to believe she wanted me, too.

She pushed me back and looked into my eyes. "This is amazing. I hardly know you, but I feel so close. You care about how *I* feel." She hesitated and looked down at her lap. "Nate, I'm gonna ask you another favor that I know I shouldn't ask."

I sat up and reached for her hands. I had no idea what she was going to ask, but whatever it was, my answer would be *yes*.

"Do you mind sleeping on the couch?"

I laughed. "Be glad to, but why should you not ask me?"

"What I shouldn't be asking you is, will you sleep on the couch, with me?"

A rush of overheated blood surged to my head. I felt faint. My vision narrowed. Heat radiated from me. "Yes. I would love to sleep on this couch with you."

Evvie's eyes were alert, as if searching for a clue about how I felt.

"I've never felt quite like this. I don't want you to disappear, but I can't have sex with you. At least not yet. I'm sorry. I'm so sorry. Can you understand that? Can you stay and just be with me without being *with* me?"

To stay all night but not have sex was a perfect solution. Now my virginity wouldn't be so obvious. I wanted her, but I could wait. This was a girl I didn't want to mess up with.

"You are the most beautiful girl I've ever met, and I want to know everything about you. I want to stay with you. If that means no sex, I'm good with it."

Evvie threw her arms around me and kissed me, then took my hand and guided it to her breast. "That doesn't mean we can't mess around. God, Nate, I didn't know I could feel like this about someone I don't even know." Then she reached back and turned off the lamp.

Chapter 5

Evvie's breast felt good in my hand. All my blood rushed to my groin, and I lost the ability to speak. I caressed her with the hand she had moved and brought my other hand to her butt.

"Easy, loverboy," she said. "We have all night."

I wasn't sure what to do next. The only other time I had touched a girl's breast was at a drive-in movie. She had fallen asleep, and I copped a feel. As soon as I touched her, she woke up and pushed my hand away. Being on the couch with Evvie was virgin territory.

She raised herself up and pulled her dress up to her waist. "Think you can let go long enough to unbutton my dress?"

"Uh, sure," I stammered, fumbling with buttons that seemed too big for the buttonholes.

"You've never been with a girl, have you?" she said.

I was burning up with passion, and now embarrassment. "Why do you say that?" I mumbled.

"Hah," Evvie laughed. "Don't be embarrassed. It's sweet. At last, I get to be with a boy that has thought about something besides my tits." Evvie pulled her dress off and threw it to the floor. "God, Nate, every time I learn something new about you, it makes me want to know more." She reached over and unbuttoned my shirt. "Take off your jeans. I want to feel you against my skin." I stood and dropped my jeans and wondered if I should take off my underpants too. They were worthless at concealing the boner I had, so I pulled them down and kicked them off.

"C'mere. Let me feel your heat."

I laid back down and stretched my body up against Evvie's. She still had her bra and panties on. Laying against the bare parts of her made me feel like Tarzan. I hoped she was loving this as much as I was.

We kissed, hard and deep. I reached behind her, undoing the hooks of her bra and slipped it off. She moaned a little when I caressed her nipple then took it in my mouth.

"Mmm. Mmm. Nate, stop." She pushed me back.

"What? What am I doing wrong?"

"I told you I shouldn't do this. I knew it was too hard."

"I can do it, Evvie. I just thought you wanted to go ahead. I mean, you were pretty encouraging." I stood back up and pulled my undies back on.

"No, Nate. It's not you. It's me. I want you so bad I can't think straight. C'mon. Lay back down." Evvie pushed up against the back of the couch and patted the clear area. "Lay right here. And take off your undies."

I pulled off my underpants and laid down. I could feel her breasts pushing against my back. I wiggled my butt into her panties and closed my eyes, resolved to try to sleep with an aching erection.

"Nate?"

"Yeah?"

"Can I touch you?"

This was my first time, but still, that seemed like a dumb question. "Uh, sure."

Evvie's hand slid across my hip and closed around my penis. "Mmm. That feels so good."

"Umm, yeah, it does. But just so you know, I can't hold off. I mean, I'm gonna cum if you keep that up."

"God, Nate, I hope so." Evvie stroked me a few times, and it was all over. And I do mean all over.

"Oh god! Oh god! Evvie, I'm sorry," I said. "It's everywhere!"

Evvie slipped her other arm beneath me and pulled me tighter into her body. "God, Nate, you're the best."

I got up, found the bathroom and cleaned up a little. When I returned, Evvie was asleep.

· · · · ·

Pressure on my bladder and a tingling in my arm woke me up. I tried to sit up, but Evvie was laying on top of my right side. "Hey, good morning."

Evvie's stretched and rolled as she raised her hands above her head. "Hey, you. Did I keep you awake snoring?"

I laughed. "I didn't hear a thing from you or from anyone else. It must have been three o'clock before we fell asleep." I leaned over and kissed her. Evvie responded, sticking her tongue deep into my mouth. The hard-on I woke up with started to throb. I pushed her away and sat up. "I gotta go."

Evvie rubbed her face. "You know where it's at."

As I entered the bathroom, I heard a knock on the front door but paid no attention to it. All I could think of was the pressure in my bladder. I heard Norma talking to someone, but couldn't make out what was being said. At the sink I tried to scrub off the remnants of last night's explosion, then washed my face and pulled my fingers through my long hair, trying to undo the snarls.

Barefoot and shirtless, I walked out of the bathroom and straight into a fist.

"Shit," I shouted. I didn't even know who I was shouting at. The punch had knocked me down. I sat, leaning on the wall, touching my jaw. When I looked up, Spider stood over me, his fist drawn back. I shook my head. The best night of my life had just turned into a nightmare.

I struggled to stand up. Spider kicked my foot out from under me, and I fell back down.

"Knock it off," I said. "What is wrong with you?"

Norma pushed Spider's arm. "Cut it out. Not in my house."

Spider took a step back and glared at me, flexing his fists.

I had learned from watching him to never take my eyes off a potential attacker. I slid up the wall until I was standing. "What is wrong with you?" I said again, scowling at him.

Spider relaxed and put his hands in his pockets. "What are *you* doing here?"

I shrugged. "Evvie needed her car fixed. She fed me supper and let me sleep here. What're *you* doing here?"

"You boys back off," Norma said then turned toward Spider. "I'm tired of you punching everyone that comes to see Evvie. She's a grown girl. She gets to make her own decisions. It's been two years since you last showed up anyway. Behave yourself."

"Aw, sorry, Norma. I hoped this dumbass was out of my life. I came to visit you and Evvie. Never expected him to show up. Goddam." Spider ran his hands through his mess of curls and glared at me.

His attention shifted back to Norma. "I ran into Evvie at her job yesterday and found out you moved out here. How're you doing?"

Evvie walked out of the kitchen. "Spider! You came!" She hugged his neck and kissed his cheek. "I have missed you so much."

"We don't all need to stand here at the door," Norma said. "C'mon in and I'll make coffee."

I made it to the living room first and fished my shirt from behind the couch. Spider and Evvie sat on the sofa. Norma took the chair. I found a place along the wall and sat on the floor.

Spider gave Evvie a sideways hug and then leaned away from her on the couch. "You sure have changed. You look all grown up now."

"Lots of things have changed. You know I graduated last year?"

"No Shit? Good for you Evvie. You always were smart, but you got distracted easy."

"What do you mean?"

"Oh, sometimes them boys tried to get too friendly. A couple of 'em I sorta suggested they oughta move on."

"You threatened my friends? Dammit Spider. That was none of your business." Evvie punched Spider then sat back and crossed her arms in front of herself.

Spider hunched his shoulders and put his hands between his legs. "All I wanted was to keep you from gettin' in a mess. Wendell and me worried that you'd end up getting' pregnant. Sometimes I sorta took it on myself to make things change course a little.

Evvie's arms were still crossed. She sat back into the sofa with her legs pressed together in front of her, looking like she was trying to keep from exploding.

Norma brought coffee, and we all sat for a few minutes, staring into our cups.

Spider leaned forward and said to Norma, "I'm sorry I haven't been around much since, you know, Wendell and all. I just didn't know what to say. When I seen Evvie yesterday, something started gnawin' at me, and I realized how much I missed you. You're the only real family I got."

Norma froze. Her face grew rigid. Her jaw tensed. Deep wrinkles formed as the flesh around her eyes contracted. Her lips pressed together. It appeared as though if her face shrunk any more it would swallow itself. Her hands were in her lap, one covering the other, veins pulsing.

Evvie looked at the floor. "Mom, Spider's right. Wendell died, but we can't let his death kill the rest of us." She glanced at Norma who sat immobile. "Oh, forget it. We've had this talk before. I'm sorry mama. I'm sorry you lost your only son. But I lost my brother too, you know. When you fade out like you're doing now, I can't get through to you. Then, it's like I've lost you, too. But I need you mom. I still need you."

Norma's face softened. She looked at Evvie and smiled. "I know. I know. I'll figure it out. I will. You know I love you Evvie. I'll do better." Then she got up and walked into her bedroom and closed the door.

Evvie's mouth formed a thin straight line as she shook her head. "Oh, God," she muttered. "I love her, but I am running out of strength to deal with her sadness."

I got up from the floor and took the chair Norma left. Spider looked at his boots. Evvie leaned back with her eyes closed. It was as if the life had walked out of the room with Norma.

Evvie looked at Spider, then at me. "I need some time. Can you guys get out of here?"

The fabulous girl I just fell in love with was asking me to leave. I'd be back with the Hells Angel and his old wise sayings. Evvie had given me a meal, a bed and a handjob. I wanted a whole lot more, but she didn't owe me anything.

Spider hauled himself to his feet. "C'mon, dumbass."

I stood and started to gather my stuff.

"Let's go. Now," he shouted.

"I gotta pack my clothes."

"Well, I'm not leaving 'til your sorry ass is gone. Shit, you'll be trying to get into Evvie's pants." Spider looked at Evvie. "Sorry, Evvie, but I know you have crappy taste in boyfriends. You'd prob'ly try to rescue this mutt."

Fire flashed from Evvie's eyes. "That is none of your goddam business Spider Kowalski." She shot to her feet and punched Spider's arm. "You walk back into our lives after disappearing for two years and start telling me what's good for me. You don't get to do that." She drew in a long breath. "Now, get out."

Spider reached out toward Evvie, but she stepped back and looked at me. "You're a nice boy, Nate. But I need some time to think, and I can't do that with you here. Do ya understand that?"

"Well, sure, I guess. Thanks for everything."

Evvie sat on the couch, folded her arms in front of herself and closed her eyes.

"Let's go, man," Spider said.

I followed him out into the Cleveland sun. A ratty Sportster sat in the driveway.

"That yours? I thought you sold your bike to open your 'business'."

"Yeah, well. Funny thing about that. When I got back yesterday, I went lookin' for the guy that bought my bike. We called him Weeds. He come into a bunch of money from a deal he'd done. Anyway, turns out, the day after I left, the guy cashed it in."

"He died?"

"Yup. Dumb SOB got into a fight at a bar. Picked the wrong dude. Guy shot him. Hadn't even transferred the title on my bike."

I didn't know anything about when titles changed hands legally, but this didn't seem legit. "So you just get your bike back?"

Spider dropped his gaze. "Don't you worry about it. B'sides, you need a ride, right? You oughta be glad I got my scooter back. Otherwise you'd be walkin'."

"What's up with Evvie?" I asked. "We were getting along great until she got so withdrawn."

"See Nate, that's what I've been tryin' to tell ya. Life isn't all about you. Evvie's brother meant a lot to her. Her mama means a lot to her. So when Norma faded out like that, well, it bothered me, but it prob'ly hurt Evvie a lot. Family may not mean a lot to you, but it's important to her. That's why I came by."

"So, you're gonna give me a lift to the highway?"

"I got stuff to get done, but yeah, I'll give you a ride." He climbed on the bike and kicked the starter. The engine roared to life, and he twisted the throttle a couple of times, making sure everyone in the neighborhood knew he was there. "I hope you can figure out how to hold on, 'cause I'm not slowin' down for you."

I threw my leg over the fender and settled onto the tiny bitch seat. I didn't want to hold on to Spider, so I grabbed the fender. Spider kicked the bike into gear and took off like a bullet. My body was thrown back from the momentum, but somehow I stayed on.

I didn't know where we were headed, but I hoped it wasn't far. My arms were sore from holding on. After ten minutes Spider pulled into the parking lot of a tavern that was built from an old house. A few cars were in the lot, and there was one other Harley.

"Let's get a beer," Spider said after he climbed off the bike. "This is a place I used to go to with Wendell."

"Is this closer to the highway?"

"Relax, dumbass. It's early. Hang with me for a while."

This was a different attitude than the one Spider had yesterday when he'd walked off. I didn't have any place I needed to be, and besides, I didn't know where I was.

"Lean your pack on my bike. No one will mess with it."

"This neighborhood doesn't look all that safe, man. They stole my underwear out of a dryer once."

"Yeah, well, my bike ain't a damn dryer. No one will touch it."

I leaned my pack on the bike and followed Spider into the dark, smoky place. The only light came from Schaefer and Carling beer signs.

Spider and I sat at the end of the bar nearest the door. The bartender was at the other end of the room placing bottles on the bar back. He glanced our way and stopped working, a whiskey bottle in mid-air. Halfway down the bar a couple of old guys were nursing beers. They turned and faced us. *I Walk The Line* played in the background. No one spoke. In another part of town this might have been termed a "Mexican standoff", but there were only old Polacks here.

"Ted, I need a Black Label," Spider said, "and bring one for this guy."

The barkeep set the whiskey bottle on the counter, grabbed the beers, and slowly walked the length of the bar, setting the sweating bottles in front of Spider. "Where you been, Spider? Who's you long-haired hippie friend? You gone queer on us now?"

Spider rolled his eyes. "Some things never change. This here's Nate. He's ridin' with me today. You do make your living selling beer, and I'm a paying customer. So be a little friendlier."

He shrugged and leaned on the bar. "So, why're you back in the neighborhood? Still trying to get that remodeling company started?"

"Naw, I gave that up. Seems everybody wants stuff done for nothin'. I've been traveling a little." Spider shot me a glance. "Just got back in town and thought I'd drop by. See who I might run into."

"Well, it might be good if you saw them before they saw you. Lotta bad feeling for you around here, man." Ted wandered away, asked the other guys if they needed anything, then went back to stocking the back bar.

"Friendly type," I whispered to Spider. "What's up with that?"

Spider took a long pull on his beer, then shook out a Camel and lit it. He blew a couple smoke rings and leaned back on the bar stool. "Well, unlike yourself, who everyone seems to take an immediate likin' to, I've pissed a few people off over the years. And some of them're slow to forget."

"Then why did you come here for beer? Is this the only tavern in Cleveland?"

"Hmph." Spider shook his head. "Look, not everybody is gonna like you. Some of the people that're upset with me don't have a good reason to be mad. I'm not gonna let their crappy judgment keep me from enjoyin' any place I damn well please. D'you hide from everyone that you've ever pissed off?"

Hide seemed like a harsh word, but I did avoid them. "Don't you worry about getting your ass kicked?"

"Hah! Look at me, dipshit. Do I look like I worry about getting into a fight? Jesus Christ, you *are* a pussy, aren't you?"

I was. I knew it, but didn't know what to do about it. I took a drink of the beer and set the bottle on the counter. "I was always told to turn the other cheek." I felt embarrassed saying that. Non-violence wasn't a matter of principle with me. I was just afraid of getting beaten. "I watched how you talked to those drilling rig workers. You even seemed in control with that crazy trucker. I was scared shitless."

He stood up and threw a few dollars on the bar. "Let's get out of here."

I downed the rest of the beer and followed Spider outside.

My pack was still leaning on his bike. I didn't say anything, but I was impressed.

We rode until we reached Edgewater Park on Lake Erie. My arms and hands were sore from holding on and my ass hurt from the lack of suspension. "How do you stand riding that thing for hours? Jesus, I feel like I'm about to rattle apart."

Spider swung his leg off the bike, spread his arms and legs like he was on a motorcycle. He shook his arms and torso. "Like that. Let's take a walk."

He headed to some large boulders lining the shore, scrambling over them to the edge of the water and sat.

I sat on the rock next to his and stared out. "This looks just like Lake Michigan. I used to spend a lot of time on the lakefront in Milwaukee, just watching the waves roll in."

Spider sat motionless, staring at the sailboats bobbing in the distance. After a while, he leaned back on his elbows and stretched out his legs. "What're you gonna do next?" he said.

"I'm riding with you, man. I don't know."

"No, dumbass. What are you gonna do next in your life?"

My life? I hadn't thought fifteen minutes ahead. How was I supposed to know what I was going to do with my life?

I shifted around on the rocks, trying to find a comfortable spot for my sore rear end while I thought about Spider's question. Giving up, I stood. "I have no idea, man. I thought I'd be on my way already, heading back to Milwaukee."

I picked up a stick that was caught between the boulders and threw it into the water. "I know you think of Evvie as your sister, and you feel responsible for her and all, but man, I got it bad for her. I've never felt like this about any other girl I've ever met. I can't just leave, man. I think I love her."

I expected a reaction, but he didn't move, just kept watching the sailboats on the lake, oblivious to what I said.

I settled back down on a rock. My arms burned with the sun's heat. The shore breeze ruffled my hair, blowing strands into my face. Squawking gulls circled, looking for a handout.

My gut ached from the feelings I had for Evvie. I stopped worrying what Spider may do and began to think about what might make Evvie want to be with me. She opened up to me so fast, but I hardly knew her. Did I mean anything to her, or was I just another guy to keep her warm for a night? She seemed so honest about it, though. I couldn't wait to see her again.

Spider looked over his shoulder at me. "What happened to you, man?"

"What do you mean?"

Spider turned all the way around and faced me. "Back at that truck stop, b'fore that crazy dude picked us up, I told you a lot about what happened to me, 'member?"

I nodded.

"Okay, so what happened to you? You usually act dumber'n dirt, but it seems like you do that 'cause you have no clue about how life works. Why're you like that? All fucked up in a thousand little ways? I mean, me? I'm a colossal fuck-up. But you? You're penny-ante shitty. I want to like you, man, but you are so strange. Somethin' musta happened to you."

I knew what he meant. I didn't understand how other people viewed life. For me, it was just one trial after another. Sometimes I got lucky. Sometimes I got beat up. I didn't seem to have any control over what happened.

"My mother always told me to walk away from trouble. She said that nothing is worth getting violent over. But I've had plenty of people get violent with me. Back in grade school kids were always goading me. There was one time when I didn't know what to do. I had walked out of school. A guy named Nico called me over.

"'Hester,' he had said. 'I need to show you something.'

"I had looked to see if I could get away, but there was no way.

"'Come on,' Nico said. 'I just want to show you something.'

"He was acting friendly. I looked at the two guys standing with him. They were all smiling. I thought, what could go wrong? I walked towards him. As soon as I was within reach, Nico grabbed my left arm and spun me around. The two other guys stepped in front of me.

"'Let's see if your undies are clean Hester,' Nico said, grabbing the waistband of my underpants and jerking them up. Pain shot through my balls as they slammed up between my legs. I was lifted off my feet. They pushed me down. I felt the blacktop scrape my face. They laughed.

"I shouted at them to let me go, they just kept laughing. The thing I most worried about wasn't that it hurt, but if there were other kids still on the playground they would see what was being done to me.

"'Oh no, Hester. I want to see if your mommy put clean undies on you this morning.' Nico continued to pull until the damn things tore loose. He pulled them all the way out of my jeans and waved them over his head. 'Clean Hester. Mommy fixed you up good.' Then he threw them at me. They landed on my head.

"I rolled over and sat up. My nuts were on fire, My face was bleeding from getting scraped. But I looked at those kids as they reached the street and *smiled*. 'Good one guys,' I had said. I hadn't wanted them to see me cry."

Spider shook his head again, picked up a stone and threw it into the lake. "Your mama didn't do you any favors with that non-violent bullshit."

"That happened to me over and over and over. I didn't know how to stop it."

He stood up and stretched. "What was different when you jammed that crazy trucker? You acted. You mighta' saved my life. Why could ya do something then and not when you got pantsed?"

"I didn't have time to think. He looked like he might kill you."

"Didn't nobody ever stand up for you? Your big brother never tried to help? No friends?"

"I stay away from my family as much as possible. My friends were just as likely to jump in to help the bullies. Nobody ever stood up for me."

"What about yourself, then? If nobody's gonna stand up for you, then you gotta do it *yerself*. I'm not sayin' that I've made a lot of bright choices, but at least I can call my mistakes my own. People do *not* get to run my life. You shouldn't let them run yours either. You're the only one you can always count on. You gotta be you're own best friend."

That was a concept that was new to me. Friends with myself? I had to learn to stand up for something. Maybe I should start with myself.

Spider walked toward the bike. "You need ta meet my friends."

Chapter 6

As soon as my ass hit the seat Spider tore out of the parking lot, driving like a maniac.

"Jesus, man. Be careful," I shouted after he swerved from the right lane to the left between a car and a pickup.

He raised his middle finger in reply.

"Seriously," I shouted. "I want to live long enough to meet your friends."

Spider twisted the throttle, and the bike roared to within inches of a station wagon, then he piled on the brakes, threw his head back and laughed. "Style, pussy boy. This tired old town needs more style, and I gotta bring it."

What the hell was he talking about? I gripped the fender harder, hoping I could hang on long enough to make it to wherever we were going.

My hands ached as we pulled into the driveway of a two-story clapboard house. The front yard was oil-soaked dirt. Three Harleys in various states of disrepair sagged in the rutted mess.

Spider shut off his engine. The leftover silence was thick and heavy. Clouds crowded the sky. The air was humid, like paste.

"Where are we?" I asked.

"Cleveland, dumbass."

Spider's talk at the lakefront was nagging at me. This wiseass answer, from my supposed friend, pissed me off. I dropped my pack and said, "You're the dumbass, dumbass. I meant whose house is this. Jeese." I shook my head and turned away.Next thing I knew, I was looking up from the ground, my head ringing from slamming into the sidewalk.

"Nobody calls me dumbass, dumbass." Spider's fists were clenched at his sides. He looked ready to drop to his knees and pummel me.

"Jesus, Spider. What's wrong with you?" I rubbed the back of my head, then checked my hand for blood. "Why'd you do that?"

"Apologize for calling me dumbass."

"Okay, I apolo-"

Spider's boot crushed my midsection.

I doubled over into a fetal position in shock and pain. "Stop." I gasped for breath. "Stop." My ribs screamed with each inhale.

"Apologize for getting in the way of my boot."

"What?"

He booted me again, though not as forcefully. "Apologize for taking up space in front of my brothers' house."

This time I didn't speak. I covered my head and rocked on the ground, forced to take shallow breaths.

Spider walked around to where I could see him. "Want me to check on your undies, Hester? See if your mommy dressed you good?"

Cold sweat broke out on my skull.

Spider's boot tapped the ground. "Why're you just layin' there." He kicked a pebble that lay on the sidewalk. "Jesus. Do something."

Nausea crawled through my gut. Shame blossomed behind my eyes. Would I never be free from this? Why was I always looking up at the shoes of my tormentors?

His boot swung back and started toward my side.

"Stop it! Stop," I shouted.

His boot stopped in mid-swing. "Make me, pussy boy. Stand up and make me."

"You're supposed to be my friend. What's wrong with—" The beer from the tavern blew out of my mouth onto his boot.

He stepped back and stomped his foot on the sidewalk. Vomit flew off the toe of his boot. "That all you got?"

My head and ribs still throbbed, but I could breathe with less pain now. Anger pushed against my sense of powerlessness. I was tired of being a victim.

I raised myself into a squat and made a show of brushing off my backside.

Spider stood with his arms crossed over his midsection.

Someone shouted from inside the house, "Hey, that you, Spider?"

He turned.

I launched myself at him with all the force I could summon, ramming my head into his belly, and grabbing him around the midsection.

He stumbled back a step.

I lost my balance as he regained his.

"Why you little bastard," Spider said. He grabbed me by my shoulders and threw me aside like a sack of dog food.

A shirtless guy ran out of the front door of the house and grabbed me around the waist. His stench wrapped around me as strongly as his tattooed arms. In a second he had me in a full nelson.

"Got 'im Spider. Whale away, brother. Kill this scrawny bastard."

I wrestled, trying to break free. The sour stink radiated off him with each jerky movement I made.

Spider took two steps toward me, drew back his fist and feinted an jab to my solar plexus, holding back an inch from impact.

The wind burst out of me. The anticipation was as bad as the punch would have been.

He stepped back. "Aw, let 'im go Horse. Least he stood up this time. I don't think he's ever done that b'fore."

The man unlocked his hands from behind my neck and backed away. He kicked me in the backside causing me to stumble. He and Spider laughed.

I caught my balance, ribs throbbing, head aching.

Spider pulled out a pack of Camels and lit one with his Zippo, then shook another one out and tossed it to the other man. Horse lit up. They both stood smoking, and staring at me.

I began to shake, sucking in huge breaths. I crossed my arms to keep my hands steady. Every breath suggested a broken rib. I needed to get out of there. I stepped toward my pack.

"Where you goin'?" Spider said.

"I'm leaving. I can't figure out the rules here."

Horse stepped in front of me, and with a menaced whisper, "There's no rules here, boy." Then grinning, "You don't mind me callin' you boy, do you?"

I took a step to the right.

Horse blocked me.

I stepped back to the left.

Horse did, too.

I looked at Spider.

He shrugged and jutted his chin in Horse's direction. "Do what ya gotta."

Spider had gone from being my best buddy to beating me up. My chest throbbed with every breath. My stomach ached with hunger. I wanted this over, but the asshole kept getting in my way. One more time I stepped to the side. When Horse blocked me again something in me let loose. A white light flashed from the back of my head into my line of sight, blurring my vision. Indignation overrode the pain and hunger. The single thing that registered was the arrogance of the pissant in front of me.

"I don't care what you call me, but get the fuck out of my way." I jammed my hands into Horse's chest, pushing him backward.

Horse windmilled back, regained his balance and rushed me.

I landed a wild uppercut to his chest.

Horse grunted but didn't stop advancing. "It's on buddy."

I backpedaled a few steps, then swung again, missing him altogether.

Horse tripped on the edge of the sidewalk and fell.

I jumped on top of him, punching his face and head, shouting, "Get out of my way. Get out of my way. Get the fuck out of my way." I swung wildly, slamming him again and again. "Get the fuck out of my way."

Horse scrabbled with his feet. He slipped out from under me and kicked, just missing my chin, jamming into my chest.

Expecting another onslaught, I sat up, sucking in great lungfuls of air.

Horse sat up on his elbows, chest heaving. Spider leaned on a corner of the house with one foot propped on the wall behind him.

I got up, swiveling my head to keep them both in sight. Anger outweighed my fear and confusion. These guys could kiss my ass. I was done with being pushed around.

My pack lay where I'd dropped it. I pulled it towards me, watching Horse and Spider. Neither of them moved. I backed a step away from the house.

"Don't leave now, Nate. I thought we was friends," Spider said.

"Fuck you, Spider. What do you know about friends?" I kept walking backward, pulling my pack along.

Horse sat up and laughed. "Well, he's a lucky sonuvabitch, that's for sure. If I hadn'ta tripped, I'd a killed him."

They both laughed.

"Thought you wanted a ride to the highway," Spider said.

I stared back. I did need a ride, but not from these lowlifes.

"I thought you was listenin' there at the lakefront," he said.

My legs were leaden, but I was determined to leave and turned away. Pain shot through my chest as I lifted the pack, so I let it fall back to the sidewalk.

"You stood up for yourself just now, man. Though, Horse is right. If you wasn't so lucky, he'd a killed ya."

They laughed again and went inside.

I hoisted the pack onto one shoulder. Shooting pain in my ribs caused me to drop it again. My aching head screamed I had to leave. But my injured body said I couldn't. I didn't know where the highway was. Even if I had, I couldn't carry the pack far.

Spider had acted like a friend while we were on the road. As soon as he got back to his own place he turned into a violent asshole. He was unpredictable, but he was my single option. I had to ask for a ride.

I limped to the front door which stood open behind the screen. Odors of spilled beer and stale cigarettes drifted out. I heard voices inside but couldn't see anyone.

I knocked on the screen door. "Hey. Spider."

The voices stopped, then started up again.

I knocked some more and waited a couple of minutes. When no one responded I decided to leave. As I turned to go, rain pelted my head and shoulders. "Oh, shit."

I didn't want to get soaked and have to sit in wet clothes waiting for a ride, so I opened the door and stepped into the dingy living room. The couch and chairs had seen better days. A pool table with a beer light above it stood beyond a plaster arch. Pool cues leaned in the corner. The carpet was grayish. And sticky.

"Drag yourself right on in."

I jerked around to see Spider standing in the hall holding a beer bottle.

I was nervous. They had asked me to stay, but I was in the house uninvited. "It just started pouring. I thought I could wait it out. Would that be okay? I don't want any more problems."

Spider leaned on the wall. "Man, we all don't want problems. But we all got 'em." He looked at the beer he held and called out, "Horse, I need a beer for your buddy."

"Look man, me and him got into it, but just let it go." I was still angry, but the pain was worse. Another go with Horse would be a losing deal. "Give me a ride to the highway."

Spider called over his shoulder, "Horse, he wants a ride to the highway."

"Jee-zus, just let it go, Spider," I said. "That guy said he'd kill me." I took a step toward the door.

Horse walked up behind Spider. "Hey there, hippie-boy. I ain't givin' you a ride anywhere." He put a hand on Spider's shoulder and grinned at me.

All of my adrenaline was gone and with it any arrogance, or even confidence. I edged another step toward the door.

"Where you goin', man," Horse said. "It's rainin'. Tough weather for ridin'."

Spider and Horse looked at each other and burst out laughing.

"Drag that shitty pack in here and close the door before the rain ruins the carpet," Spider said. "You might as well stay a while."

I didn't want to stay. But, my chest ached, my head throbbed and I had nowhere to go. I slammed the door and leaned my pack against the wall.

"C'mon to the kitchen and drink a beer, man," Horse said. "Beer is what makes fightin' both possible and worthwhile." He tipped his head back and downed what was left in the bottle he carried. "Ahh," he said. "Quiets down the pain and makes me want to kick your ass all over again."

Spider pushed me from behind.

Horse faked a jab in my direction. I leaped back. He cackled like a crazy person, then put his arm around me and pulled me into the kitchen. "Welcome to our house, little shithead. Spider told me you saved his ass the other day. Now, we're going to save yours."

The walls and stove wore grease and spatters from long-gone attempts at cooking. Spider and Horse stood with their arms crossed, their muddy jeans matching the kitchen's décor.

"What do you mean, save my ass?" I said, looking from one to the other.

Horse took a chair on the opposite side of the table. "Spider, *pul-lees* get this young man a goddam beer. For some reason he's actin' nervous."

Spider shoved an open beer in front of me. The smell triggered the same spasm that had sent vomit all over his boot a few moments ago. I swallowed back the bile in my throat.

"Drink up, amigo. We're all brothers here." Horse leaned back in his chair and stretched his legs to the side. "'Least most of us."

His was smiling, but his eyes bored into me. "C'mon, man. You need to quench your thirst after all that scufflin' out front." He pushed the beer closer to me.

I took a long swallow.

Horse clapped his hands. "There you go. See? We ain't so bad."

"Yeah, Nate," Spider said. "We're the best friends you'll ever get."

Spider used my name. All he ever called me was dumbass and shithead. Hearing him call me by name was nice, but no one was nice for nothing.

Spider sat up in his chair. "Horse here is our chapter president. Me an' him have been through some shit together. I told him how lethal you was swingin' a truck door, how you knocked that hopped-up trucker on his ass. That's our way. If somebody swings on Horse, they're swinging on me." He paused a minute and leaned toward me. "And that's dangerous," he said, chuckling.

Horse joined in. "When you went off on Spider, well, I had to go after ya, see? We're a family. Better'n family. You could use some o' that from what Spider tells me."

"Family hasn't done much for me, it's true. But, I'm not from here, and I need to be leaving."

Spider pulled out his pack of Camels, shook one out and tossed the rest to Horse. They both lit up, inhaled, flicked ashes and blew smoke rings; silent while they watched me.

I slid back my chair, then started to stand up. As I did, my ribs and stomach screamed in pain. "Awww, shit." I slumped back into the chair.

"Give it a couple days," Horse said. "You prob'ly have a couple bruised ribs. I got in a few fights while I was on I&I during my 'Nam tour. Didn't want to see a doc, man. You only had five days. Didn't want to waste a minute away from the poon tang."

I leaned back in the chair trying to find a position that didn't make me hurt. "I&I? What's that?"

He raised his eyebrows and leered at me. "Intoxication and intercourse."

Pain cut my laugh short. "I&I." I gasped for breath. "That's hilarious." I drained the beer and set the bottle back down. The alcohol dulled the pain and warmed me. Leaving didn't seem so urgent anymore.

Spider got me another beer. This time I didn't let it sit. I tipped it back and drained half the bottle. "I&I. Aye, aye."

Horse grinned and shook his head. "Spoken like a true Marine." He leaned forward with his elbows on the table and frowned at me. "Speakin' of which, hippie-boy, are you a goddam war protester?"

Uh-oh. Horse had been in Vietnam. I wasn't political, but my draft status was 1-A and I didn't want to go. The whole non-violent idea seemed logical and right, especially because getting killed in a jungle halfway around the world scared the shit out of me. But I couldn't admit that. I took another long pull on my beer. "Uh, well..."

Rain beat on the window screens. Horse drummed his fingers on the tabletop. Spider's chair creaked.

"Well, it's all right if you are, man," Horse said. "That fucked up invasion is killin' a lotta good men for no goddam reason."

I let out the breath I had been holding and threw back the rest of my beer.

"I used ta buy all that 'love it or leave it' shit," Spider said. "Wendell dyin', made me think." He hung his head. "Wendell, he's one a' them good men. And he's dead, for no goddam reason."

Horse got up from the table and rubbed the back of his neck. "Well, hang around for a while, man. Life's too short to waste it worryin' about no-count shit." He stepped toward the hallway. "Drink another beer and relax. That highway'll be there t'morrow."

Horse walked out of the kitchen and Spider set another beer in front of me.

"You can crash here for a few days. There ain't no fancy couch like at Evvie's, but it'll keep you outta the rain."

The first two beers had me feeling warm and comfortable. This third one made me feel like everything was right with the world. If I didn't move too much, my ribs didn't hurt too bad. Having a dry place for the night was a good idea. There was nowhere I needed to be. This was like a brotherhood, right? Why not stay?

"My ribs hurt bad when I move," I said. "I suppose I can spend the night here."

"I just said that. Just don't act like no pussy boy." Spider leaned in the doorway. "Horse is bein' extra nice to you."

"Extra nice? He said he woulda killed me if he could have."

"And he coulda." Spider sat down again. "Guys come around here all the time askin' how to join the Hells Angels. Huh! We jump 'em and thump 'em. If you gotta ask, then you don't belong. If they stay anyway, we figure they might be worth keepin'. Most of 'em just ride away."

"So, Horse trying to beat on me was like an initiation?"

Spider grunted. "Initiation. Yeah, I guess so. But most guys he sends to the hospital. Like I said, he's bein' extra nice to you."

Somehow, the idea of being favored by Horse felt good. "Why? Why's he bein' nice?" Before Spider could answer I asked, "Can I have another beer?"

"Get it yerself."

Forgetting the shape of my ribs, I leaned onto the table as I tried to get up. "Owwww, fuck." I slipped back down. Pushing the chair back from the table, I stood up using my legs.

Spider grunted again and shook his head. "You'd best learn how ta move around in pain, man. Life's full o'pain."

I grabbed another bottle and hobbled back to the table. "I'm gettin' used to it, though the beer's makin' me a little sleepy." I sat back down, gingerly.

Spider narrowed his eyes and studied me for a minute. "I got somethin' for that."

"For what?"

He pulled a pill bottle out of his pocket and shook it. "You're hurtin', so I'll let you in on this. But don't expect me ta give you these all 'a time."

"What're those?"

Spider rolled his eyes. "Aspirins." He reached across and rolled four little white pills onto the table. "These'll help some."

"They're small for aspirin," I said.

"Just take 'em, goddamit."

I scooped the tablets up and washed them down with a swallow of beer. "I just never saw aspirins that were so small," I said. "Jeese."

He hooked one arm over the back of his chair and regarded me from the corner of his eye. "You are shittin' me, right?"

"About what?"

"About them pills."

"What about 'em?"

Spider faced front again and leaned his elbows on the table. "So, I'm guessin' you've never done any drugs…of any kind."

I considered Spider's bemused expression. "I've tried marijuana a couple times. Made me sleepy, so I wasn't too wild about it. Why?"

Spider eyed me. The edge of a grin formed on his lips. "Oh, nothin'. Those weren't aspirin, though. You ain't gonna get sleepy for a while."

My stomach sunk. "Did you give me drugs? What's gonna happen to me? How long will this last? Am I gonna get addicted?" Every public service poster, TV commercial and magazine ad I had ever seen flashed before me. Sickness, injury, insanity, death. Drugs were evil and dangerous. And now I was a user. "What about your first rule? You told me drugs were for chumps."

Spider laughed. "Easy, man. Who's been plantin' nonsense in your head? I been doin' drugs since I was ten years old. What I meant was don't let yourself get too hooked. Ever'body needs a little boost now an' then."

He sat back again and relaxed. "Shit, that beer you've been pourin' down's as good a drug as any."

"But it's legal."

"Big fuckin' deal. So's them pills you just took. Least as long as some pinhead doctor prescribes 'em."

We sat for a while, not talking. A few guys came to get beer, but none of them spoke to me.

After about fifteen minutes Spider asked, "How're you feelin'?"

Though my ribs still hurt, I felt powerful, energized. I no longer cared what Spider or anyone else in this shitty house thought. "What's it to you?"

"Ooh, you're feeling better now," Spider said. "So, here's the deal. I gave you some bennies to help you feel better while your ribs heal. But if you injure 'em again, it'll only get worse. You'll have a lot a energy for a few hours. Have another beer or two or three to even out your excitement. I got somethin' I need your help with later on." He stood. "I'm gonna run an errand. Stay here and try to keep your mouth shut."

A moment later the screen door slammed, and a bike roared to life in front of the house.

I ached when I moved, though the pain wasn't localized anymore. Alertness, clarity, determination circulated through me. Spider needed my help in a few hours? No problem. Stay and be a part of the brotherhood? Got it. Drink more beer? Oh hell yeah. Take more shit from Spider? Well, he had given me these wonderful pills, and things were getting better by the minute. So, sure, I could put up with him, too.

Motorcycles roared into the yard. The noise level in the house rose as the place filled up. Guys came and went through the kitchen to the back door. Women with big, black, frizzy hair and eyes circled with smudgy black eyeliner wandered by. Most of them ignored me, but one stopped and stared. Her tongue circled her lips slowly until the guy she was with slapped her and pulled her away.

"Watch yerself, dickhead," he said to me.

I started to rise up and answer him, but my ribs still hurt too much, and I sat back down. "I'm watchin'," I said.

The woman chuckled.

"What's funny, bitch?" the man said, dragging her toward the back door.

Smoke wafted through an open window. The smell of roasting meat filled the kitchen. Plates of sausages and ribs were carried past.

Horse walked through and pointed at me. "This here's a hang-around. Make sure ya treat him well."

Everyone in the kitchen snickered. One of them made kissing sounds. "Can't wait to taste you, pretty boy," he said. Then everyone carried on getting food, ignoring me.

My head began to droop. All I could think of was sleep. During a lull in the parade through the kitchen, I wandered upstairs, found an empty room, and passed out on the floor.

•   •   •   •   •

The clack of billiard balls and the curse accompanying a missed shot woke me from a sound sleep. The odor of dust and neglect stirred when I moved my head to the side. I was on old carpet. No light came through the window on the opposite wall. The house was quieter than before.

My midsection throbbed as I sat up. I could see my pack leaning on the wall. I shut my eyes and tried to remember where I was, what day it was. Parts of memories crawled through the molasses in my brain. Spider brought me here. Then he stomped me. Then he fed me beer. And aspirins. But the aspirins weren't aspirins. And I felt real good. For a while. I couldn't leave, and now I didn't want to. This would have to be home, at least for a while.

A loud slap echoed off the sheetrock. The door flew open and slammed against the wall. A small woman fell through the doorway, landing hard on the carpet.

"Get your skinny ass in there."

"Aww, not here, ba-bee. You said we could go."

A short man in a leather jacket leaned on the door jamb. "I said get your ass in there."

I wrestled myself to a standing position, aching with every movement. "Who're you?"

The man's head jerked up. "Huh?" He tried to stand taller, but wobbled and fell onto the door casing. "Who're you?"

Chapter 7

"Let's just go ba-bee." The woman struggled to her knees. "There's lotsa things I wanna do for you, sweetie."

The man took a step into the room and backhanded the woman.

"Oww, aww...stop it ba-bee." She rubbed the side of her face. Why're you hurtin' me?"

"Whad'd you say?" He reached back as if winding up for a pitch.

I grabbed his arm and pushed him out of the door. His feet tangled up, and he slammed face-first into the wall opposite.

I turned to help the woman off the carpet and walked straight into her fist.

"Oww. Damn!" I said.

"Back off my man, you bastard." She pushed by me and started stroking the arm of her attacker. "Are you all right, ba-bee? You want me to kick his ass, ba-bee?"

The man turned around, still leaning on the wall. He jammed his finger toward me. "You be careful, man. You're fuckin' with the wrong hombre." He grabbed the sleeve of the woman's jacket and pulled her down the hall. "C'mon, bitch. We're gettin' outta here."

I watched as they lurched down the stairs, the woman rubbing the man's arm and cooing "ba-bee, ba-bee." Near the bottom of the steps, he pushed her away. "Get offa me, woman. Goddam."

The beer and bennies were gone, leaving headache and nausea. Voices and the click of pool balls drifted up the stairs. Occasionally a laugh cackled above the conversation. Most of the crowd from earlier must have left.

I bent over carefully. Pain was everywhere, but not the sharp pain of earlier. I felt stiff, my movement was restricted. If I could get Spider to spot me some more of the little white pills, I'd be all right.

Feeling every step, I crept down the stairs, minimizing the movement. At the bottom, I heard, "...lose 10,000 bennies, man. He's gotta be scramblin' even if it was an independent deal."

"Aw, that lucky sumbitch always lands on his feet."

I could see into the room with the pool table. Three guys in t-shirts and Hells Angels colors held pool cues.

"Oh, he's scrambling, all right," said a tall, blond-headed guy. He lined up his shot and fired the three ball into the corner pocket. "He's working on it as we speak, I think."

The guy that had referred to a "lucky sumbitch" looked my way. He had a big nose and a black eye. "Hey, the hang-around woke up."

The other men looked at me and chuckled.

"Spider's partner in crime," Black-eye said. "Well, let's hope you ain't changed his luck. He's gonna need alla the good luck he can get."

Spider had lost some pills and Horse referred to me earlier as a hang-around, but I didn't know why I was Spider's partner or what I was hanging around for.

"Join us and play pool, rookie," the blonde man said. "I'm Dieter. The talkative one is Rumble, mostly for the sound his ass makes, not his fighting ability." He pointed to the third man. "That's Bobby."

Bobby nodded at me.

"Hope yer ready, fella." Rumble held out his hand. "We love new members, but we like ta make sure their good material."

I reached my hand out.

He grabbed it and pulled me toward himself.

I stumbled.

"Just testin' yer balance. Cuz most of us here're a little off." He cackled at his joke.

I hugged my ribs, aching from the sudden movement.

Spider and Horse walked in the front door carrying a case of beer. "Hey, hang-around. Come put this beer in the fridge," Horse said.

"But don't drink any," Spider added. "You got work to do."

I took the beer into the kitchen, then came back to the front room and sat down. "Work?" I asked.

"Well, yeah. What'd ya think? You could just stay here fer free?" Spider scowled at me.

"Damn, man. I just woke up," I said. "What time is it? Can't this wait 'til tomorrow?"

"'Member the pills them dickheads stole from me?"

I nodded, then regretted having moved my head.

"Well, I needta replace 'em. And you're gonna help. You don't mind helpin' me out do ya?"

What was he asking me to do? I didn't want to get arrested. "I'll help, but I don't want to get into any trouble."

"Trouble? Naw. You'll be aidin' a friend who'll be helpin' a lotta folks feel better. It's like charity work."

Everything in me hurt, and Spider wasn't making any sense. "Suppose you could give me a few more of those aspirins?"

Spider pulled the pill bottle out of his jeans, shook out some pills, and handed them to me. "Now, let's go."

•　　　•　　　•　　　•　　　•

Outside the rain had stopped but the air was still heavy with humidity.

"So, you kin ride, right?" Spider asked.

I stared at the white Harley "Police Special" parked in the dirt outside the front door. "Yeah," I said. "I had a Honda 90 for the last two years."

"Well, this is a whole lot different. I guess there's nothin' easy with you." Spider climbed onto the bike and raised it off the kickstand. He twisted the left handgrip. "This's the spark advance. The other side is the throttle. Your left foot is the clutch. Once ya get it runnin', do not take yer foot off this clutch 'til you're ready to go." He tapped the lever on the left side of the gas tank. "This model has a shift lever, so even dumbasses like you can tell what gear you're in. So, turn the spark advance, stand up on the starter pedal and turn the throttle when you come down. Got it?"

He leaned the massive Police Special over onto the kickstand and climbed off. He mounted his Sportster and kicked it to life. The bike roared as he revved the engine. Each time he eased off the throttle backfires popped like gunshots. "Git on that hog and follow me."

"I need the key," I said.

Spider pointed to a tangle of wires just below the gas tank. "Wind them together and kick it. We gotta go." He revved the Sportster's engine again.

A spark leapt across the gap just before I wound the wires together. I stood up on the bike which was still resting on its kickstand. I rose up on my toes and shifted most of my weight to my right foot, pushing down the starter pedal as hard as I could.

Bl-bl-bl. The bike hadn't started.

"Twist the spark advance, shithead," Spider said.

"The what?"

"Yer left hand. C'mon, man. I just showed ya."

Even with the bike on its kickstand, I didn't think I could control it. My head was clearing, but I wasn't feeling strong, just irritated. "I'm still hurtin', man. I can't start this thing."

"Quit yer bitchin'." Spider's scowl made plain his irritation. "We gotta go."

The bike still rested on its kickstand. I sat astride it and folded my arms.

Spider slammed his hands into the handlebars of his bike and stared straight ahead. "I'm almost done with you, man. I've been tryin' to help you, but you're such a fuckup."

"Fuckup? What're you talking about?" I rose up on the foot pegs. "What have I fucked up? I didn't lose them pills. Quit bitchin' at me, just because you're mad at yourself."

Spider shoved the kickstand on his bike back down and dismounted.

I jumped off the other side of my bike and backed up a few steps wishing I kept my mouth shut.

Spider walked around the Police Special, reached across the tank, twisted the left-hand grip, stepped onto the starter pedal and brought his weight down hard. The motorcycle spat once. He jumped on the starter again. The motor caught and the bike settled into a steady chug. He goosed the throttle a couple of times, then walked back to his own ride.

"Let's go, man," he said, getting back on his bike. "We got people to meet." He kicked the bike into gear and pulled off to the street where he waited for me to follow.

I swung my leg over the Harley and raised the kickstand. My hands shook as I grabbed the handlebars. I stepped on the clutch, pulled the shift lever into first gear, twisted the throttle and let the clutch back out. The bike responded with a jerk, but I was moving.

Spider took off.

As long as I kept moving, the power of the bike transferred into me. Balance wasn't a problem. I shifted into second and cranked the throttle. The engine blatted as power rushed to the rear wheel. The Honda had never felt like this.

In front of me, Spider kept accelerating, and I was determined to keep pace. I jammed the shifter into third and turned the accelerator to the pin. The old Police Special's motor was half-again as big as Spider's Sportster. The engine thundered as the gap between the two bikes closed. I kept the gas on until I was alongside Spider. "Goddam! Goddam!" I hollered. "This is the shit, man. This is fuckin' style."

Spider glared at me like I was a bad odor, then his cycle howled as he pulled ahead.

I kept pace behind him, high on the amphetamines and drunk on the sensation of power. The wind, the noise, the vibration were hypnotic, excluding everything that wasn't there and then. I was helping a drug dealer I had just met to replace 10,000 hits of amphetamine. What would my mother think of me now? I didn't care. The police? Well, what was the worst they could do? Was I going to Hell? Fuck that notion. Life was exciting for the first time. I was riding with the Hells Angels and duty-bound to help my new-found brother. I wanted to make Spider proud.

We rode across the Cuyahoga River, turning off onto a road accessing the riverfront. The big Police Special was a handful on the loose gravel, but I managed to let gravity take the bike down the steep slope to the river's edge. We pulled into a narrow space between the riverbank and the concrete support of the bridge we just crossed.

The space was dark and smelled of piss and shit left behind by drunks and junkies who had nowhere else to do what they had to do. Spider killed his engine and got off his bike. I pulled the wires apart, stopping mine. I lowered my kickstand, knocking a broken bottle into the river. After the splash settled, the 2 A.M. hush of the city descended on us.

"Think you can get that bike started again?" Spider asked.

"Wires together, spark advance, throttle, kick. Yeah, I got it." Spider's condescension rankled me. "Why're you raggin' on me?" My hands and arms still resonated from the vibrations of the Harley's engine. The aspirins had kicked in. I was ready for whatever might happen.

He looked left and right then left again. "You gotta start it is all I'm sayin'. We're waitin' on some folks that you're gonna meet with. Then you're gonna carry the box they give ya back to the house."

"Folks that I'm meeting with?"

"Yeah." Spider raised the palms of his hands. "That's why you're here, right?"

"I'm here to help, not to do some drug deal on my own. What the hell are you thinkin'?"

"Don't worry. Nothin' can go wrong. I've done this a hunnert times."

"Okay. Then you do it. Or, I want a piece."

His eyes were hidden in the murky light. He stepped toward me, fists at his sides. "You want a piece?" Leaning into my face, he whispered, "Sure, buddy. Pull this off, and I'll see you get a piece."

Spider straightened up, stepped back and relaxed his fists. "Here's what's going to happen. Do not fuck this up."

Chapter 8

The way Spider laid things out left a lot of holes. Two men would arrive on foot, carrying a box. They were supposed to open the box and hand me a bottle from it. The label was supposed to match the one Spider kept his bennies in. If they matched, I was to take the box, get on my bike and take it back to the house.

Spider had been gone for what seemed like an hour. With nothing to do and a full load of amphetamine in me, anxiety was rising. The Cuyahoga River smell mixing with the ammonia stench of urine added disgust to my anxiety. I paced the shadowy area, kicking at rocks, bottles, broken syringes. Who would come here on their own? It was pathetic. Fucking Spider. Where the hell was he?

Rock skittered down the embankment. I held still. Hot wind blew off the river as I looked for the source of the noise. A bead of perspiration dripped down my spine.

A small avalanche of gravel broke loose as a skinny guy wearing white Levi's slid into view.

I was covered in a cold sweat. "About time," I said. "What took so long?" My eyes were darting from the man to the river to the open space behind him. I was terrified, but punched one fist into the other trying to look tough.

Gravel crunched as another man carrying a cardboard box made his way down the hill. His surfer-blond hair was shaggy, but not long like the first man's.

"Whoa, man. Easy," he said. "I sorta slipped up. Er, down, I guess. We're here, right? This here's my good buddy, Chad, and he's got the goods to make you glad. Right, Chad?"

"Shut up, Brian," Chad said.

Brian's teeth reflected white, even in the shadows of this stinking spit of land. He moved easily. The spot under the bridge was disgusting, making Brian's fresh-scrubbed appearance ridiculous. But something else about him bothered me.

"Just bring me the box."

"No problem amigo," Brian said. "Show me the cash, and we'll be on our way."

His voice seemed familiar, but all I could think of was, what now? "That's between you and my partner." Spider left me alone to do this deal, and I wasn't leaving without the box.

"See Brian," Chad said. "I told you this was a bullshit deal."

"Easy, brother," Brian said. "We'll work this whole thing out." He bent over and picked up a stone the size of a large apple and hefted it in his hands. "I mean, we're all friends here, right Mr.... I didn't get your name."

Chad took a couple steps, moving behind me.

I glanced over my shoulder, keeping him in view.

Brian stepped closer to me. "Your name. I asked your name." He wasn't smiling anymore as he fondled the rock. He stopped. "Oh, wait. You're the other dude from New York."

The amphetamines were peaking. The river smelled worse than before. The hush of the city in the distance throbbed. What little light penetrated the shadows was magnified in my mind. I looked closely at Brian. "Oh, shit. You're the motherfucking driver."

I could see Brian nod his head toward Chad. I heard the box land with a thud and the sucking of the mud when Chad shifted his weight.

I clasped my hands together and swung to my left, twisting from my torso, connecting with Chad's head and knocking him on his side.

Brian flung the rock, but he was too close. It glanced off my shoulder.

I charged at Brian, head down, smashing into his midsection, forcing an audible gasp from him. I kept pumping with my legs, forcing him backward until he slammed into the concrete bridge support. His head snapped against the concrete with a crack. I stepped back, and he crumpled to the ground.

I stared at him, expecting him to get up. From behind, Chad grabbed me around the neck and threw me onto the mud. My bruised ribs deflated and I sucked for air.

Chad grabbed a rock and raised it above my head. I covered my face, expecting the rock to slam into me. Instead, Chad cried out, "Aw, no." He fell to the side.

I saw a flash of metal and Dieter bending over Chad, smiling and wiping the blade of a knife on Chad's shirt.

"Are we paid up now, asshole?" he said to Chad's writhing form.

Brian was still knocked out. Spider stared at him. "This guy. I fuckin' know this guy. This is the dickhead that was drivin' that car last week."

Spider kicked him in the ribs.

"Uuhhn" leaked out of Brian, then he rolled on his back.

"How'd you get here?" I asked Spider.

He ignored me. He kicked Brian again. "You just had the worst luck of your life, Mr. Shiny Car, Mr. Smooth Mickey man. You worthless piece of shit. Yer dead motherfucker. You are dead."

"Chill, man," I said. "We got other problems right now."

Spider looked at me like he had forgotten I was there.

Chad was dazed, holding his hand to his face. Blood dripped through his fingers.

I looked at Dieter. "Is he gonna die?"

Dieter shook his head. "Oh no. I just cut his cheek from his mouth to his ear." He smiled and rubbed his own cheek. "Some ladies think scars are sexy. But this guy is so ugly, I don't think it will help him."

"Where'd you guys come from? I thought I was supposed to get the box and leave."

"We were never far. See, Spider needed the bennies but didn't have the funds. I needed some funds myself so we partnered up. We never planned to make payment to these clueless rookies."

I staggered back a step. "Why involve me? You put me in the middle of a fuckin' scam that could have gotten me killed."

Dieter laughed. "Oh my little friend, you are so dramatic. Spider said you needed some experience. Well, *this* is experience. See how it worked out? Hells Angels two, stupid rookie drug dealers, zero. What could be better? Oh, and we have the drugs. It's the very best we could hope for."

"I could have died, goddamit. It was me them guys attacked. Not you. Not Spider."

Spider walked over at the mention of his name. "What're you bitchin' about now? Jesus, you'd think we'd a left ya to die."

"You told me I'd get the drugs and ride away. You never said—"

"You got the fuckin' drugs and you're about to ride away. Just like I said."

Spider was staring at Brian, shifting his weight from foot to foot.

"The hang-around is leaving?" Dieter said. "Wouldn't he be the perfect one to weigh down the bodies, so they sink when we throw them in the river?"

Spider looked at him but didn't speak.

Dieter was smiling now. "Or perhaps he could cut them up and leave the pieces for the wild dogs that will soon be attracted to the smell of blood."

"This isn't funny," I said. "We need to get out of here before the cops come or someone else finds us out."

"You know, he is right." Dieter put his knife into its sheath. We need to be moving along."

Brian sat with his back against the concrete wall. His head hung, his elbows rested on his knees.

"You messed up, man," Spider said. "You ripped off a Hells Angel. No one lives through that, you know."

Brian shook his head, then looked up at Spider. "Yeah, that was some ugly bad luck. But look, it wasn't personal. You didn't have your colors. How was I supposed to know?" Brian hung his head again.

Spider stared at Brian for another minute, then sighed, picked up a rock and threw it into the river. "God, I'm tired. I wanna kill ya and get it over with, but I'm so goddam tired."

Brian looked up. "Well, hey. Then we're on the same page, see. I don't want to die, and I think I can help you out with your distribution problems."

Spider scowled. "Shut up. I don't have distribution problems. I got 10,000 bennies and you just have a death wish. Quit talkin' through yer ass."

"Look, we have something you need."

Spider kicked him in the thigh. "You don't seem to understand the shit you're in."

Chad sat up, holding his cheek together. "We may have something you want."

Everyone turned to look at him. The bleeding had slowed, though he was covered in blood from his forehead to his lap.

Dieter said, "What could two dead men have that we would want?"

"A steady supply of pharmaceutical grade drugs. Benzedrine, Dexadrine, Librium, morphine. Brian only stole your drugs 'cause he's a worthless piece of shit who thinks life is a joke."

"Shut up, Chad. You don't seem to mind the stuff I supply you with," Brian said.

"Will you two pecker heads stop this constant yammerin'?" Spider said. "Goddam! My head hurts."

I'd never heard a conversation like this. I'd never seen anyone so close to committing murder. I'd never heard criminal activity discussed like plans for a party. I was scared, and the bennies were wearing off. I wanted to leave. "Spider, let's get out of here. There's a pile of problems sitting at our feet. Let's go."

Spider looked at Dieter, then said to Chad, "You two have a car close?"

Chad said, "Up on the street."

"Here's the deal." Spider pulled a small, black revolver from the back of his waistband. "Nate is gonna ride his bike up and park behind you. Dieter and me are gonna get our rides. Do not stop unless we do. Do not pass us, or turn, or drive too close to us. Yer dead men right now. You need to walk real careful. When we get to where we're headed, you better have a plan that's worth hearin', or you'll be right back here at the river, only in pieces."

Chad struggled to his feet and stood, wavering. Brian got up and walked up the rocky embankment without looking at his supposed friend. Chad headed up, followed by Spider and Dieter.

"Tie that box to the hog, Nate," Spider said. "Then fire it up and park behind these assholes. We'll be there in a couple minutes."

The box of drugs was about the size of a rectangular watermelon and weighed about the same. I set it on the Harley's rear fender and strapped it on with rubber tie-downs.

Wires, spark, throttle, kick. I stood up on the kick starter and jumped hard on that pedal. The bike caught on the first try, and my mood soared.

Feeling the bike's power brought back the thrill I felt earlier. The fatigue that had begun to settle on me flew off as I eased the clutch up and the bike moved up the rocky path.

Brian and Chad walked to a new Corvette parked on the street. I idled the Harley behind them until they reached the car. Brian climbed behind the wheel. Chad moved carefully, holding his face as he got into the passenger side

I heard their bikes before seeing where Spider and Dieter came from. They motored up side-by-side. Spider pulled in next to me, and Dieter pulled ahead of the Corvette.

As soon as Dieter was in place, Spider called out, "Hey, look back here."

Brian's head stuck out the driver's window.

Spider held up his pistol, not aiming it, just showing it. "Follow that guy. Got it?"

Brian nodded.

Dieter pulled away from the curb, and the 'Vette followed. Spider and I trailed them to the Hellhouse. Spider pulled alongside the car. "Back it in the driveway. Turn it off and gimme the keys. Don't get out. Neither of ya. If you can follow directions good, ya' might be around for breakfast."

Chapter 9

Spider asked Dieter to watch the boys while he went inside. "Hang-around, you come with me."

I didn't like being called "hang-around," like I was something less than everyone else. It reminded me of those schoolyard bullies calling me "pussy" or "wuss." I loved that feeling of invincibility the amphetamines gave me. In all my life I'd never known such feeling. But at this moment I could barely keep my eyes open. I just wanted everyone to leave me alone, so I followed Spider into the house, aiming to find my way back to the bedroom upstairs.

Horse was sitting in an easy chair in the living room, his leg bouncing like a jack-hammer. When we walked in he stood and paced back and forth. "What happened? You get the drugs? You get rid of them sorry amateurs?"

"Better," Spider said.

"Better? You got drugs and money? Hand it over man. We got bills to pay here. Hand it over."

Spider rubbed his chin and watched Horse's nervous movement. "How 'bout the hang-around gets you a beer and we talk about it?" He motioned toward the kitchen with his head.

I didn't move. I was thinking about that bedroom and sleep.

"Move, goddammit," Spider said. "Get Horse a beer. And get me one. Now!"

I got the beers and handed them to Spider who in turn gave one to Horse who was still pacing back and forth. I sat down on the floor and leaned against the wall. "Relax, man," Spider said to Horse. "You're a little fired up."

Horse stopped and stared at Spider. His jaw clamped, and he squeezed his lips together.

"Easy, Horse. I'm yer buddy. I'm here to help ya, man."

Horse rubbed his face with his free hand. The tension in his face eased, and he sat back down in the easy chair. His leg was still jumping. "Watcha got, amigo? Better be somthin' good."

"Yeah, I think," Spider said. "They showed up with the box of drugs."

"So, you got 'em."

"Yeah."

"Where'd you lose the bodies?"

"Well, that's what I was sayin' was better. We got 'em outside."

"What? Jesus Christ, you brought 'em here? Are you whacked out, man? Are you trippin'? You can't bury 'em here. What the hell is wrong with you?"

Spider pulled a folding chair close to where Horse sat. "Naw, man. Not bodies. We got them guys outside, still breathin'. They say they got a line to a reg'lar highway of top-shelf drugs, man. No Mexican shit. Not counterfeit. The real deal from the real makers. You know, the stuff we could get top dollar for."

Horse's leg stopped moving. He sat back in his chair, drained his beer then rubbed his chin, looking past Spider. "Hmm."

Spider sat back also and drained his beer. He waved the empty bottle at me.

I brought two beers and handed them to Spider. "I'm going to sleep," I said.

"Oh no yer not," Spider answered. "We're not near done."

My head was swimming. My eyelids felt like sandpaper against my eyeballs and too heavy to keep open. "I can't keep going. I feel like I'm gonna drop right here."

Spider held my gaze for a moment, then reached into his pocket. "Well, you got to keep goin'." He threw me the bottle of amphetamines. "Take four o'these. Don't drink any beer. You'll be okay in a while."

I shook four pills into my hand and threw them into my mouth. While I swallowed, I shook a few more pills into my hand.

"Oh no. Put them goddam pills back. I'll give 'em to ya when ya need 'em. Don't be a piggy."

I held onto them and looked at Spider. "I'm gonna need 'em if I gotta work, right? Can't expect me to work all night on nothin'"

Spider grunted. "Okay, dumbass. Keep 'em. That's the cut you wanted from the deal you worked on. Enjoy 'em, but go slow."

I counted on the pills fixing me. No need to go slow. "What do we need to do?"

"Them guys outside need babysittin' while we figure out what we're gonna do with 'em. Go tell Dieter to get his ass in here. You watch 'em for a while."

"You can't leave me alone with those guys. What if they try to leave?"

"Well, then you'll just have to shoot 'em," Spider replied.

"I can't shoot 'em." Cold sweat spread across my forehead. "I don't have a gun."

Spider reached behind his back. The pistol looked like a tarantula in his hand. "Take this," he said, holding the gun butt-first toward me.

I took another step back. I'd never fired a gun before and didn't want to. "I don't know how to shoot."

"'Bout time you learned then," Horse said. "If they try to move at all, shoot 'em in the fuckin' head. Now get outta here."

Spider stood and handed me the pistol. "It's simple." He pointed to the barrel. "Make sure this end is pointin' away from you before you pull the trigger."

I took the gun. It didn't weight much and was smaller than the six-shooters the cowboys had on TV. The amphetamines were beginning to kick in, and I didn't like how I was being pushed around. "How's this little shit gun supposed to do anything? I need a decent gun if I'm supposed to guard them by myself."

Spider snatched the gun from me and jammed it into my belly. "Look shit head, you need to get your ass out there and watch them guys. If you don't wanna do that, I'll shoot you in the gut right now and let you bleed to death on the carpet. Waddya say badass? You wanna be a guard or a corpse?"

"Jesus Christ. Jesus Christ. Gimme the gun. Yeah, sure, of course. I'll get Dieter."

"This here gun will do just fine, right?" Spider pushed me back and looked hard at me. "You're in the big leagues now, dumbass. We ain't playin'. I'm gonna give you this gun. If you make a move to aim it at me, I will break your fuckin' arm. Understand?"

"Ye-Yes?"

Spider handed me the pistol. "You're hangin' with the Hells Angels now man. You've been accepted as a hang-around. You gotta do what it takes from here on out. No more shit from you."

"O-okay. No more shit from me." I shoved the gun into the back of my jeans and walked out. I had almost peed my pants when Spider threatened me with the gun. Now I felt like a badass. Let those bullying pricks from middle school try me now. I'll kick their ass and steal their women.

Outside the air was even more sodden than in the house. As the pills ramped up, more and more sweat leaked from my pores. I was soaked from head to foot.

The windows were rolled down on the Corvette. Brian was in the driver's seat looking sleepy. Chad sat upright, his hands still pressed to his cheek.

Dieter leaned on the Police Special. "They sent the hang-around."

"You're supposed to go inside," I replied. "What're those guys doing?"

"Hoping they get to live another day." He looked at the car. "Aren't you boys?"

Brian sat up. "When you hear my offer this'll all be straightened out."

Dieter shook his head, tossed me the 'Vette's key and headed into the house.

Brian's gaze followed Dieter. As soon as the screen door slammed he said, "You and the other guy are partners now, huh?"

I stared at him.

"A guy like him acts like he's doing you favors, but really, he's setting you up to do his dirty work."

"Shut up. You're the one in deep shit."

"I knew the minute I saw you sitting by the road you were ready for somebody to own you."

Chad elbowed Brian. "Shut up, man. These guys aren't going to fall for your BS. We're in serious trouble here. Your daddy won't be able to extract you from this. He'll only be able to claim your body."

Brian reached behind himself and pushed Chad away, never taking his eyes off me. "Never mind him." He smiled. "You and me? Pretty soon we'll be partners. I can help you out more than the other guy. What do you say? Work with me."

My brain was on fire with amphetamine, heat and humidity. The streetlight in front of the house had been shot out, and I was glad. The light from the one further down the street made my eyes ache. Even the gray shadows had sharp edges as the bennies flooded my brain. Brian's chatter made me want to slug him.

"I don't know what you're talking about, man," I said. "Just shut up."

"Now that's no way to treat a business partner. You and the other guy are partners, and he and I are about to become partners. You and I need to get along."

"You ripped Spider off, man. You're gonna pay for that."

"I told you, Brian." Chad said. "These guys aren't playing around."

Brian kept his gaze my way. "Hey, hanger. I need to take a leak. So, I'm going to get out of the car for a minute. Okay?"

His words hit my ears like relentless BB's. Each word stung just a little, until my anger was too much to ignore. "Hanger? Did you call me hanger?" The vivid contrasts of the shadows melded into a curtain of black.

When my vision returned Brian had one foot out of the car door. I took two steps, raised my right leg and kicked the car door, scissoring Brian's leg in the gap between door and frame. "Hanger? Who are you talking to, you sorry piece of shit?"

"Damn, watch it." Brian tried to pull his leg back into the car. I grabbed the door and slammed it into his leg again.

"Ow, fuck!"

I slammed the door into his leg again. "Who's a hanger?"

"Shit! Fuck! You're hurting me." He pulled his leg back into the car. "Goddam. You're *already* doing the dirty work for those guys. You're pathetic."

My vision went black again for a moment. "You called me pathetic? I'll show you who's pathetic. Take this motherfucker. I'll kill you, you worthless—"

"Nate, let him go. Nate!"

My vision returned as I was pulled off Brian. Spider's pistol was in my left hand. Brian's face was scraped raw and bleeding. At least he wasn't talking anymore.

"Get a grip on yourself, man. Don't let 'em get in yer head. I'm takin' over."

Spider leaned on the door and looked in at Brian. "Does your face hurt?"

"Of course it hurts," Brian said. "Look at what he did to me. He's psycho."

"How 'bout yer leg? Does that hurt, too?"

"That crazy asshole slammed it with the car door. Yes, it hurts."

"Brian is it?" Spider said.

"That's my name."

"Well Brian…" Spider straightened up and opened the car door. "Step out of the car."

Brian put his left leg out.

Spider pulled the door all the way opened and then slammed it into Brian's leg.

"Fuuuck! Stop! God, it hurts. I think it's broken."

Spider still held the door. "Put yer leg back in."

Brian moaned as he hoisted his leg into the car with both hands.

Spider closed the door then sat on his haunches with his arms on the top of the door. "Man, yer fancy car smells like piss. How's it feel to pee yer pants, fancy-ass?"

Brian sat immobile, staring out the windshield.

"Not so great to be in the spot yer in is it? I don't know what you did to tick off my soon-to-be Hells Angel brother, but it was a mistake." Spider stood. "You mess with Nate, you mess with me."

Brian drew a ragged breath. "I can get money. I can get drugs, good drugs. Don't hurt me anymore."

Spider stepped back. I leaned on the parked Harley, the gun still in my hand.

"What about yer partner, there. What's he got for us?"

"Chad? Never mind Chad. He's just along for the ride."

"What?" Chad said.

A smile crossed Brian's lips. "Never mind him. I'm the one with the connections."

Chad punched Brian's arm. "What a douche, man."

Spider leaned onto the car door. "So, yer friend is no good to me?"

Brian shook his head. "He's nobody."

Spider straightened up and started to turn away from the car, then wheeled around and backhanded Brian's face.

Blood erupted from his nose. "Awww..."

"Your friend, who came with ya, to back ya up, is now nobody?"

Brian didn't move.

"Nate, come 'ere."

I stepped up next to Spider. Everything was sharp and crisp, even in the dense humidity. I was on the winning side, and it felt terrific. "Yeah?" I said.

"Shoot him."

Chapter 10

I looked at the gun, then at Spider, then at Brian.

"Shoot him, man," Spider said. "You can't deal with a guy that'd sell out his partner. This asshole needs to die."

I raised the gun and pointed it toward Brian's chest. My hand was shaking. The angry adrenaline had been diluted. I wanted Spider to know I was Hells Angel material but I didn't want to kill anyone.

"Don shoo me. Pleah, don shoo me." Tears cut tracks through the bloody mess that was Brian's face. "I don wanna die. Don shoo me."

"He's a dead man, no matter what, Nate. We can't let him survive with what he done to us. Get it over with."

"Hold on, hold on, hold on," Chad said from the passenger seat. "If you fire that gun somebody'll call the cops."

"I give a fuck," Spider said.

"Look man, hear us out. Maybe we can help you."

I leaned in to hear Chad better. Brian grabbed the barrel of the pistol. I pulled my arm back.

I heard a pop and the gun jerked in my hand. Brian's eyes got wide. His lips moved soundlessly as he stared at me. Blood trickled from a small hole in his forehead. Then his chin hit his chest, and his shoulders slumped forward.I looked at Spider. "I shot him. I shot him." My legs folded underneath me. I sat cross-legged on the ground staring at the pistol in my hand. The sweat on my forehead froze into crystals.

Chad opened the passenger door and climbed out of the Corvette. "Oh shit. Oh, shit," he said to no one in particular. Even in the darkness, his face was ghostly white. "I didn't mean you any harm. I thought it was a straight-up drug deal. Brian's crazy, man. I mean, he *was* crazy. Let me go. Let me go, and I won't say anything to anybody."

"C'mere," Spider said. "Pull your buddy's body outta the car." He looked down at me. "Get up."

I stood.

Spider took the pistol from me. He watched Chad walk around the car. "Speed it up."

Chad pulled the door open and stared at the body.

"Move," Spider said. "We gotta git 'im outta here."

Chad started to reach in, then straightened up and punched Brian's shattered nose. "Fuck you, Brian. Fuck you. You deserved this you prick."

Spider pulled him back. "Shut up and move the body," Spider said. "You can be mad later."

The silence of the street weighed on me. I heard air moving in and out of my nostrils. The dead man's eyes were open. His mouth yawned, as if struggling to breathe with a broken nose. I had done that. I had killed that man. Turning away, I doubled over, stomach clenching. I had killed a man. There was nowhere to go, nowhere to run.

Chad grabbed Brian's shirt and pulled him from the car, pushed the door shut with his foot, then dropped the body. The head slammed onto the driveway with a dull thud.

"Hey, be careful," I said. "Have some respect." Little bits of old teachings about the dead swirled in my thinking. Didn't we owe a dead body something?

"Grab the feet, Nate," Spider said. His voice was quiet. "That sorry asshole has gone to his just deserves."

Chad lifted the body under the arms, and I grabbed the feet.

Spider followed us as we carried the dead weight behind the house. He pointed to a pile of used lumber. "Drop him there and pull that tarp over him."

We laid the body down. Chad tugged at a canvas tarp that lay in a heap. Rainwater ran off as he pulled it toward Brian's body. Musty, sour smells erupted from the fabric as we placed it over the dead man. I felt like puking, but swallowed it back.

I was shivering in the humid heat. A dead man lay on the ground in front of me. A man I killed. I hadn't intended to kill him, but no matter. I held the gun. The gun fired. I killed him. The night was silent, but my mind was screaming.

Spider walked down the driveway.

Chad and I followed, our soft footsteps echoing against the side of the house. "What happens now?" Chad said.

"I have no goddamn idea," I said. "But it ain't gonna be good for you."

Spider led us into the house. The front room was empty. "Siddown and shuddup." Spider held out his hand. "Gimme the key for the car."

He took the key and walked to the kitchen.

I slumped down onto the carpet. Guilt at shooting Brian, fear of having to run from the law, fear of going to jail, fear of God's wrath swirled in my thinking. Beneath it all a layer of tiredness tugged at me. I fished in my pocket for the pill bottle and shook two into my hand. I looked at Chad, then threw the pills into my mouth.

"Can you spare a few, brother?" Chad asked. "I need something bad."

"We're not brothers. You best shut up. Look what happened to yer buddy."

"You did that."

I swung around onto my knees, grabbed Chad's hair and slammed his head into the wall. The impact shook the house. "Don't speak to me. Shut up. Shut up."

Spider walked back from the kitchen and Horse staggered down the stairs, pulling up the zipper on his jeans. "Jesus Christ, what happened?"

Neither of us spoke. Chad sat, rubbing the back of his head. I slid back down to the floor and leaned against the wall.

"So, ever'things all right?" Horse asked.

A naked woman followed Horse down the stairs. "What's up, honey? Come back upstairs."

Horse looked over his shoulder at her, then walked to an easy chair and sat down. The woman followed him and sat across his lap, crossing her legs. She kissed his cheek, then passed her eyes my way. "The hang around's cute, honey."

Horse ignored her, but I couldn't.

Her face and hair weren't great, but her tits and ass made up for whatever she might have been lacking. I stared back at her. All the crazy thoughts took a step back in my mind. The amphetamines gave me invincibility. In the middle of all my fears, my dick got hard.

"You like her, hang around?" Horse said.

I looked Horse in the eye. "Yeah. She's beautiful."

Horse's head reared back, and he laughed. "Yer bee-u-ti-ful Annette. Bee-u-ti-ful."

The woman's face turned red, and she looked down. "Yeah, well, I was once."

"C'mon, man. Come take this mama. She belongs to the club."

The woman unwound herself from Horse's lap and walked toward me. Her black hair was tangled and matted. She had on mascara that was a mess and traces of lipstick. But her tits. Oh my god, her tits were perfect.

I slid up the wall, reaching into my pocket to adjust my hard-on.

Annette put her arms around my neck and kissed me, then put her lips to my ear and whispered, "Let's go upstairs. Share a little speed with me. We can go a long time, sweetie."

Her breath smelled of sour beer and cigarettes. Her body smelled like sex. I took a deep breath. I wanted her.

She took my hand. "C'mon," she said and pulled me toward the stairs.

We ended up in the same room I had woken up in several hours before. The only furniture was a mattress on the floor. I kicked off my sneakers as we crossed the room.

Annette pushed me onto the bed and pulled at the waistband of my jeans. "Where're the pills sweetie? Gimme four or five will ya? Ooh, I'm gonna make you happy, so make me happy, okay? Give me a few pills, sweetie."

She undid the button and pulled my pants down to my knees. She caressed my erection a few times then stopped and stared at me.

"What?" I said.

She held out her hand.

"In the left pocket."

Annette dug around and came up with the bottle. She shook four pills into her hand and threw them back, then shook out four more and held them out to me.

"Oh, no. I just took some," I said.

"So, take some more." She held the pills out again.

"Ah, what the hell." I downed them and lay back on the bed with my hands behind my head.

Annette pulled my jeans all the way off, then worked her hands down my chest and cupped my balls. She scraped her fingernails from my lower belly down, slowly, around my crotch and the tops of my thighs. I spasmed in anticipation of her touching me. But she stopped, laid her head down on my stomach and sighed.

"What's wrong?" I asked.

"How old're you?" she said.

"What? Why?"

Annette laid still.

I didn't want to move, to break the mood, though I didn't know what the mood was. After a few minutes I asked, "Are you all right?"

She sat up and said, "I gotta pee," and walked out the door.

The excitement of having a naked woman take me to bed leaked away. The second dose of uppers was coming on. Pictures of Brian's bloody face and the neat little hole in his head slid into my consciousness. My hard-on went flat. My hands shook. My stomach lurched. I sensed I was being watched. Someone would turn me in for killing Brian.

I took a few deep breaths, but couldn't stay down any longer, so I sat up and looked for my jeans. As I stood up, Annette breezed through the bedroom door.

"Whoo-hoo," she hollered. "Them magic pills are workin' now. We're gonna have us some fun, lover-boy." She pushed me back onto the bed and fell on top of me. "Where were we?"

She slid off to one side and began stroking my cock. "C'mon, sweetie. Let Annette make it all better."

I batted her hand away. "Stop it."

Annette didn't miss a beat. "Okay, sugar. I know what you want." She slid down and took me into her mouth.

Nothing happened. No erection. I tried to push her shoulders away. "Stop, I said. Stop it."

She didn't stop.

I brought my knees up and pushed her with my feet knocking her off the bed.

"Goddamn, man. What's wrong with you? Are you a faggot?" She pulled herself up, grabbed a pillow and swung it at my head. "I'm the best woman you'll ever have you bastard. Nobody else's ever gonna do you like me. You push me away? You gotta be queer."

I slid off the bed and pushed her back with both hands. "I told you to stop. Don't you speak English, you fucking whore." I pushed her again. "You talk this shit to me?" I took another step and pushed her back into the wall. "You can't talk like that to me, you slut." I pinned her arms against the wall and leaned into her. "Next time I tell you to stop, you stop. Got it, bitch?"

Annette's eyes flashed anger. She looked straight at me. "Whadda ya gonna do if I don't? Shoot me?"

I jumped back and threw my hands up as if she had thrown a punch.

She crossed her arms below her breasts and leaned against the wall. Her foot tapped a million beats a minute. Her jaw was set. She stared at me with her lips squeezed shut.

I dropped my quivering hands to my side. My whole body shook. My legs felt like rubber. My mind felt as exposed as my body. I had killed a man, and it seemed the whole world had witnessed it.

Life as I knew it was over.

Chapter 11

Annette pushed herself up from the wall. "Better get goin' hang-around. You can knock me around, but them guys downstairs'll eat you for lunch." Her upper lip contorted into a look of contempt as she headed to the bathroom.

I couldn't find my underpants, so I slipped my jeans on my naked butt and pulled my shirt over my head as I headed toward the stairs. At the end of the hall, I realized my shoes were still in the bedroom. I turned back, but stopped when I heard Horse's voice from downstairs.

"…so we'll have the hang-around move the shit." His voice was high-pitched, like he was holding back a laugh,

"Quiet down, man," Spider said.

"Aw, that horny bastard won't hear nothin' while Annette's up their blowin' his mind."

I sat on the top step.

"We don't wanna send 'im to the Outlaws. He won't come back in one piece," Spider said.

"Look, we don' have much choice. We need them drugs outta here 'til things cool off."

A chair creaked. A Zippo clicked open and then shut. The smell of fresh tobacco smoke drifted up the stairs.

"C'mon Spider," Horse said, "I know he's kinda your buddy, but Jesus Christ man, we all gotta pay our way. Them Outlaws are bad motherfuckers, but who can we afford to send? All our other guys got their colors. They ain't gonna do it. Your guy? He's made for this run. Too stupid to be afraid."

"True, that boy seems to have missed out on every lesson there is. Sometimes he don't see what's right in front of his face. But he's learnin' fast, man. He's learnin' fast."

Another Zippo flipped open. More smoke climbed the stairs.

I tip-toed back to the bedroom. Annette wasn't there. I stepped to the window and looked out. The drop was more than I could survive without breaking something.

"Nate, goddamit. Get down here," Spider called.

There was nowhere to run. I pulled on my sneakers and headed downstairs.

"'Bout time." Spider elbowed me in the ribs.

"Ouch. Watch it."

He leered at me. "Annette'll make you lose track o' time, right?"

I was ashamed I had attacked Annette and embarrassed I hadn't had sex. I was scared the police would show up to arrest me for killing Brian. I was even more afraid I would die in some drug deal that everyone else was afraid to handle.

"Whatsa matter, Nate? Annette suck all the life outta ya?" Spider said.

They were sending me off on some suicide mission and he's making jokes? "Why don't you shut up?"

Spider's head snapped in my direction. "What did you say, hang-around?" He took two steps toward me and pushed out his chest until it brushed against mine. "You wanna shut me up?"

I stepped back and fell into a chair.Spider bent at the waist, his face level with mine. "Answer me." His breath smelled like beer and raw onions.

Exhaustion pulled on my body, but the amphetamines honed my thoughts to sharp points then hurled them at me like a barrage of arrows. I wanted Spider to be my friend and help me, but he was letting Horse send me off to get killed. I wanted to apologize, and I wanted to spit in the stupid motherfucker's face.

My head dropped, and I stared at my lap. "Back up."

"That's no answer, you little shit."

Adrenaline flowed into my shoulders and arms. My muscles stiffened, ready to fly up into his face. My leg began to bounce up and down. "Back up," I said in a voice just above a whisper.

Spider punched my arm. "Make me."

I clasped my hands together and swung them straight up into Spider's chin. His teeth clacked as his uppers and lowers collided.

He stumbled back but didn't fall. He stared at me as he rubbed his tongue along his front teeth. "You all of a sudden got a death wish?"

"What's the difference? You're gonna send me on some errand that I likely won't come back from. Might as well make a stand here."

Spider ran his finger across the bottom of his upper teeth, then wiggled the front two. He looked at Horse. "I told you."

Horse laughed. "What're you talkin' bout, Nate?"

"I heard you guys sayin' you were going to send me on a run that I wouldn't come back from in one piece."

"You was right, Spider. Little fucker has x-ray hearing, too," Horse said.

"Yeah, I told ya he was getting' smarter. I think we need to level with 'im. Tell 'im what needs done and let him do it. See if he's prospect material."

"He don't even have a scooter. How're we gonna make him a prospect?"

I sat there listening to these guys talk about me like I wasn't in the room. Spider told Horse I should ride the Police Special. Horse said that wasn't his to give away. Spider said the guy hadn't come around for three months and was either dead or in jail. Horse said how would he feel if—

"Shut up! Shut up! Shut the holy fuck up!" I shouted. The room became silent. "Tell me what you need done. Let me choose to do it or walk away." The wide-awake-I-can-go-forever feeling was at its peak. "Tell me."

Horse looked from Spider to me then back to Spider.

Spider shrugged and shook his head. "Do what you wanna, Horse."

Horse turned to face me straight on. "I guess fuckin' Annette made yer balls grow. Okay, here's the deal." Horse took a glass vial from his pocket and tapped some white powder onto the side of his hand then snorted it. "Hah! Ah! Okay, okay."

He shook his head twice and leaned back for a moment before focusing on me again. "We got that box o' pills from them two idiots. We're havin' to deal with a couple of bodies."

The mention of the bodies made my gut twist. I hated Spider for dragging me here. I hated Horse for suggesting these guys were like a family. I hated that my insides were jumping, running full-tilt, like my head might explode. "Wait. Where's Chad?"

No one spoke.

"Where's he at?" I looked from Spider to Horse.

"He went for a ride," Horse said.

The front door slammed, and Dieter walked in. "Done and done, sir," he said to Horse.

Horse nodded once, but didn't speak.

"Why is everyone so glum? I leave for an hour and the party ends?" Dieter scanned the room. "I guess the legends are true. I *am* the life of the party."

He was smiling, full of energy. He looked like he'd just taken a load of speed, but his eyes were clear, not glassy.

"I see the hang-around is still hanging around. How's your first killing? Thrilling, right?"

"Are you talking to me?" Understanding knocked me back. "You killed Chad."

Dieter laughed and raised his hands, palms up. "Was that his name?"

"And you're excited about it." My brow furrowed. "You're turned on."

"Again, what of it?"

I couldn't look at him. The memory of killing Brian made my stomach twist. Yet here was Dieter, just back from murdering a man, acting juiced. I couldn't believe anyone could be so perverse.

Dieter walked to the pool room whistling and picked up a cue. "One quick game before bed. Anyone want to take me on?"

I assumed Dieter was taking speed, or something else, like Horse and Spider and me. His mention of bed reminded me it had been two days since I slept, but I was too jumpy to lay down. "How can you think of sleeping?" I asked him.

He shrugged his shoulders. "When I am tired, I want to sleep."

"Don't the pills keep you awake?"

Dieter laughed. "You think everyone has this weakness? Not me. I am strong and pure. I don't need those pills we sell."

Horse grunted. "Yer strong, all right. 'N twisted."

"Oh well, call it what you want. I won't subject my body to such torture."

I was getting confused. "You don't use drugs because you're pure. But you think it's fun to kill people?"

"You ask a lot of questions for a nobody," Dieter flipped the cue, so the thick bottom faced up. "I think it might be fun to kill you, you little *schwein.*"

I jumped to my feet and balled my fists. "You're a psycho."

Horse got between Dieter and me. "Nate, you need to shut up. Your goddam mouth is causin' a lot o' shit. What say you go sleep for a little while before you go see the Outlaws?"

"Now you say get sleep. I'm on a full load of bennies, man. I'm not sleepin'. No way."

"Yeah, man. An' that's why yer mouth is about to get you in some kinda trouble. You can sleep. There's sumthin' for that." Horse looked at Spider. "You got any reds?"

Spider narrowed his eyes and stared at Horse.

"Well?" Horse said.

"Yeah," Spider answered.

Horse tilted his head in my direction.

Spider stared at Horse, not moving for a moment. He pushed himself up from his chair and walked out the front door.

"Dieter, how 'bout you go play with yerself, or go to sleep or whatever."

Dieter put the pool cue in the corner, smiled at Horse, glared at me and walked to the stairs. "Sweet dreams, little hang-around. You'd best sleep with your eyes open."

I wasn't sure where Spider went to and being alone with Horse I was unsure of what to say. I'd pushed back on these guys. I'd tried to assert myself which seemed to get Spider's and Horse's attention. Was this what I'd been missing since grade school? Balls?

Horse went back to his chair. "That Dieter. Man, what a piece of work." He rubbed his nose and chewed on his fingernails. "Sometimes you do what you gotta, but he does seem ta like it too much. Know what I mean?"

I shrugged. What could I say? Dieter acted like a sadist.

Spider came through the front door and handed me four red capsules. "I'm takin' a ride," he said and walked back out.

"What're these?" I asked Horse.

"Them's good medicine for whatever ails ya. Take a couple of 'em with a beer and go upstairs. You'll sleep good for a while. Save the other two. You might need 'em later."

I grabbed a beer from the fridge and tiptoed up the stairs. At the top of the stairs I washed down two of the four capsules with the beer. The cold beer felt so good in my throat I went back down to the kitchen, got another one and walked back up.

Annette was waiting in the hall wearing a t-shirt and panties. "You back for more, sweetie?" Her tone was sweet and relaxed.

"Annette, look—"

She put her finger to her lips, then took my hand, led me into the same room as before and closed the door.

"Sorry about before." I hung my head. I'd never pushed a woman. "You were great. It was other stuff, ya know?" The beer and the capsules were having an effect. My speech was slower. I felt heavy all over.

"Okay, okay. You think yer the first man to get mad at me?" She slid down and sat on the floor. Her head sagged. "I can be a handful when I get cranked up." She held up a pint bottle. "I been sippin' on this vodka. Sorta mellows me out. I just wanted you to be quiet, 'cause Dieter came up a while before ya. He's a creepy motherfucker." She shivered. "So I sorta hid in here hopin' he'd walk on by and go to sleep."

She took a swig and held the bottle out to me.

"No, thanks. I'm drinkin' beer. I need some sleep. Spider gave me some red capsules and I'm getting sleepy." I laughed. "I just noticed the sun's up. Must be time for bed."

Annette took another pull on the vodka. "You got any o' them reds left?"

I fished the pills out of my pocket and handed them to her.

"I need some sleep, too." She tossed the capsules in her mouth and swallowed them with more vodka. "Shouldn't be a problem now."

"Do you have trouble sleeping?"

"Hah. You could say that. But I get along with some help from my friends."

"Well, I gotta find a place to lay down. I'm so done. I don't even know what I'm sayin'."

Annette struggled to her feet, took my hand and pulled me up. She led me to the mattress. "We can stay here."

"No offense, Annette, but I need to sleep."

"I know. Me, too." She laid down and scooted to the far side then patted the empty space. "C'mon, baby. Lie with me. I'll hold you while you sleep."

•   •   •   •   •

When I woke up, it was light outside. The room was stuffy and hot. Annette, still in her t-shirt and panties, was snoring like a Harley with no muffler. I sort of remembered where I was, which was okay until my full memory kicked in. I was in a strange town with people I hardly knew, two men were dead, one of them shot by me. I was being sent on an illegal run that might cause my death, and yet I was incapable of making a decision that didn't suck me further into this mess.

My mind was muddy, but fear cut through my hangover. I reached down and found my jeans. The bottle of little white pills was still there. I took three of them and laid back waiting for the fog to clear. I had no idea of what time it was, but another day had begun.

Chapter 12

I scooted to the edge of the bed and got up carefully, not wanting to wake Annette. I couldn't bear speaking to anyone as confused as I was. I went down the hall to the bathroom. Voices drifted from downstairs. I didn't recognize any of them. After I peed, I listened at the head of the stairs. No one mentioned my name, or "hang-around," so I crept down. Four guys were playing pool.

They didn't pay me any attention as I got a beer from the kitchen then leaned on a wall in the living room. My throat hurt and my mouth was dry. An uneasy dance between hunger and nausea chittered in my stomach. Exhausted, I slid to the floor, hoping the speed would come on soon.

The events of last night marched through my thoughts. Or did those things happen yesterday? Or two days ago? What about Brian's body? What was it that Horse was going to have me do? Why was I so tired when I slept so hard? Why wasn't the speed kicking in?

I dug into my pocket for the pill bottle and shook out a couple more. I looked at them wondering if I should be taking these so early. I threw them in my mouth and washed them down with beer.

A short hairy dude walked into the room. "Hey, fellers, it's the hangy-hangy-hang-around. How're you doin', man?" He bent towards me. "Word is yer turnin' out to be a badass."

I looked up and tried to remember who this guy was. The amphetamines were beginning to hum. Complete thoughts were forming. "Hi, Rumble. You were here a few nights ago."

"I'm at Hellhouse 'bout every night. I'd be here even more if I didn't hafta work. You been a busy SOB, huh?" Rumble rubbed the side of his ample nose, "Dieter told me you kilt a guy, which's 'bout the only thing he seemsta respect. But he don' like you much."

Dieter's name sent a jolt of anger and disgust through me. "Yeah, well, the feeling is mutual."

Rumble cackled. "You do got a lotta mouth for a new guy. No wonder Dieter don' much care for ya."

Someone called from the pool room, "Rumble, get yer ass back in here and take yer shot."

"What time is it?" I asked,

"Dunno, man. There's a clock in the kitchen." Rumble walked back to the pool table while I went to look for the clock.

The tiny dial on the stove read 7:20. My body couldn't tell whether the sun was rising or setting. I didn't know what day it was. I could remember eating barbeque but didn't know if one day had passed or three. I was hungry when I first woke up, but now food didn't matter. I was feeling fine.

The back screen door slammed, and Spider walked in. "'Bout time you woke up."

"It's only 7:20."

Spider glared at me. "At night."

"Oh," I said. "Hey, man. Where'd you disappear to?"

He looked at me as if considering his answer. "No business of yours." He walked past me toward the living room.

A Harley roared up out front and idled a moment before the engine went silent. The screen door slammed and someone hollered, "Nate."

Two seconds later Horse strode into the kitchen. "Just the guy I'm lookin' for."

"Me?" I asked. "What did I do now?"

"Oh no, sonny. You ain't done it yet. But I got somethin' real special I need done, and yer the man for the job."

This sounded familiar. "Does this involve me getting killed or anything like that?"

Horse smiled. "A course not, Nate. A course not. We just have a little run for you to make. See, yer not a well-known individual like myself or Spider. An' we need somebody ta make a little delivery on the quiet side. I'd do it, but I can't." He rubbed his nose. "Besides, you need ta get yer patch, man. We don't give 'em fer just nothin'."

I studied Horse's face. His mouth formed a soft grin, but his eyes looked like glassy balls.

"What patch?"

"Are you shittin' me boy? You don' know what a patch is? Goddam, where was you raised?"

"Milwaukee."

"Well, that explains a lot. No wonder yer so stunted." Horse shook his head. "Them Outlaws are from there."

I couldn't imagine how being from Milwaukee disqualified me from common sense. But I knew I didn't understand how things worked like everyone else did. Maybe it was Milwaukee's fault. "I used to see Outlaws ride, mostly on the south side. I thought they were just like you."

"Oh no, man. They ain't nothin' like us. They're a bunch o' thieves."

"So, what's the patch you talked about?"

"It's a honor bestowed only on a few. It's the next step fer you to become a Hells Angel. You don't wanna be a hang-around fer ever. When you get yer patch you'll be a prospect. If ya work it right, you'll be a full member in six months. But all that's a ways off. Ya gotta do somethin' tonight, right now. Then we'll see what we see."

"What do I need to do?"

Spider came back into the kitchen with a bulging canvas satchel slung over his shoulder. He swung the satchel onto the kitchen table and sat down.

Horse took out his little glass vial and tapped out a pile of white powder onto his left hand between his thumb and first finger and raised it to his nose.

"Yer getting' pretty serious with the blow," Spider said.

Horse glared at Spider, snorted the cocaine, then licked his hand and ran his tongue over his teeth. "Mmm-mmm good, motherfucker. Ha! Good stuff." His hands tightened into fists. "You got a problem with that, you sorry junkie ass?"

Spider sprung to his feet knocking over a chair. "That was then."

"Easy, amigo. I didn't mean to rile ya. It's just we all got our little helpers," Horse said.

Spider grabbed the satchel and looked at me. "C'mon."

"Where're we going?" I asked.

Horse held his hand up. "Nowhere right now, hang-around. Yer gonna do somethin' fer me, first."

"I'm takin' 'im on the run," Spider said.

"You can't Mr. Wiseass. Them Outlaws all know yer ugly face. They'll know who to come after when this all turns to shit." Horse rubbed his nose again. "I'm sendin' the boy."

"No disrespect, but yer not thinkin' right on this one. I'm takin' the whole box o' pills and deliverin' em to them sorry goddam Outlaws."

"No yer not, big shot. This here's the perfect chance to stick it to 'em. They'll never see there's a few pills missin'."

"Half of 'em, Horse. You pulled out half of 'em. They're gonna know. That's when the shootin' starts."

"This's the life, amigo. Ain't they tried rippin' us off for all that new meth they were makin'? We owe 'em." Horse got up and spat into the sink. "Cuttin' that shit with bakin' soda. Bunch o' thievin' animals."

"I get it, but we got too much heat our ownselfs." Spider lowered his voice. "People are startin' to take interest where the two boys are at. We need to get rid o' the drugs the cops seem ta be trackin'. Let them dumbasses from Milwaukee start peddlin' 'em. The F-B-fuckin'-I can shine a light up their ass."

Horse pursed his lips and narrowed his gaze, staring at Spider. "Well, okay then. But I don' like it."

Spider smiled at Horse as he walked past him. At the door, he said to me, "C'mon, let's ride."

I didn't understand how these two could be all buddy-buddy, then face off with their fists up, then move ahead like nothing was wrong.

The sun was descending as I wrestled the Police Special to face the right direction. Spider had his bike started and was rolling down the driveway. He gunned his Sportster as soon as he reached the street. I didn't want to be left behind.

It had only been a few days since I first saw the Hellhouse. I couldn't remember where I was in relation to anything. I didn't know what we were going to do, or with whom, or where. When we reached the top of a hill overlooking Lake Erie, I saw we were back at the place where Spider and I had talked. My whole world had changed since then.

The temperature dropped as we followed the road winding down to the lake. We pulled into the lot, left the bikes and walked out onto the rocks, just like last time. I was still feeling strong. The double-dose of uppers was performing its magic. I didn't know why Spider had come back here, but I wasn't going to be a victim again. Not in the stories I told. Not in the present moment. Just to be sure I was up for what Spider had to say, I shook a couple more amphetamines out of the bottle and swallowed them. Spider would see the real me. The strong guy. The one who could be counted on.

"Hey, dumbass, get over here." Spider stood on a boulder near the water.

My muscles tensed. Why had he brought me here? Paranoia gripped me. I wanted to call him out for treating me like I was stupid, but I remembered the little gun he had in his boot. I wondered if he'd brought me here to shoot me. I was frozen in place.

"Nate! Come over here. Now."

The edge in Spider's voice shattered my fearful hesitation. I walked toward him, stopping a few feet away. "Why're we here? You gonna shoot me and throw me in the lake?"

"What?" He threw up his hands. "What are you sayin'?" He dropped his hands. "I saved yer ass. I vouched for ya to Horse and them. What're you talkin' about, shoot ya?"

The paranoia was persistent, but if he wanted to get rid of me, he'd had better chances. Still, my heart pounded and fear dominated. "I don't know, man. You guys have been talking about this drug deal with the Outlaws and me doin' a run and not coming back. What am I supposed to think? Dieter is a sicko. Horse goes from quiet to crazy. You keep disappearing. I'm not exactly getting me a sense of security. Geeze. Rumble seems like the most normal person of all you. And he's goofy as a cartoon."

Spider stared at me as I ran out of words.

Every heartbeat made a rushing sound in my ears. My head felt like it might explode. Thoughts swirled too fast for me to decode. I was vibrating hard enough to make the boulders we were standing on shake.

"Sit down," Spider said.

I hopped from one rock to another. "I believe I'll stand."

"Suit yerself. But, you need to pay attention. An' fer you, that's no small feat."

Spider's tone was different. He stared at me, his forehead was wrinkled. "I went to Evvie's last night."

"So?"

Spider started to speak, then went silent for a moment. He adjusted his position, then settled back. "Evvie's worried 'bout you."

"Why? What'd she say?"

He pushed his lips into a thin line. He shook his head and looked at his lap.

"What?"

"She went nuts when I told her I'd taken you to Hellhouse. She was pissed you was still with me."

"She doesn't know about Brian, right? She doesn't know about the drug deal."

Spider took a long breath. "She don' need ta know any partic'lars. She knows you're with me and she takes it from there. She's got good reason to think what she thinks. I've been a fuck up my whole life."

Spider hadn't sounded so defeated since he'd found his drugs missing. There was no time to feel bad for him, though. Evvie was asking about me. That's what mattered.

"So, tell me more."

Spider stood up. "I gotta figure out how to let you take a walk without Horse gettin' up in my face."

"Take a walk? What're you sayin', Spider. We need to do this deal. Then, what's done is done."

"You don't get it, man. Yer gettin' in deep. This is a way o' life. Ya can't just come n' go. You deliver those pills with me, and you're in. Look at yerself, livin' on speed, fuckin' with the likes of Annette. Yer drunk when you ain't flyin. I don' know if I ever seen someone take to it so fast."

I was bewildered. Spider was lecturing me about drinking and drug use? "So, you're saying all these things you got me started on are bad? I should quit?"

"Lookit. You showed up, and I felt a little sorry for ya. Not knowin' anythin' 'bout how things' work n'all. I wanted to show you a better way ta think. To stop bein' a goddam victim. Only trouble is, I don' know shit about livin' right."

"That's no revelation, man. I mean the first thing that happened was you losing all your drugs."

Spider's face grew dark. "That ain't funny, son. It was that mess that got us here. Them rich kids that stole the pills have some kinda connection."

"Had."

"What?"

"Had. They're dead now."

Spider looked out on the lake. The sun was down, and the wind was dying. Water lapped gently on the rocks. He blew out a long breath and sat back down. "Only one of 'em's dead."

"What?"

"The guy who was with Brian when they drugged us wasn't Chad. His name is Sean. His uncle is Tommy Boyle."

"Who's he?"

"Tommy's a big mobster. When they got back to Cleveland the kid sent Brian and Chad to unload the drugs. Now Sean's pissed cause Brian's disappeared. That's why me 'n Horse wanted to get the drugs to the Outlaws. Take the heat offa us whenever it got clear Brian wasn't comin' back. Seems ever'body is watchin' for them pills. A friend tol' me the FBI was interested' cause a who had 'em in New York. All I wanted was to get my drugs back. All the rest o' this hit later. And now, we gotta watch our asses from two directions. Neither of which is a good choice."

"What was Horse arguing with you about?"

"That crazy fuck wanted to take half the bennies and replace 'em with saccharine pills 'cause they're about the same size. Said we needed to increase our margin. What the fuck? We need to stay outta the way of Tommy Boyle. He don't play."

"So what are we doin' now?"

"We're gonna give them shitty Outlaws full value. We're gonna wholesale them the pills the way we told 'em we would." Spider grinned. "Funny thing is they'll never stop wonderin' what our angle was."

"So, doing this will get us off the hook with this Tommy guy?"

"Naw. Not really. It'll just give the mobsters somebody else to be pissed at. They'll still be shootin', just not at us." Spider stood up and brushed off his jeans. "Let's go find them sorry wannabes and unload these pills. We got another stop later."

"Where're we going'?" I asked.

"Someplace you only think you wanna be."

Chapter 13

Spider and I took off from the lakefront heading toward downtown. We crossed the snaking Cuyahoga River three times before we reached an area with streets lined with neglected red-brick buildings with shattered windows.

There were no streetlights, at least none that worked. The sound of our motorcycles hammered the sides of the buildings which threw the noise back at us, amplifying it to a deafening roar. If there were other noises, we couldn't hear them. If anything else was moving, we couldn't see it.

After a dozen blocks, we pulled into an alley which lead to a courtyard of sorts. A half-moon came from behind clouds and offered a grayish light. Spider killed his engine, and I did the same, leaving an eerie silence. The skin in the center of my back turned icy.

I walked the Police Special around to face toward Spider. "So, what now?" I whispered.

He pulled a smoke out of the pack rolled into his sleeve and lit it before he answered. "We sit and wait."

My body pulsed with the noise and vibration of the ride here. Sitting and waiting seemed like an awful idea. My ears throbbed in time with my heart. I felt like I were being watched. "What are we waiting for?"

Spider drew on his cigarette. "Be quiet, Nate. We're here early, so's we kin hear how many bikes roll up. It's basic shit."

The thought had never occurred to me, but I could see the wisdom of the plan. "So, we're meeting them here?"

He glanced at me then shook his head. "No dumbass. If we was meetin' em here, they'd ride up and we could count 'em. We're meetin' 'em close t'here. But we'll listen to 'em comin'. Once the racket stops we oughta know about how many bikes showed up."

"Man, you are one evil genius. I see why you can stay ahead of this shit."

He held my gaze for a few breaths. "That there's the problem. I ain't always stayed ahead of it." He turned away, took another drag and smashed the butt with his boot.

I was, as usual, baffled. Spider seemed like the master of his environment. My stomach was doing flip-flops. Between the speed and the fear, I couldn't process what he was trying to tell me. So, I said nothing.

We sat enveloped in silence and half-light for what seemed like half an hour, until the sound of motorcycles drifted in from the distance. "Is tha—"

"Shh!" The sound increased until we could hear at least three, maybe four bikes navigating the industrial wasteland. Their engines slowed to an idle. Voices rose above the engine noise, then two of the bikes roared off, while two more remained at idle. They sounded like they were a street over from where we waited.

Spider leaned close. "The two that left prob'ly aim to wait on us to go so's they kin steal back the money." A shiny pistol appeared in Spider's hand, a chrome plated automatic. He held it up for me to see. Then he bent down and took the little .22 out of his boot, turned it butt first and extended his hand. "Take it."

"Oh, hell no!" I said.

"Shut up!" Spider hissed. "You'll get us kilt. Take the piece. You got no choice. You ain't getting a walk like I wanted, but I gotta keep you alive. This might help." He shoved the gun into my hand.

The little revolver felt heavier than the last time, like the weight of Brian's life pressed down on it. It didn't seem like a stupid toy gun anymore. It felt like a responsibility I didn't want to have. I stuck it in the waistband of my jeans anyway.

Spider turned his head to hear the idling motorcycles more clearly. After a couple of minutes one engine died, then the other, leaving the tangible silence of before. Only now I was more scared and warier. I didn't see how we were going to get out of this without violence. And the last violence I had been a part of ended in someone's death.

Once more, Spider leaned in and whispered, "They're one block over. There's a alleyway we kin go down. But we gotta walk these bikes, man. Ya up ta that?"

My ribs were almost recovered. I'd had some sleep. Besides, there was no other choice. "Sure."

Spider climbed off his bike and pushed it toward what looked like a dark space in the wall. I got off the Police Special, but left it on its kickstand while I freed a few bennies from my pocket and swallowed them. Then, I said to myself, "Now I'm sure," and followed behind Spider, pushing the 700-pound machine.

As we got closer, the dark space revealed itself to be a passageway. There was room for one bike with not much left for someone to push.

At the entrance, Spider stopped. "Don't let it scrape," he whispered. "The other end comes out in a corner. If we're quiet, they won't see us 'til we're right behind 'em. I'll do the talkin'. Got it?"

I nodded.

Spider entered the tunnel-like passage, just avoiding the brick walls with both his back and his bike.

As soon as the front fender of my bike was in the passage, I saw there was no room for me be beside the beast without scraping. I mounted the bike and walked it into the tunnel. After a few steps, I waited, counting breaths from one to ten and then back to one. I listened in the total darkness for any creak, scrape or bump. I gripped the handlebars tighter to keep my hands from shaking and resumed walking the bike.

At the far end, two motorcycles sat, their riders facing the street, smoking and talking about some party where there were strippers who were pretty and the one guy fucked one of 'em, and it was the best, blah, blah, blah.

Spider was out of the tunnel. He motioned for me to bring my bike alongside his and to get ready to flip on the headlight. He counted down soundlessly, waving first one finger, then two, then three. We both flipped on our headlights.

"Oh shit. Who's there? Cut the fuckin' lights, or I'll shoot 'em out." The guy talking wasn't holding a gun.

Spider stepped just to the side of his bike and held his pistol in the light, then said to me, "Shut 'em off."

In the blackness, he and I had an advantage, not having been blinded by the headlights. Spider walked to the Outlaws, swung the canvas satchel and let it land at their feet. "$5000. Now. No negotiation, no bullshit, or I shoot both of you." He called over his shoulder, "Give us some light again."

I turned on the Police Special headlight. The Outlaws still seemed dazed.

"Where's the money?" Spider asked.

"We got it," the larger of the two said. "We need to see them pills first."

"The pills are in the bag at yer feet. Open 'em up. Take a few. Shit, take 'em all. But I need that fuckin' money."

The big guy said, "Pick 'em up and try some, Johnny."

The smaller man pulled open the satchel, grabbed a bottle and shook out half-a-dozen pills. He threw them in his mouth and crunched them before swallowing. He ran his tongue around the inside of his cheeks. "We'll see." He threw the pill bottle to the other man. "Now you, Maurice. Then you can be a lab rat, too."

Maurice did not look amused. He shook three pills out and dry swallowed them.

Spider raised his pistol. "In the meantime, show me the money."

Maurice pulled out the wallet chained to a belt loop on his jeans and removed an envelope. "Fifty $100 bills." He held it toward Spider.

"Get it," Spider said.

I grabbed the envelope, lifted the flap and counted the bills. "Looks good." I handed the cash to Spider.

Johnny was looking amused. His eyes were glassy, and his speech was fast. "So, you badass Hells Angels are getting out of the drug business, huh? Why else would you sell us these brand-name pharmaceuticals at such a bargain price?"

Spider's grin covered his whole face. "Why, you must surely be correct, there Johnny. We are getting out of the business so we can spend all our time riding. We're just recruitin' lower tier clubs like Outlaws to do the dirty street work."

Maurice stiffened. "Outlaws don't do anybody's dirty work. You better watch yer mouth big man."

"What you gonna do, Maurice? You think them other two riders are coming to help out? Look, me 'n my partner here are gonna git on our ponies and ride. If you or Speed-freak Johnny or the clowns you got waitin' try to take back this cash, I will kill you all."

Spider looked at me. "Give me your pistol and start both bikes."

I gave him the pistol, and he gave me his. I fired up both bikes and climbed on the Police Special.

Spider walked to Johnny's bike. The pop of the .22 echoed as he shot a hole in the front tire. Then he walked to Maurice's cycle and fired into its rear tire. Looking at Maurice, he said, "You pissed me off." Then he climbed on his Sportster, and we left through the front entrance.

After a few blocks, I pulled alongside Spider and asked, "What about the other two bikers?"

"They're still waitin' ta hear two more bikes leave. They may be waitin' a while."

We motored out of the industrial neighborhood with no problems. After a few minutes, it became plain Spider was headed back to Hellhouse. "What's up?" I shouted over the noise of our engines.

"I'm takin' the cash ta Horse, then we got a visit to pay." He cranked his throttle wide and pulled away from me.

I followed at a distance. He hadn't told me where we were going, but I could guess it was Evvie's. He was right about me wanting to go.

I realized the sun had been down for an hour or better and I knew it would take a while for us to give the money to Horse, then ride all the way to Evvie's. The pills I had taken earlier had done their job. I still felt okay, but I wanted to be sharp when I saw Evvie again, so I fished the pill bottle out of my jeans and tried to unscrew the cap one-handed. The bike hit a pot hole and the handlebars jerked. I dropped the bottle of pills to grab the other handle and steady the bike. The bottle shattered as it hit the street. "Oh shit!"

"Shit, shit, shit," I said. Spider had gotten a block ahead of me, so I twisted the throttle wide open to make sure he didn't lose me. I didn't know what I was going to do now with the pills gone. There weren't that many left anyway. It didn't matter. Spider would have more.

I pulled alongside. "Hey man," I hollered.

Spider turned toward me and raised his chin.

"You got another bottle of them pills?"

"What? You're through them first ones?"

"Just dropped 'em back there. Can you help me out here? I went on this run like you 'n Horse said to. Don't I get a cut or something?"

He responded by gunning his bike and pulling ahead.

I sped up and tried to pull even, but he drifted in front of me. I backed off for a moment, then tried to pull up again. The Sportster once again blocked my way. So, I dropped back and followed him the rest of the way to the house. We both parked our bikes on the dried mud in front.

"Stay here. I'll be right back," Spider said.

"What about the pills?" I asked.

He stepped close and said, "Think about it, chief. What was in the satchel I gave them thievin' Outlaws?"

"Pills?"

"Yup. So, if you need a bump that bad, go see them bastards. They'll be happy to sell you a few," he said, and walked into the house.

The only noise on the street was coming from inside. A bunch of bikes were parked in the front yard, and the driveway. Loud conversation and laughter flowed out of the open windows. Steppenwolf played in the background with several drunken voices joining in, "Born to be wild…"

I was going to Evvie's, I was pretty sure, and that was going to be wild, but my energy was draining from me waiting for Spider. I needed a bump. I couldn't see Evvie like this. I was so tired I could fall over

I got off the bike and went in the house. The crowd reminded me of the barbeque day, but I couldn't remember most of them. I wove my way to the pool room, "Hey, Rumble, have you seen Spider?"

Rumble spun around. "Hangy-hangy, how's it hangin'?"

Before I could answer, Dieter walked in from the kitchen. "Oh, it is you, little big mouth. Why are you still here? I thought it was past your curfew." He was smiling, but there was no mirth in the coldness of his eyes.

I stepped to the side, trying to walk past him, but he grabbed my arm.

"Watch yourself, little schwein. Watch your backside."

Dieter released my arm, and I made my way to the kitchen.

Spider wasn't there, but Horse was. "Well come on in, brother. Good job on the deliv'ry. All your brethren appreciate yer efforts."

I sat at the table, grateful to not have to support my body, which seemed to get heavier moment-by-moment. "Uh, thanks. You suppose I could get another bottle of the pills for my effort? I mean, after all, I did do the run."

Horse studied me for a minute. "That's all you want? A bottle 'a uppers?"

This sounded like a trick question. Who wouldn't want a bottle of these pills? "Um, yes?"

Horse stood up. "No! You don't just want a bottle of pills. You were born to be wild." His left arm shot out, and he strummed the air in front of his waist with his right hand. "Born to be wiiilld," he croaked out. Then he laughed as he reached in his pocket and drew out his glass vial. He tossed it to me. "This is what you want, amigo. You done good tonight. That there is yours."

I looked into the small bottle. It was full of white powder.

"Shake a little out on yer hand and snort away, man. Yer blues are sure ta flee."

I'd seen Horse snort this a couple of times. It always seemed to give him energy and put him in a good mood. I shook some out onto the edge of my hand.

Horse leaned forward, grinning. "Go on, son. This'll put starch in yer undies."

I held the powder up to my nose and inhaled. "Whoo-hoo. God A'mighty. Damn." This was the feeling I was born to experience. This was what was missing from my life. With this, nothing could stop me.

Horse laughed again and fell into a chair.

I screwed the top back on the vial and slipped it in my pocket.

Spider walked in. "There you are. I told you to wait outside. Let's go." He walked out the back door.

I looked at Horse, and we both burst out laughing. Horse put his finger to his lips and said, "Shh," tossing his head in the direction Spider had left.

I nodded, giggled and walked out the door.

"What're you so cheery about," Spider asked.

"Oh, nothin'. Seeing Evvie, I guess."

"Yeah, I figured. Fair warnin', though. Yer about ta wade into a hornet's nest."

"Why?"

Spider climbed on his bike and kick-started it. When he had it idling, he looked at me and said, "Don't say I didn't warn ya." He gunned his engine, slammed his bike into gear and tore off.

I didn't know the way, and I wasn't going to miss out on seeing Evvie, no matter what, so I took off after Spider.

He slowed down some after we had ridden south for twenty minutes. He drove the speed limit through the residential streets, slowing to just above idle after the last right turn.

The house looked inviting, as we rolled onto the driveway. It was hard to believe all that had happened since I slept there. I was a different person.

"I wanted to roll up quiet," Spider whispered. "Norma might be sleepin'. You stay here for a minute. And I mean it, dammit. Stay here 'til I come git ya." He walked toward the front door.

As soon as he was around the corner, I grabbed the vial of cocaine, did a pile off my hand and pocketed the bottle. God, the rush! Everything was enhanced, the crickets, the buzzing of a streetlight. I could hear the bike engines creak and crack as they cooled. I wanted to be ready and alert to see Evvie, and now I was, but I never heard her coming. I turned to face the front of the house and heard the "crack" before I felt the burn where Evvie had slapped me.

Chapter 14

Evvie's eyes glistened in the low light. She bent at her waist, feet shoulder width apart, arms rigid at her sides. If there ever was a stance for trying to hold back from throttling a person, this was it. "Why're you here, hangin' with the likes of Spider?" She stared at me unblinking until a tear broke free and rolled down her cheek.

I reached out to pull her into my arms. "Are you all right?"

"Aaauugh!" she shrieked and took a step back. "What is wrong with you? Why can't you grow up and see what is happening to you?"

I stepped back. "Why are you crying?"

Spider walked around the corner of the house. "She's cryin' 'cause she's a caring person, 'cause she worked her ass off to not get sucked into the way she was raised, 'cause Wendell helped me get straight, and she thinks I fucked it up again." He tried to put his arm around Evvie's shoulder.

She pulled away and squared off in front of him. "Don't touch me. I could kill you right now. When you told me you'd taken Nate to that ratty dump of a biker's house I wanted to tear your eyes out."

Spider hung his head like a swatted puppy.

Evvie took a deep breath and held it for a few seconds then whispered, "Let's go in. I don't want the neighbors hearin'." The back door of the house squeaked as she pushed it open. "Be quiet. Norma's sleeping."

We walked through the kitchen and into the living room. Light shone from a single lamp. Spider slumped into the easy chair while Evvie and I took opposite ends of the couch.

The cocaine rush was already dissolving and, with it, any confidence I felt. No one spoke. The silence sat on me like a millstone, waiting for criticism, for rejection. I was on edge, and I knew just the cure. "I need to use the bathroom."

"You know where it's at," Evvie said.

As soon as I shut the door, I pulled out the vial of cocaine and snorted half a capful. The drug smashed into my brain, shattering the uneasy dread I felt a moment ago. Now I was ready to hear Evvie out. Bring it on. I'll show you who I really am.

I walked back and bounced onto the couch. Energy pulsed through me. I drummed a quick beat on my leg.

Evvie faced Spider. "Tell him why I asked you to come here."

He sat up straight, hands clasped in his lap. I'd never seen Spider look so nervous. He raised his hands and opened his mouth, then dropped his hands back to his lap and closed his mouth. Then he did it again.

The third time was too much for me. "Spider, goddammit, what?"

"He was in bad shape four years ago," Evvie said. "Wendell came home on leave before he left for Nam. He went to that shitty house lookin' for him. They'd kicked him out."

"I'll tell it," Spider said.

"Well, then do it," Evvie said.

"Let me take my time. This ain't easy fer me." He lit a cigarette and exhaled toward the ceiling. He stretched his neck left and right. "The Angels took me in when my momma disappeared. They was good to me. It was the first time I ever felt like a part a somethin'. Like I said, we're family. I learned how to take care o' myself and not have ta be afraid. After a while, they needed me to pull my weight, and I was scramblin' fer cash. A guy at a bar said he could show me how to make a pile o' money." Spider drew on his smoke then smashed it out in the ashtray. "He started talkin' about makin' a thousand dollars a week, and drivin', Cadillacs, and havin' women hangin' offa me. Man, I was ready ta walk to the moon for what he was offerin'."

Spider rested his elbows on his knees. "The guy took me outside to show me his caddie. It was all gold and chrome and shiny. Then he asks me if I'd like to try somethin' that'd make my troubles disappear. Hmmph. We climbed into that car, and he showed me how to smoke heroin." Spider closed his eyes and shook his head. "And that was where things went to shit. 'Chasin' the dragon' they call it. Well, pretty quick the dragon turns around and takes everything ya got."

He sat back in the chair with his eyes closed. "So I started sellin' that shit. Horse tol' me, 'be careful'. I thought I could handle it, thought I was in charge. I'd taken all kinda drugs. Smoked dope, popped pills, drank 'til I puked. Never had no problem. An' I was makin' big money. But pretty soon somebody showed me how to use a needle. It bothered me to think about it, 'cause I knew the Angels didn't put up with needle users. But man, I wanted more of that feelin', and the needle was the way ta get it." His head sagged almost to his knees. His voice got so soft it was hard to hear what he said. "Hells Angels don' allow no needles. We get fucked up a thousand ways, but if you stick a needle in yer arm, yer out."

The coke had me flying. I liked the way it made me feel. So my Hells Angel guru was a goddam junkie. He was just whining. Drugs weren't the train wreck everyone tried to make out. "But you're back in with 'em now. What's the big deal?"

Sparks flew from Spider's eyes, but he didn't speak. He looked away, his jaw working like he was chewing a tough piece of meat. "I never showed up at the house stoned, but the guys saw me wearin' my colors on Green Road where I scored, and at the lake shore where I went to shoot up. After a while, they seen enough and tossed me out." He shook his head. "Can't be mad about it. I had it comin'."

We sat in silence. At least no one talked. My brain screamed opinions and judgments and random ideas. Spider's expression had me trying to keep my mouth shut, but my coked up brain won out. "So, everything turned out good, right?"

Spider scooted forward in the chair and sat on the edge. "The rest o' the story is comin', you jackass." He squinted at me. "Just how cranked up are ya?"

"What d'ya mean? I haven't taken any pills." *Just cocaine.*

"Yeah, I don' know why I'd think that. Yer always runnin' yer stupid mouth." I stood up.

"Where ya goin', dumbass. Siddown. Listen ta the rest."

"Yeah, Nate," Evvie said. "This isn't funny. You're bein' a total jerk." I sat back down.

Spider settled back and drew a long breath. "Like Evvie said, Wendell came lookin' for me. I'd been shootin' for about six months by then. I'd sold my bike. I had one pair o' jeans. My boots had been stolen. I was livin' in a stand o' trees in the park by the lake." He rubbed his arm as he spoke. "Wendell found me in the woods, layin' on the ground shakin'. I didn't know how long I'd been there. My money was gone, and the big shot with the Caddy was lookin' for me to collect what I owed 'im. 'Let's go' Wendell said, and he helped me to his car. I fell into the seat and threw up. The stink was nothin' you ever wanna smell." He wrinkled his nose like he was smelling it again. "Wendell didn' lecture, or ask me why, or tell me what a dumbass I was fer endin' up like that. He took me home and helped me clean up." He looked at Evvie. Tears pooled in the corners of his eyes. "Wendell saved my life."

Evvie face was frozen, eyes narrowed, lips pursed. "And now he's dead. And what are you doin'? You're runnin' with the Hells Angels. Sellin' drugs. Gettin' drunk. Dammit, *Wendell saved your life*. Act like that matters." She drew a deep breath. "His birthday's coming up. We oughta do something to honor him. You especially. Maybe we could visit where he found you. Might make you think twice about what he did for you and what you're doin' with your life."

Spider wiped his eyes and looked away from Evvie. "You don' get it. I can't jus' walk away. Them guys took me back, too."

"And now you're draggin' unsuspectin' young guys in to do your dirty work. To take chances that the old guys are too smart to take. You're just using Nate." Evvie grabbed one of the cushions from the back of the couch and swung it hard into my chest and face. "And you're following him. You idiot. That man does not care about you. Run! Get out! Don't become who he is."

"You don' know that, Evvie," Spider said. "I do care about what happens to him. I just got no clue about what to do. I know you think I'm a fuck up for runnin' with the Angels, but I got nobody else. You don' know what it's like. They're the only family I got."

"You use bennies. You drink beer. So maybe you're skating the edge." I said. "So what? You seem like you handle it all right."

"You ever seen me use bennies?"

I must have. After all, he'd given them to me. "I can't remember," I said. "But you're all around drugs. You sell drugs. Why are you doing that if this's all so bad?" I was pissed. The drugs I'd taken the past couple of days were awesome. They made me confident and alert. Colors looked sharper, music sounded better. Sure, I'd felt a little paranoia, and I'd gotten short-tempered. Nothing's perfect. "What could be so bad about a little speed."

Spider snorted and shook his head. "Man, yer as ignorant as you was when I first seen ya. Any drug can take ya down. It's just smack was the one that got me. Sooner or later they get everybody fool enough to mess with 'em. You're not exempt neither."

Evvie scooted up. "That's a nice lecture, but your words don't mean anything. You got your ass in a crack, then Wendell got it back out. That's why I'm so mad at you for pullin' in Nate. What're you thinkin' Spider? What goes around comes around. You *are* skating the edge, and you'll fall off again."

Spider rolled his eyes. "Aw c'mon, Evvie. I was tryin' ta help. I was tryin' ta do a good thing."

"And look how it turned out."

"Why'd you ask me to come back here, then? Why're you so damn concerned about Nate? Not long ago you didn't know he even existed. I'm sorry if yer pissed, but all I wanted was to help this boy out."

"How? By takin' him to your friends so he can learn about drugs and bein' drunk all day?"

"No! I wanted him to learn to stand up fer himself, to quit gettin' his ass kicked by every douche that sees 'im standin' there with that lost look on his face."

"Hey," I said. "I'm sitting right here. I'm hearing everything you say. I can take pretty good care of myself."

Evvie and Spider spoke in tandem. "What?"

"You're stupid if you think that," Evvie said. "You think those assholes are helping you for free? You think they're your friends?"

Her words were arrows hitting a bullseye in my brain. When Spider called me stupid, I chalked it up to his general demeanor. When Evvie said I was stupid, it pierced my every defense. I crashed. "I need to use the bathroom again," I said, and jumped up from the couch.

"Again?" Evvie asked.

"Mm-hmm." As soon as the bathroom door closed I tapped a pile of coke onto my hand and snorted it. Then I tapped out some more and snorted that. "Mm-umm-mm-mm-mm-um." My mood soared again.

I flushed the toilet and turned to go when I saw blood on my shirt. It was dripping from my nose. I stuck some toilet paper up my nostril and tried to rinse the blood out of my shirt with cold water. Most of the blood came out, but a big wet spot was left. I looked at myself in the mirror. This was a little setback, nothing anyone would notice. I pulled the TP out of my nose and headed back to the living room.

"What happened to your shirt?" Evvie asked.

"It's nothing," I said.

"Look at me," Spider said.

I turned, and he leaned in to me, staring at my eyes.

"Hmph. Evvie's right, but I already knew it. You are stupid."

"What is this? Pile-on-Nate-Day?"

"Oh, shit," Evvie said. "You're high on coke." She grabbed the couch cushion again and swung it hard into my head. "You stupid, stupid idiot." She slammed me again.

"Hey, easy," I said, laughing.

Evvie sprung up. "Get out of my house."

"What?" I said.

"Get out!"

"Calm down. You'll wake Norma."

Evvie pushed me toward the door. "You were supposed to be the good one. You were the one who was going to do all right. But you're like all the rest. Wendell woulda tried to make you see. But not me. I don't have time to waste on losers." She turned toward Spider. "I told you your idiot friends would take him down to their level. You get out of my house, too."

Spider got up and shuffled towards us. "I'm sorry. I didn't mean to—"

"But you did. And you can't take it back." She swung her arm toward the door. "Get out."

She was the girl I hoped to get with, and she called me an idiot. Her words hurt like hell, and I couldn't stand to hurt. The coke turned the hurt into anger. I pulled the door open and leaned on the jamb with my arms crossed. "What makes you so special? Who're you to act like you're better than me?"

Evvie's head jerked like I'd slapped her. Another tear rolled down her cheek.

"Nate, shut up," Spider said.

"Why should I? She acts so high and mighty, but she slept with me the first day she ever met me. Now she's acting all perfect. It's bullshit."

Spider grabbed me by my shoulders and threw me out of the door. I stumbled down the stairs and fell onto the grass. The front door slammed hard enough to shake the house. So much for not waking up Norma.

When I rolled over, Spider's boot was swinging toward my thigh. I shot my arms out and grabbed his leg. I didn't want a repeat beating of my ribs. "No!"

Spider bent his knee and dropped onto my stomach, knocking the wind out of me. My arms flew apart, releasing his leg. He stood up and kicked my backside.

"Auugh, Stop!" I rolled onto my side and held my belly.

Spider took a step back and looked down at me for a moment, then walked to his bike and climbed on.

I dragged myself up and swung my leg over the Police Special.

He turned his bike to face the street.

I did the same with the Police Special. I was waiting for Spider to kick his bike over, but he just sat there, staring over the handlebars.

A streetlight half a block away was the only light. It didn't even cast a shadow where we were. The neighborhood was quiet, except for the faint hum of distant traffic. The night was still hot, and the humidity was stifling. I was jumpy. "Where we going?" I asked.

Spider didn't move.

My eyes were on him, but my mind was on the little glass bottle of white powder. How long was he going to just sit there? "Spider."

He didn't turn his head. Didn't move a muscle.

"Hey. We goin' or what?"

He glanced over, stood on the kick starter and his bike barked to life.

I kicked mine, but nothing happened.

Spider roared off.

"Hey, wait," I called as I kicked the starter again. No response.

Spider's taillight disappeared around the first corner.

I kicked the starter yet again. When it failed to catch I remembered I hadn't connected the wires. I wound the wires and started the bike. I took off, turning where Spider's taillight disappeared, but he was nowhere to be seen. I twisted the throttle, racing several blocks, aiming to catch up, but all I saw were little houses set back from the street. For the first time in Cleveland, I was on my own.

Chapter 15

I zig-zagged, block after block, looking for Spider. I gave up and pulled into a coffee shop. It seemed the bar crowd was arriving. People got out of cars and staggered into the restaurant, laughing and cursing.

I didn't feel like laughing. The shame I felt made the sweaty night feel lonelier. I was wild about Evvie. Why had I taken the sweetest thing any girl had ever done for me and turned it into a weapon? Why was she so against Spider and the Hells Angels? They felt like brothers. They seemed okay to me.

I put the kickstand down and walked to a dark corner of the lot that was edged by a stand of trees. I tapped the rest of the coke into the cap of the vial and snorted it.

"Hey. Got some for me?" said a female voice.

I spun around but couldn't see anyone except a couple walking across the lot. Moths dove at a streetlight on the opposite side. Humidity clung to me like a blanket.

"How about it?" The same sexy voice.

"Where are you?" I asked.

"Come find me, and bring that snow."

The voice was coming from the woods. The shadows grew sharp edges as the coke hit my brain and my senses tuned in. It was only a girl. She sounded nice. What could go wrong? "Where are you?"

"Naw, naw, naw. Find me. Bring the goodies."

I was out of cocaine, but she didn't know that. Evvie had thrown me out. This girl sounded so inviting. Maybe my luck was about to change.

Walking into the trees, shadowy images changed to solid black. I moved carefully, taking short steps. "Where are you?"

Silence.

"Hell-lo-o. I'm coming to find you. Help me out a little. Say something." I stopped to listen for her, but all I heard was crickets. Then, *whap!*

•   •   •   •   •

My head pounded with each heartbeat. The trees were dark gray splotches, standing out from the lighter sky. The streetlamp in the parking lot stabbed the corner of my eye causing sharp pains in my forehead. I felt the lump at the back of my head. No blood came away on my hand.

The pockets of my jeans were pulled out. I felt for my wallet. It wasn't in my back pocket. Then I remembered I'd left it in my pack at the biker's house. I sat up. My body ached, my head throbbed, my vision blurred. I had nowhere to go, didn't even know where I was. I was totally screwed.

Gray light shone through the trees. My body was a ball of pain, my thoughts dark. The euphoria, the brilliance of the cocaine had departed. Spider was gone. Hope of winning Evvie back faded to nothing, taking with it any desire to live.

Not knowing myself or how I fit into the world was normal, as was having no purpose or direction, feeling empty. But this was worse. Breathing seemed a waste of air, the rising sun an insult. Why not just sit here and die? I'd never be so lucky. I would have to keep breathing and feel this deadness. Sadness and pain were all I felt, the only things telling me I still lived.

Light overtook the silent gloom. Traffic noise drifted across the parking lot. The tree pressing into my back forced me to squirm, making my head swim. I laid back down on the dusty ground, caught between the need to do something and the nausea and pain that prevented me.

I lay there until I heard the sound of Harleys approaching. Listening to the engines rev and backfire told me there were at least two bikes. Could it be Spider and Horse looking for me?

I struggled to my feet and leaned against the tree to brush the moldy leaves off my t-shirt and jeans. Pain pulsed through my head and neck and down to my ribs. Would I ever stop hurting? Where were the pills when you needed them?

I pushed away from the tree and reached one foot out, gauging my balance. Then I took another step. I could stand. I could walk. Every step caused pain, but I had to get out of these trees so Spider could find me. I kept my head down, squinting, watching for tree roots. Tripping scared the hell out of me. I wasn't sure I could get back up.

Through the edge of the clearing, I saw two guys facing each other next to a couple of motorcycles. "Spider," I called, and waved.

The men turned and looked at me. Too late, I saw the larger man sported Outlaws colors.

The smaller man took a few strides toward me. "You wouldn't be callin' me Spider, would ya? 'Cause that'd be a insult I couldn't let pass."

I stepped back and hit my head on a tree. The coffee shop door was thirty paces away. I wouldn't make it in before he caught me. A minute ago I'd wished for death. Now, it seemed to be staring me in the face. Something in me snapped. My vision cleared, the pain muted by the rage rising in me. "Yeah, I called you Spider, but I don't know how I could have made that mistake. You sure ain't him."

The guy was maybe 5'8", and skinny with a concave chest and arms like sticks. He punched his right fist into his left hand and stared at me. "You got that right, dickhead."

I stepped off the curb and stared back. "Because Spider's not goddam Twiggy."

The skinny biker puffed out his chest. "What're you sayin'?" His jaw gyrated, but he didn't move towards me. "I'll kick your ass."

"Oh, I'm sorry. Are you sensitive about being skinny?"

His face turned purple, but he still didn't move.

This guy was all mouth. My confidence soared. I ran to him and swung my elbow into his throat. The impact sent him reeling. His partner, who had been standing near the bikes, caught the guy then let him drop and advanced toward me.

"Come on, badass," I said. "Come on and fight this pussy's battle."

He ignored my taunt, striding toward me.

My mind felt like it was on cocaine again. I had no pain. The man coming at me was like a piece of steel, a blunt object about to collide with my soft flesh. But the adrenaline drowned out my fear. I stared into his eyes. "Come on," I repeated.

Only a step from me, he clasped his hands and raised them above his head. My foot shot out and connected with the side of his knee. He gasped as his leg gave way and he staggered to the left. I clasped my hands, just as he had done, and brought them down with all my weight onto his shoulder. He stumbled and fell to the pavement then scrambled to his knees. He got up on one foot. I kicked him in the ribs. He gasped and wrapped his arms around his midsection.

"Okay, okay," he said. "You got us."

"Got you? I own you." Why was I taunting this guy? Some part of my mind was telling me to leave well enough alone, but I wasn't listening. "You two best get back on your bikes and get outta here before I really hurt you."

The biker's jaw clenched. He stared at me as he got to his feet and walked backward to where their motorcycles were parked. "Come on, Sal."

Sal stood, rubbing his throat. He tried to say something, but only a croak came out.

"Save it, man. This guy here might *really* hurt us," the big man said.

Sal raised his eyebrows, then shrugged and turned toward their bikes.

The other man backed all the way to the rear of his cycle. He unbuckled a saddle bag and stuck his hand inside. "You sure got us good, man. You're a real badass. I respect that."

He yanked his hand out of the bag gripping a three-foot length of chain. He raised it above his head and swung it around as he ran at me.

His moves didn't register right away. When they did, I turned to run but stumbled and fell to the pavement. I could hear the chain whistle as he whipped it around. The first blow slammed my back and shoulders. "Ahh, fuck!" I shouted and curled into the tightest ball I could.

The chain thumped into my butt and arms. My head was spared because I had wrapped my arms around it. Every blow forced me to cry out in pain.

"You threatened me." He was panting. The chain hung from his hand. "You better *respect* me motherfucker. I will kill you dead."

"Stop! Stop! I'm sorry. Just stop."

A siren started up somewhere not too far away. The man stood back. "C'mon, Sal. We gotta go."

Sal kicked me in the thigh. "You're a dead man next time I see you."

"Let's ride," the big man said.

The cycles fired up and roared off. The siren grew louder. I finally made the connection. The cops were coming. Even though I was the victim here, they'd find a reason to haul me in.

I rolled onto my belly and got to my hands and knees. Everything ached. My fear of the cops outweighed the agony, and I struggled to my feet.

The Police Special was still where I left it seven or eight hours ago. I cranked it up and rode out of the lot. The police cruiser pulled in with its lights flashing as I turned onto the street. The cop looked at me, but kept driving. This was incredible luck. If someone had called in a fight in progress, I was proof one had taken place.

Pain wasn't my only problem. Killing Brian haunted me anytime my brain slowed down enough for me to hear what it was chattering about. Guilt burned in my stomach. As frightening as getting caught felt, in some ways I wished it was over. I almost wanted to turn myself in. Spider would be arrested, though, and likely Horse. I had that to think about, even though Spider had taken off and left me.

I rode aimlessly, looking for landmarks, for anything to point me towards Hell house or the lake or even Evvie's, though I knew better than to knock on her door. I ended up riding north, knowing I'd reach Lake Erie sooner or later.

I pulled into Edgewater Park where Spider and I had our talk. I parked the bike near the boulders that lined the shore, then sat down on a narrow strip of grass that separated the walkway from the rocks.

The lake was choppy in the sunlight. A stiff lake breeze whipped up whitecaps. Pain throbbed, the price of standing up for myself. I found the most comfortable position I could and let the sight of the water wash over the thoughts sloshing around in my head.

I had known something like brotherhood with the Angels. They'd given me speed which made me feel confident, better than I had ever felt. Then there was cocaine which brought euphoria, made life seem worth living. Spider thought the drugs would be a problem for me, but I just didn't see it. His story of woe seemed over the top. How bad off could he have been? That would never happen to me.

"Excuse me."

I turned to see a skinny woman standing on the sidewalk. She looked about thirty. A tangle of dull brown hair surrounded her windburned face. Her fingernails were chewed to the quick.

"Yeah?" I said.

"Ya got any spare change?"

"You got me on a bad day. I don't have a cent."

"It's not what ya think, see. I just lost my job, and my rent was due, and I got no money to buy food. You can help me, can't ya? Please?"

"I said, I don't have any money."

"That's what everyone says, see? But I'll buy food. I swear. Just help me."

I studied her. She was sweating, yet wore a gray hooded sweatshirt with mud and grass stains on the sleeves. Her eyes were vacant. She was rubbing her arms.

"You're a junkie," I said before I could rein in my mouth.

She started trudging down the path, hands in her sweatshirt pockets, shoulders slumped.

"Wait. I want to talk to you," I said.

She kept walking.

"Wait." I managed to get on my feet and follow her. "I want to talk to you. I didn't mean to insult you. What's your name?"

She turned around. "Jane, as in Jane Doe and I ain't got time, man. I'm already sick, and if I don't get the rest of the ten dollars I need, it's gonna be a bad day for me. You got a dollar? Gimme a dollar. If you got four dollars, I'll blow ya. I need it bad. C'mon, man. Help me out."

I pulled the pockets of my jeans inside out. "I don't have a penny, lady."

She turned and started walking, this time a little faster. She approached a middle-aged couple sitting on a blanket on the grass. "Excuse me, please. I just lost my job and need a few dollars to get some food for my baby. Can you help me?"

The man shook his head, but the woman pulled a dollar out of her purse and handed it to her.

"Why, thank you, but I need four dollars."

The man shook his head again. The woman took out a ten dollar bill and handed it to the lady. "Take care of your baby, sweetheart. It must be hard to be on your own and with a child."

"She's a beggar, Doris. That money will go straight to the liquor store," the man said.

"You can't know that, Paul," the woman answered. She looked at Jane. "You be careful, hon. Your baby needs you."

I was touched by the woman's kindness. She didn't seem to care where the money went, she just wanted to help, so she did. Jane nodded, turned back in my direction, and double-timed past me.

I tried to jog after her, but it hurt too much. "Slow down. I'll go with you."

At this, she stopped and looked me over. "Huh. Showing up broke won't get you anything. Besides, you don't wanna go with me." She shook her head and walked away.

Chapter 16

I sat back on the grass and watched her hurry away. She was a mess for sure, but that wouldn't happen to me. She must have liked using when she started. Why had she let it get away from her? Once again I let the water drown out the tribe of monkeys swinging through my brain. The repeated swoosh of the breaking waves lulled the monkeys into a stupor. I blinked at the sun's reflection. With each blink, my eyelids grew heavier until I laid back and slept.

•   •   •   •   •

"Hey."

Something prodded my leg.

"Wake up. This is public land. You can't camp here."

A cop stood over me twirling his nightstick.

"I'm not camping," I said.

"You're camping. Don't get smart with me, you long-haired bastard. The ordinance says you can't sleep on the grass."

Several people were sitting or laying on blankets under the noon sun. Some of them may have been sleeping. I swung my arm in a wide arc. "Looks like you need a lot of tickets."

The cop's face turned red, and he thumped the bottom of my tennis shoe with his baton.

"Ow! Damn. Stop," I said.

"You're a smart ass to boot. Stand up." I had been sleeping deeply, and my bruised muscles weren't ready for me to leap up. I rolled onto my hands and knees and put one foot flat on the ground, trying to get up.

"Are you stoned? Get up, dammit. I ain't got all day to fuck with you lowlifes. You worthless hippies ruin this place for the decent folks."

I got to my feet.

The cop brandished his nightstick. "Show me yer arms."

I held my arms out in front of me. "What're you looking for?"

"Take off yer shoes, you sneaky bastard. I'll find yer tracks, and you'll be on your way to jail."

"Jail? For what? I haven't done anything."

He whapped the side of my thigh with his stick. "Did that hurt?"

"No."

"Take yer fuckin' shoes off or the next one will."

I pulled off my tennies and held them out to the cop. "There's nothing in them. Go ahead."

He whacked them out of my hand. "I don't need to see your shoes, and you'd best quit actin' so cute. Take your goddam socks off and let me see your feet."

I sat back down, pulled my socks off and held my feet up.

He bent over and inspected the tops and between the toes. After a few seconds, he straightened up. "Yer a lucky son-of-a-bitch, I'll say that. Stand back up and pull out yer pockets."

Oh, fuck. I didn't have an ID or a single penny.

Fear replaced irritation. I'd read where criminals were caught by accident. A traffic stop, a domestic call. I figured this bastard was going to find some reason to haul me in, and Brian's death was bound to come out.

I wrestled my way to my feet again and pulled the pockets of my jeans inside out. Bile churned up from my gut.

The cop stuck his billy club through the ring on his belt and started to pat me down when the radio in his car came to life. "Forty-two, be advised 10-18, respond 10-39. 10-32 officer down at Seventh and Herschel Court."

"Son of a bitch." He ran to the car and reached for the radio. "Forty-two 10-76 to Seventh and Herschel Court, ETA 6 minutes." He threw the mic into the front seat, put one foot in the car and pointed at me. "You get yer ass outta this park. Find somewhere else to do yer fuckin' drugs." The car's tires squealed as he pulled away with lights flashing and siren wailing.

My heart hammered in my throat. Panic at the prospect of being arrested for Brian's death pulsed through me. I grabbed my shoes and socks and sank down to the grass. My hands shook as I put my tennies back on. I faced the lake, hoping the waves would calm me one more time.

My hands stopped shaking. It was easier to breathe, but dread dragged on me. The cop said I couldn't stay here, but he was gone, and I had no place to go. I laid back down and let the sun hit my face. On a beautiful day in August, on the shore of a majestic lake, the contrast was blatant. The world was a place full of beauty and love, but I would never know any of that. My life may as well be over at eighteen. Brian's death would chase me forever.

"Hey."

Jane stood next to me. She was dressed the same as earlier, but was almost smiling. Her hair was combed. She seemed calm.

"Hey," I said. She interrupted a perfect stream of mental misery. I didn't like the misery, exactly, but at least I could feel it. I didn't want to deal with anyone. I looked away.

"You said you wanted to talk." She sat down next to me. "Let's talk."

"That was then. I don't have anything to give you."

"Maybe you do and don't know it."

What the hell was this crazy woman talking about? I shook my head.

"Look, I'm set for now, and I'm lonely. I'd like someone to hang with. To talk to. You can give me that, can't ya?"

She slid closer until her hip touched mine. She was much calmer than before. Her touch felt good. "What's with you, Jane?"

She laughed. "Yeah, let's keep it at Jane for now. What's your name?"

"Nate."

"Okay, Nate. Nice to meet ya."

She leaned into me and slipped her arm through mine. Aches from bruises all along my side reminded me I'd been beaten twice this week. But I didn't flinch, or move away, or tell her to stop. Her touch found an empty place in me. I was lonely and glad to have any kind of comfort, no matter where it came from.

I squirmed to find a more comfortable position, and she let go of my arm. "You don't have to move," I said.

She leaned her head onto my shoulder.

"You said you were 'set for now,'" I said. "What did you mean?"

"You know, set. I scored for a whole day." She tapped me on the arm. "I even got a little extra, just in case."

"In case what?" I asked.

"You know... you said you wanted to go with me earlier. I thought you were looking for a connection. I was runnin' then. I couldn't think about anything but getting a fix. But now I'm okay. Been to heaven, fell back to earth. Still mellow, under the influence. And I'm set. So, what do you say? Want to get high with me?"

I leaned away from her, causing her to sit up straight. "What's it like?" I asked.

"Heroin? It's the best feeling ever. Keeps me coming back. Come on, let's go see Tony."

I was curious about heroin. This was the drug everyone said would ruin your life. But, they'd said things like that about amphetamines and cocaine. Those drugs had made me feel alive and in control for the first time. Maybe all the information was wrong. I wanted to try heroin no matter what they said, but Jane's actions earlier in the day slowed me down. "All I want to do is try it, not to end up high all the time."

Jane rolled her eyes. "Shut up and kiss me." She put her hand behind my head and pulled me into her. Her lips were wet and warm and wonderful. Her tongue plunged into my mouth and probed. I forgot my pain. Then she pulled me onto my back and straddled me, resting her ass on my groin.

"Come with me," she said.

"Go with you? Where?"

"I have a friend." She stood. "We can go there."

I struggled into a sitting position and looked at her. "And do what?"

Jane's eyes widened. "What the hell do you think, lover boy? Get your ass up. Let's go."

Annette leading me upstairs to get bennies from me and the sexy voice in the woods telling me to 'bring the snow' were fresh on my mind. It was clear there was no free ride. But none of that mattered. "Sure," I said. "We can take my bike."

The Police Special started on the first kick, which I took as a good omen. Jane, or whatever her name was, guided me through the streets to an old section of town. The houses were two-story, with porches and yards that spoke of better times.

"Right there," Jane said, pointing. The house's second-floor porch railing had fallen into the front yard. The place was a mess.

I pulled the bike to the curb in front of the house. A bearded guy stumbled out the front door and down the stairs to the sidewalk. He shrugged his shoulders as he passed us.

"Who's that?" I asked.

"Dunno," Jane answered. "C'mon.." Her gaze was fixed on the house as she walked up the stairs. "Come on!" she barked.

I hustled to catch up with her, then followed her into a high ceilinged room devoid of furniture. A staircase cut a slash down the far wall. There wasn't any trash on the floor, but the place felt dirty.

"This is your friend's place?"

"Hey, Tony," Jane called.

"That you, angel?"

"Yeah. I brought the guy I told you about. You know, uh, uh..." She looked back at me. "What's your name again?"

"Nate."

"Yeah. Nate is here. We're gonna crash for a while, then party. So, you got me covered, right?"

A slender man of about thirty walked down the stairs. He was clean shaven except for a mustache and small goatee. He wore a white button-down shirt and a cardigan. "Hello, Nate. Welcome to my place of business. Doreen says you're looking for a connection. Well, look no further." He clasped his hands in front of himself and smiled.

His wispy voice was creepy, but I liked him in spite of it. "Well, Jane, er, Doreen, invited me." I didn't know what she told him, but I wasn't looking for a real connection. I wanted to get laid and maybe try snorting heroin.

"Yes, she told me earlier today you wanted to try my product. I have the best in Cleveland. Hell, the best in all of Ohio. Ready?"

Doreen, stood in the middle of the room, looking up the stairs, rubbing her arms.

I tapped her butt. "I thought we were-"

"Yeah, yeah, Nate. We will. But first things first. C'mon Tony. Hook me up. You said we were square for today and tonight."

Tony looked at Doreen and smiled. "You're dependable, sweetie. That's what I love about you." Tony took my arm and led me up the stairs.

Doreen followed on my heels. "Yeah, Tony. Dependable. I always come through."

Tony ignored her, speaking to me in quiet tones. "I see you're walking stiffly, and you have some bruises. Been in a fight?"

I nodded. Tony's patter was soothing, like I could tell him anything. "Yeah. I got jumped. It's been a long day."

Upstairs was a different world. The carpet was clean. There was a recliner and a huge couch. A bar ran along one side of the room, separating it from the kitchen.

"Nice place, man," I said.

"Have a seat here," Tony said. "I'll get you something for your aches."

"What about me, Tony?" Doreen said. "Don't forget about me. C'mon man."

Tony's eyes narrowed. "You're acting like an addict, Doreen. I hate that."

Doreen raised her shoulder and lowered her head like she'd been slapped. "Yeah, Tony. Sorry, Tony, but I'm getting a little shaky, you know?"

Her transformation was remarkable. In the park, Jane/Doreen was calm. Now, she was jumpy, unable to stand still. She chewed her lower lip and shifted her weight. She alternated from wringing her hands to rubbing her arms. She was sweating. We wouldn't be having sex anytime soon.

Tony returned from a room off the side with a small packet and a syringe. He picked a rubber strap off the bar and knelt beside my chair.

"I don't have any money, man. Jane, er, Doreen said she had some extra stuff. I just wanted to snort it, that's all."

Tony pulled a spoon out of his pocket and tore open the packet. "This is easier than people think. We just have to cook it, liquefy it, then we'll be ready to go."

His voice was so calm. He seemed so confident, so in charge. If he was going to give me a free ride, I wasn't going to say no. I felt safe.

Doreen stared at Tony's hands as he heated up the heroin. "C'mon, man. What about me? I mean, you promised. I brought him here. You promised."

Tony stuck a cotton ball into the bowl of the spoon and pulled the liquid into the syringe through the cotton. He put the syringe in his teeth while he wrapped the rubber strap around my bicep and pulled it tight.

"Tony! Dammit! You promised me. You promised!"

Doreen was almost doubled over as she yelled at Tony. Her arms wrapped around her midsection as if she were holding herself back from grabbing the syringe out of Tony's hand and plunging it into her own vein. She slumped to the floor and cried. "I need it, Tony. I need it."

Tony glanced at her, then thumped the crook of my arm a couple of times and slid the needle in. He pulled on the plunger, drawing a blur of blood into the syringe, then pushed.

Ooohhh. Yeaaahh.

He handed me a trash can.

"What's this for?" I asked.

"You'll need it." Tony smiled.

My insides lurched, and I vomited into the can.

"It only gets better from here," he said.

Chapter 17

After my stomach settled, a hazy, blurry, cottony sense of contentment came over me. Doreen was laying on the couch with a needle still sticking out of her arm. As bizarre as being in a heroin house was, it felt normal, like this is where I should have been my whole life.

Tony sat in an easy chair opposite me. "There you are, my friend. Are you enjoying the ride?"

I laughed. "Oh, yeah. Man, this is like world peace, and the end of poverty all rolled up in one. This is truth."

Tony smiled a grim smile. "That's great. Remember, I'll be here for you." He crossed his legs. "Doreen tells me you're broke. That true?"

Uh-oh. "Yeah. I'm broke." But that was okay. *Everything* was okay.

"Well, maybe we can help you out. Why don't you stay here for a while? Let's see if there isn't something you can do for me."

Doreen stirred, then sat up on the couch. "Yeah man. Do it. Tony always takes care of me, don't you baby?" She got up and knelt in front of the dealer. Her hands slid up his thighs and rubbed his groin.

She started to unbuckle his belt, and Tony backhanded her, knocking her on her side. "Get away, bitch."

Doreen lay on the floor, rubbing the side of her head. "Yeah, Tony. You're right. I'm sorry. But don't hit me, okay?"

The drug had me in a calm space, but addled. Doreen had asked me here to have sex, then went down on Tony. Tony hitting her wasn't right, but mom always said you get what you deserve, so it must be okay. Doreen even said so. Ah, I didn't give a fuck. Everything was fine, just fine.

"You won't act like this slut, will you?" Tony ground his jaw.

I was blissed out and could barely shake my head.

"Good," he said. "I hate it when people act like addicts."

What does an addict act like? I wasn't going to blow him, that was for sure. Doreen had gotten pushy, even desperate before. Her addiction was plain. *No way*

I'll let this own me. Fuckin' Spider with his pay attention bullshit. I am payin' attention, and I'm seein' life from a whole new angle.

"Yeah, I'll stay here," I said. "I mean, if it's okay."

Tony's head snapped up. "Yes. Good. Stay here. There's always something that needs doing." He stood up and rubbed his hands together as if to warm them, but the August heat was oppressive, even with the windows open.

"I'm a good worker. Tell me what you need, and I'll do it. But not just right now."

He rose and walked to a doorway at the rear of the house. "No, no. Don't worry, Nate. All in good time." He went into the rear room and closed the door behind him. Two deadbolts clicked into place.

"Far out, man. All in good time," I said to the empty space where he had stood.

I wandered to the oversized sofa along the wall opposite the bar and slouched at one end. Dull throbbing reminded me of the beatings I'd received. Like the physical pain, guilt and fear about Brian's death pulsed in edges of my mind. The drug had numbed my concern. The emotions existed, but I did not care. I would handle them later, if at all. For now, for this moment, all was right. This is where I wanted to stay.

Doreen pulled herself up from the floor and lay down on the other couch again. A red welt swelled on her cheek where Tony had slapped her, but she seemed unfazed even as she rubbed it.

I tapped her on the shoulder. "So, what do you say?"

"About what?" she replied.

"C'mon, you know."

Doreen sat up. "What? Are you twelve? If you're talking about sex, forget it." She slid back down and stretched out. "Leave me alone, Ned."

"Ned? Who the hell is Ned?"

"Ned, Nick, Nestor, whatever. Leave me alone." She shifted around, curling into a ball.

She couldn't even remember my name. What a loser. I leaned back and closed my eyes. It felt good not worrying about anything.

"Where'd Tony go?" I asked.

Doreen stirred. "Wherever Tony goes. I dunno, Nate." She sat up and laughed. "Nate! That's your name." Then she laid back again.

"So, what now? I came along with you, and you scored, and I scored, and Tony's gonna let me stay here. So everything's perfect, know what I mean?"

Doreen shifted around and covered her head with her arm. "Mm-hm."

I fell into a trance-like state. It'd been a while since Tony had pushed the plunger on that needle. Thirty minutes or thirty hours, it was hard for me to tell the difference. The peace and relaxation that calmed my every cell overrode eighteen years of anxiety and negative reinforcement. There was this weird upper room in a dicey part of Cleveland and a woman who had led me here by my dick, who was now sleeping across from me, but not with me, off in her own world of happy-happy. I still wanted to fuck her, but didn't have the energy to make the effort.

Tony had to be one of the good guys, giving me a free ride, and a place to stay, away from the confusing double standard of Spider and his Hells Angels buddies. I guess I ought to have taken their bike back. Aww, fuck 'em. It could wait. I was dry and off the street in what seemed like a safe place. What more could I want?

Tony reappeared, closing and locking the door behind him. He looked around. The sun was going down and the room filled with shadows. Tony flipped a switch, and the shadows disappeared.

"Looking for something?" I asked.

He fixed me with a stare, eyebrows and lips relaxed.

After a minute, I grew uncomfortable. "What's up?"

Tony cocked his head. "I think you're the man for the job."

Job? The thought of doing much of anything made me laugh. I felt capable of anything, but motivated to do nothing. "Oh, yeah? I think so, too."

Tony set down a briefcase, sat opposite me. "I can see you've been around some. You came in here a little beat-up, but not bitching about it. You weren't asking for a free ride. I like that. Shows character. You do have character, don't you?"

Wow. He thought I had character. "Yes, sir. I have great character. And you're right. I've been around some." I thought of all that had transpired since I'd gotten to Cleveland. Sure, I'd had my ass kicked several times, but I was still alive and fighting. I'd learned to not run away at the threat of violence. And look at the guys who had become my friends. I mean Spider had taken a liking to me, though he was missing at the moment. And Evvie. I mean, sure she was mad at me, but that was a temporary misunderstanding. A few weeks ago I had been a scared boy with no direction, no purpose, no experience in life. And now? I was blissed out on H. Things were great.

Tony eyed me. "So, you ready to do something for me?"

My body felt welded to the couch, but I was eager to please this man who had spotted my abilities. I wanted to prove him right. "Yessir. What do you need?"

Tony held the briefcase out to me. "We have a few deliveries to make. You ready?"

Make deliveries? What could be easier. "Sure. Let's go."

A metal staircase led down to a small enclosed backyard. A beautiful burgundy car with a white vinyl top sat amidst the trash cans hidden from street view by a six-foot fence.

"Nice ride, man," I said as I walked around to the passenger side.

Tony snorted. "It ought to be, for what it cost."

I slid into the white leather bucket seat and put the briefcase under my legs on the floor. The door closed with a solid "thunk."

Tony turned the key, and the car came to life, purring like a contented lion.

"Awesome, man. Totally far out." I'd never ridden in a car so fancy. The dash lights had everything glowing. Even the ashtray was spotless.

Tony slid the car into gear, and we glided onto the street.

"This car is far out. What kind is it?"

"It's the '71 Riviera. I've got the only one in Cleveland. Had to pay a big premium to get the dealer to sell me his demo." Tony leaned his head back on the headrest. "Perks, my man. The finer things." Then he sat up and fiddled with a red plastic cartridge, pushing it into an opening in the dash. "Eight-track stereo. State of the art." He turned the knob, and Gary Puckett and the Union Gap came blasting out of the speakers. *"Young girl I'm outta my mind..."*

Tony drove to a more commercial area, and pulled into a burger and shake drive-in. He backed the car into a spot in the rear. A carhop skated up and took our orders.

Tony pulled the cassette out and didn't replace it. He reached behind his back and pulled an envelope out of the waistband of his slacks. He hefted the package and tapped his hand with it. As the carhop skated up with our food, he slid it out of sight.

I was curious, but didn't want to seem over-eager, so I concentrated on my burger and fries.

"You have a healthy appetite, Nate. Enjoy. Next time we'll go for something decent, like steak."

I was thrilled to be eating at all. I would've been content to have burgers for a long time. I shrugged. "I guess that'd be good. I like steak okay."

As we talked, a cream-colored Lincoln pulled into the drive-in and rolled to where we were parked, blocking the Riviera.

A man in an open shirt and slacks got out of the passenger side and walked to Tony's window.

Tony handed him the envelope.

The man hefted it, then opened the flap and riffled through the contents. He leaned into the car window. "You got it all this time, right? Cause we don't need a repeat of your last performance."

"Paddy, come on, my friend. I told you, my deliveryman got into the envelope and slid a few hundred out. He no longer works for me. And, I made it right with Mr. Boyle. So, I trust that's the end of the problem. The boss is okay now, right? He's knows I'd never stiff him."

Paddy didn't move a muscle.

"Really, man. He's okay with me now, right?"

The gangster straightened up. "You've got eight lives left, Tony. Maybe fewer than that. Don't fuck up again." He walked back to the Lincoln and climbed in. The huge auto idled a few minutes, then pulled away.

Tony drew a deep breath and pursed his lips as he let it out. "Welcome to the world of business, my friend." He looked at me and smiled. "That's how I pay my bills. Now, I'll show you how I make my money."

I was still stoned from the heroin, but watching Paddy and listening to his suggestion that Tony was in big trouble worried me. I mean, I knew drugs were sold by criminals. Hell, Spider told me about what had happened with the stupid amphetamines that started me on this raft of crazy shit. I was in way over my head. Who was "the boss?" Tony seemed to be in business for himself, but he answered to someone. "What just happened?"

Tony started the car. "Don't worry about what doesn't concern you." He grabbed my upper arm and stared at me. "And that does not concern you. Understand?"

"Uh, sure, man. Sure." But it did concern me.

"We're heading to Hough."

Hough didn't mean anything to me, but as we drove the streets got dirtier and the buildings rougher. People walked alone and in pairs, heading to corner stores or just sitting on the curb smoking. There wasn't a white face to be seen. The car attracted a lot of attention, young men craning their necks as we drove by.

We made a right and pulled up in front of a green house. At least what was left of the paint looked green. Graffiti covered the lower walls. The windows were boarded up.

Tony turned in the seat to face me. "It's a little late to be asking you this, but you seem like a guy who's been in a scrape or two, right?"

I had been in a few scrapes, though all of the serious ones had taken place since I'd arrived in Cleveland. And I had lost almost all of them. I had some swagger now, though. So I let him think I was a tough guy. "Yeah, sure. I've had my share."

"Good, good. I have a little business of my own to conduct, not unlike what our friend Paddy had to do. Are you with me?"

My head was beginning to hurt, and the food was bubbling in my stomach. I didn't like the way this was headed. "Uh sure. I'm with you, I guess. What do you need me to do?"

"It's simple. There is a man in that house who is supposed to have $3000 in cash for me. Last week he owed me $1500, but didn't have it. So, I gave him some time to make it right. I need you to go get the $3000 he owes me."

"So, this guy's expecting me?"

"No, he's expecting me, but I'll be where he can see me. He'll know what you want."

I didn't move. All I could think of was overhearing Horse planning to send me on a suicide mission. "Okay. I'll do it, but why me?"

"Hey." Tony jabbed a finger at me. "You said you'd help me out. Like I told Paddy, the last delivery guy I had is no longer with me. He lacked character. I hoped you would serve as a good replacement."

Through the haze in my mind, I realized Tony was beginning to own me. Bile shot up my throat. I climbed out of the car, staring at the decrepit house. I was coming off my first hit of heroin, having decided that drugs were the most mind-expanding thing I'd ever experienced. I'd used drugs, sold drugs and now I was about to collect a pile of money for a drug dealer. As I slammed the car door vomit shot out of me, some through my nose. It burned like hell.

"Oh brother," Tony said. "Go get my damn money."

I straightened up and spat, trying to get the foul taste out of my mouth.

A cracked sidewalk led to the front door, or rather to where the front door had been. A sheet of plywood covered the opening. There was a square hole about four feet up covered by another piece of plywood on hinges.

I raised my hand to knock, but before I could, a voice sounded from within. "What do you need?"

"I'm here for Tony's money."

The flap swung open. A pinched face eyed me up and down before snorting a laugh and slamming the flap shut. "Send Tony. I don't deal with nobodies."

I looked at Tony seated in the car and shrugged. "He wants to see you."

Tony got out of the car, opened the trunk. When he stood up, he was pushing a chrome automatic into his waistband. He pulled his sweater over the pistol and strode toward the house. He bounded up the stairs, pulled the pistol and shot three rounds into the lower portion of the plywood. *Boom, boom, boom.*

"Open the fucking door, Elwood, or you are a dead man." Tony, the mild-mannered, quiet drug dealer had become Al Capone.

"Geez, Tony, the cops, man. What are you doing?" I said.

He ignored me. "Elwood, you have until I count three to open up. One. Two." *Boom.* He fired another round. "That was three, asshole. Are you ready now?"

A frantic banging came from behind the reinforced opening. "Hold on, Tony. I'm tryin'."

Tony replaced the pistol in his waistband, looked at me and smiled. "Gets them every time."

I was bewildered. The effect of the heroin had faded leaving a mess of conflicting voices in my head. Speed gave me courage and cocaine gave me confidence, but heroin! Heroin cured every anxiety, every regret, every fear. But that feeling was muted now, and I wanted it back strong.

The noise from behind the plywood grew louder and more frantic. "I can't get this open, man. The guy that made it done too good."

The plywood covering the window to the right of the door cracked under repeated blows from the inside. At last a boot smashed through. "Hold on, man. Keep that shooter in your pocket. I'm comin'."

A man with long, matted gray hair pushed the shattered wood aside and climbed onto the porch. His crotch looked wet, like he had pissed his pants.

Tony's fist slammed into the old man's face.

"Ah, shit," he cried. "What're you doing, man? You know I always come through."

Tony raised his hand again.

The man staggered back and held his hands in front of his face. "Okay, okay. Let's talk about it, then."

Tony lowered his fist and adjusted the pistol in his waistband. "There's nothing to talk about. You stiffed me last week, and that made me light for Mr. Boyle. Mr. Boyle doesn't accept excuses, and neither do I. Elwood, we go way back, but we won't go too far forward if you don't do things right."

The old man looked at his boots and shuffled his feet. "I haven't been light before. Doesn't that count, man? I hit a rough spot."

"It is plain to me that the 'rough spot' you have hit involves sampling your own product. There is practically a groove worn in the sidewalk leading to your door from the masses of desperate people who bring you your wealth. You're light because you're using."

The old man looked at his feet. "Well, yeah. But, really, it was quality control. Don't you see? And, I'm over that now. No more, man. I've conquered this shit. I've come out on top."

Tony peered into the man's eyes. "Why are you acting so squirrelly? Why didn't you open for my collector?"

Elwood shifted his weight from one leg to another. "Well, you ain't used a collector before." He took a deep breath. "And I ain't got the money."

Tony pursed his lips and shook his head. "You do not have my money?"

Elwood stared at the porch floor.

"Well then, You are going to die."

Chapter 18

"Goddam, Tony. Wait a minute, man." Elwood shielded his face with his hands, as if that would stop a bullet. "I have *some* of the money. And I can get the rest pretty fast."

Tony shook his head.

Elwood slumped against the wall and stared at the porch floor.

"What should I do, Nate?" Tony asked. "You've seen the pressure my obligations have me under. How should I handle this untenable situation?"

Why was he asking me? "I dunno. If he hasn't got it, he hasn't got it, right?"

"See, Tony, that's the voice of reason," Elwood whined. "Listen to the guy." The old man pushed away from the wall. "Let me get what I've got for you." He pried the plywood further from the window and climbed back inside. "Don't go anywhere. I'll be right back." The wood slapped against the siding as Elwood disappeared.

A lone streetlight shone from across the street, leaving the porch in shadows.

"What do we do now?" I asked.

Tony stood, hands on hips, staring at the plywood that covered the front door opening. "Elwood," he called.

No response.

"Elwood! Do not make me come looking for you."

Silence. "Shit!" Tony yelled and kicked the plywood. "Run around to the back. Make sure that deadbeat isn't running."

I jogged around the side of the house. The first-floor windows and the back door were boarded over. Elwood was leaning out of an upper window bathed in moonlight. He tossed out a canvas bag which landed with a thud.

"Tony, he's back here," I yelled.

Elwood straightened up. The moonlight framed him in the window. He pointed a pistol at me. *Pow.*

I stood, frozen in place, not comprehending that he was shooting at *me*.

Pow. Dirt exploded to my right.

Oh, shit." I ducked around the side of the house. "That motherfucker is shooting at me, Tony! Where are you?" I ran back to the front entrance. "Tony?" The car was still parked at the curb, but there was no sign of him. What the fuck do I do now?

A brief scream followed by another thud came from the rear of the house.

"Nate, get back here!" Tony shouted.

I hustled along the side of the house until I reached the rear corner, where I stopped and peeked around. Elwood lay face down on the ground.

Tony leaned out of the second-floor window. "Grab the bag and wait for me."

Elwood gasped for air.

I walked to where the bag lay, keeping my eyes fixed on Elwood.

"Bastard...pushed me. Get...my...pistol," Elwood said. "We can...take...it all."

"Fuck you. You tried to kill me."

The bag was packed tight and heavier than it looked. I slung the strap over my shoulder and scanned the ground for the pistol.

"*Uhn.* C'mon, man...get the...goddamn gun."

"Shut up."

Tony walked around the corner. "Where's his pistol?"

"I don't see it."

"Here it is." Tony picked up the pistol and held it out to me. "Take it."

I stepped back and raised my hands. "I don't want it."

Tony snarled at me. "*Take it.*"

I was nervous. The last time I handled a gun, I killed a man, but seeing Elwood made my fear morph into anger. He had tried to shoot me. I pointed the pistol at him and pulled back the hammer.

"Easy there, Nate," Tony said. "I'll handle this." He pointed his gun at Elwood. "You have finally bought the farm. Are you ready to meet your maker?"

Elwood, still gasping for air, didn't speak.

"I guess that means yes." Looking at me, he said, "Pull him over to the wall and sit him up."

I aimed the gun at Elwood, frozen, wanting to pull the trigger, but unable to.

"Come on, Nate. Do what I say." Tony waved his gun at the rear wall. "Lean him up there."

"I don't want to touch him, man. I mean, he fell out of the window. He might be hurt bad."

Tony laughed. "You're aiming a pistol at him and now you're the son of Albert Schweitzer?" He pointed the pistol at me for a moment, then waved it at the back wall again. "Move him!"

I jumped at the intensity in Tony's voice and pocketed the gun. Elwood groaned when I rolled him over, but his breathing seemed easier. I stood behind his head and reached down to lift him by his arms, but before I could get a grip, Elwood grabbed my hair and yanked me head over heels to the ground beside him. He held the tip of a four-inch switchblade against my neck. "Let me...walk, Tony." He coughed and groaned. "I've fucked it all up...but I don't deserve...to die...neither does this stupid kid. Just let it be."

Tony lowered the gun to his side. "Why?" he asked as he rubbed his chin.

Elwood scraped the blade along my neck.

My bowels felt liquid. "Aw, shit. C'mon, don't hurt me, man."

Tony raised the gun again. I guess he was aiming at Elwood, but it looked like he was aiming at me.

"Okay, Elwood. You get a pass. So, how do we handle this?"

The pressure of the knife tip on my neck eased. "Get up." Elwood eased his hold on me.

I rolled sideways out of Elwood's reach and stood up.

"Come over here," Tony said. Once I was next to him, he said to Elwood, "You're free to go. A luckier man I do not know."

Elwood struggled to get up. Perhaps adrenaline masked the extent of his injuries, but his grunts and groans made it plain that he hurt. He took a step toward the bag.

"You are kidding, right?" Tony said.

Elwood stopped. "Yeah, I knew better." He turned back, facing us. "Any chance we can start over? You know I got nowhere to go."

Tony leaned his head to one side, like he was studying Elwood, as if trying to see something deeper than the wreck of a man that showed on the surface. Then the pistol flashed in the moonlight as Tony swung the butt of the gun into the back of Elwood's head.

Elwood fell in a heap as his knees collapsed.

"Drag him over to the wall," Tony said. "Pull him up to a sitting position."

I tugged at Elwood. "What're you going to do?"

The dealer picked up the satchel Elwood had thrown down and pulled a tinfoil wrapped brick from it. He made a tiny slit, prying some white powder out of it. He pulled a leather case from his pocket and took out a spoon and a Zippo.

Elwood moaned, and his head rolled.

"We're going to send him to heaven, Nate, and he won't be coming back to earth." Tony cooked the heroin with the lighter, then pulled a syringe from the case and injected Elwood. He stood up and put everything back into his pocket. "He'll never know what took him out. I would say that was a kindness. Wouldn't you agree?"

"He's going to die?" I asked.

"Yes he is." He tossed the canvas bag to me. "Come on, let's go."

Tony took off toward the street, and I followed. "You're just going to leave him there?"

Tony kept walking.

"Won't somebody get suspicious?"

"Get in the car," Tony said as we reached the sidewalk.

I climbed in, stashing the satchel between my feet. The car purred as we pulled away from the house. The leather seats and the cushy ride felt good, but my mind still reeled. I didn't understand what Tony had done to Elwood. It looked just like what he had done to me a few hours ago. "What did you do to him?"

"I gave him what he wanted."

"Um, you shot him up, just like you did me. Won't he come to in a few minutes?

Tony laughed. "Oh, my goodness. I fear I may have misjudged you. You don't know anything, do you?"

"Why do you say that?" When Tony was asking me about being in scrapes, and if I knew how to handle myself, I'd been in the sweet spot of a heroin hit. Everything had seemed alright. I didn't want to tell him I'd only been high a few times, and high on cheap amphetamines and some good cocaine. Now, I was way past that point of bliss. Nothing felt right.

"I liked what you did for me is all. But now you say Elwood is going to die. I don't get it."

We drove on in silence for a few minutes.

"Okay Nate. I'm going to fill you in. But, trust is paramount in this business. So, what I share with you is privileged. I tell you what you need to know and you never, ever lie to me. Understand?"

Something sounded off about what Tony said, but I was in his car, had eaten his food, still needed a place to stay and a way to make a few bucks. And, I was sure I wanted to try heroin again—not to get hooked, but to feel that utter contentment.

"Sure, Tony. I get it. You can trust me."

"So, you're being straight. You're from Milwaukee, and just passing through, and need a few bucks. You haven't lied to me about that, right?"

All of this was true. I was just passing through, never even meant to stay, had no ties, didn't know anyone here. The Buick's AC was blasting. Sweat popped out on my forehead and felt like beads of ice. The questions still seemed odd to me. Why would he care where I was from or where I was headed?

Tony glared hard at me. "Right? I need to know my associates are straight with me."

I leaned against the door, trying to add some distance from this guy. "It's all true, Tony. I swear."

Tony resettled into the seat and put his hands on the wheel. The corners of his mouth turned up. "That's what I'm talking about, Nate. Trust." He shifted into gear and pulled away from the curb.

After a while, I asked, "Where are we headed?"

"We've got a few more stops. They won't all be like that one. Elwood's been sinking for a while. It was just a matter of time before he lost it."

Risking Tony's disdain, I asked again, "So, what'd you do to him?"

The passing streetlights illuminated Tony's placid smile. "Do you know who Paraclesus was?"

I shook my head.

"Paraclesus was a philosopher ages ago. He said, 'The dosage makes a poison or a remedy'. Heroin is a wonderful drug. I gave you a remedy. I gave Elwood a poison."

I rode in silence, watching streetlights, parked cars, houses, people go by. Everything looked like the Milwaukee neighborhood I'd grown up in. Some places were real nice, some were dumps, most were in-between. I couldn't imagine

Elwood in the backyard of one of the houses in my neighborhood, unconscious. Dying. For a few dollars, even a few thousand dollars.

"So, you left him there to die?"

"Yes, my friend. When the body is found tomorrow or the next day, the police will assume this was just another junkie overdosing. They all want to die, you know."

I was on overload. Anxiety shredded my thoughts. Tony's demeanor no longer calmed me. His lack of emotion made him seem like a psychopath from a horror movie. He'd just killed a man, and now he's quoting dead philosophers. He did have heroin, though. And I wanted more of that. The deep serenity of my last hit was gone, and I was longing for more.

We left the main drag and meandered through several winding streets in a neighborhood where the houses were in good repair, and the lawns were mowed. The Buick glided to a stop in front of a low, ranch-style house.

"Where are we?" I asked.

Tony glanced at me. "Bring the bag. Keep your mouth shut and your hand on the pistol in your pocket. Is that clear?"

I tried to answer, but fear tightened my throat, so I nodded my head.

"Good. This is business, and it pays to be alert."

Tony and I got out of the car. I tried to swallow, but my mouth was too dry. I wanted to ask questions, to understand what we were doing, but I couldn't. So, I followed him toward the house.

He knocked on the door and stood back and to the side.

"What do you want?" came from within.

"It's Tony."

A series of clicks and clanks sounded, followed by a scraping noise. The door opened a crack. A curly-headed man with his shirt half unbuttoned stuck his head out. "Yeah?"

"You do have Mr. Boyle's payment?"

The door swung open the rest of the way, and the man stepped aside.

Chapter 19

Tony nudged me in the back, and I stumbled into the cramped living room. A single lamp lit one corner of the room. A plaster archway revealed the dining room. TVs, stereos, car radios and assorted junk were piled around the walls. Looked like a pack rat lived there.

The door slammed, and the locks clicked back into place.

"Who's here?" someone called from the back of the house.

The man who had opened the door motioned for us to follow. "It's Tony."

Tony hadn't said a word, and I kept my mouth shut like he told me to.

The man half turned. "You do have the product, right?"

Tony nodded. "Of course. You have cash money, right?" He pointed at the piles of stuff. "I used to take all kinds of items from my retail customers, but no more. I'm not a fence, I'm a pharmacist."

"We got cash, Mr. Wiseass. Bert's back here. He'll wanna test a couple of the bricks."

Tony looked at me and shrugged. "What can I say?"

We were led through the dining room into a large family room which was empty save for a large wooden desk with a balance scale perched on one corner. A flabby man, his face illuminated by a green-shaded banker's lamp sat behind the desk. "Bring it here."

Tony stepped in front of me. "Show me the cash."

Bert reached behind him and flipped a switch on the wall. Fluorescent fixtures flickered to life, filling one corner with harsh light. He leaned on the desk as he pushed his large body up, then waddled toward the lit area and kicked back the carpet revealing a floor safe. "Jack," he said to the man who let us in, "come here. You know I can't bend over that far."

Jack crossed the room and lifted the top from the safe.

I felt for the gun in my pocket. In my mind, the only thing coming out of that safe was a pistol.

But, when Jack straightened up, he held several bundles of wrinkled bills wrapped in rubber bands.

"Satisfied?" Bert asked.

Tony took the satchel from me and held out the brick he had slit open earlier.

Bert put the dope on one tray of the balance scale and a brass weight on the other tray. The weight bobbed up and down a few times, then settled about even with the foil-wrapped brick. "Looks good weight wise. How's the purity?"

"It's open. Test it."

Bert pulled out a pocket knife and worked some of the powder out through the slit Tony had made, then sniffed the white substance. He held it under the banker's light and moved the blade back and forth while peering at the crystals. Finally, he licked his pinkie finger, dabbed at the heroin and tasted it with the tip of his tongue. "Seems pretty good."

Tony snorted. "You doubted? How long have I been your vendor of choice?" He stacked the rest of the foil-wrapped bricks on the end of the desk. "Six kilos total. You better step on this pretty hard, or you'll kill off your customers."

"Hah," Bert said with a wave of his hand. "I know my business. Pay the man, Jack."

Jack handed Tony several bundles of the rubber-banded bills. "You know you're not the only act in town anymore. We had someone else approach us offering a better deal."

Tony ignored the comment and counted the bundles. "Twelve bundles, twelve thousand?" He raised his eyebrows. "Do I need to count this now?"

Bert leaned back in his chair. "You know me better'n that. It's all there."

Tony nodded. "Okay, Bert. I know you know better than to mess with Mr. Boyle." He looked at Jack, then back at Bert. "So, what's this about competition? Mr. Boyle will want to know."

Bert looked at Tony from the corner of his eye, then scowled at Jack. "Oh, you know, dipshits come and go. Forget Jack said anything."

"Keep me informed, Bert." Tony pointed his finger at Jack and dropped his thumb, like the hammer of a pistol. "You too, Jack." He turned to me and said, "Let's go."

We made our way to the front of the house, Jack shadowing us. He unlatched the door and stood aside.

Once we were back in the car I asked Tony, "What's that mean, 'step on it'?"

"We get heroin in a pure form. Before use it needs to be cut, adulterated. A number of things are used. Powdered sugar is popular."

"So, that's why Elwood died from the shot you gave him."

"Mm-hm."

"Don't you feel a little bad about all this?"

Tony started the car and pulled away from the curb. "Feel bad? About what?"

"Well, you killed him. That doesn't bother you?"

"He was stealing from me. He had to go. I'd do it again. I'll bet you would, too."

"No. I don't think I would." Guilt for killing Brian, shame and dread about watching Tony inject Elwood closed my throat. I couldn't swallow, much less speak.

"Hmph," said Tony. "I thought maybe you were a little more experienced. I need someone I can count on to make good decisions, to help me out." His voice was calm, emotionless. "You seemed like that kind of guy, but, maybe not."

With the heroin out of my system, the full impact of what transpired was ice in my gut. I hadn't killed Elwood, but I handed the Tony the poison. I was as guilty of killing Elwood as I was of killing Brian.

"We killed him, Tony. What if the cops find out? I'm a dead man."

"That's a little dramatic, don't you think? There's nothing to implicate you, or me, for that matter. This is the life I live. Look, people have needs I can fulfill. But because there are laws against it, I need to handle my own problems. I can't call the police when someone tries to steal six kilograms of pure heroin." Tony laughed. "Feeling guilty will put you out of business. Or even get you dead."

I watched the neat little houses as we passed them. Straight people lived there, people with kids and jobs and hopes and dreams. I used to live in a place like this, but not anymore. I had committed murder. Twice. Nausea and fear doubled me over. I would have done anything for relief.

"I do feel guilty. I mean, I'll get over it, I guess, but what do I do until then?"

Tony laughed again. "You won't turn yourself in, will you?"

The night I spent in the woods flooded into my memory, how close I was to confessing to shooting Brian and to asking for the punishment I knew I deserved. I shook my head.

"Answer me. You wouldn't, would you?" Tony's voice was half an octave higher.

"No, of course not," I said staring into my lap. But I wasn't sure. Maybe confession offered relief.

Tony drove out of the neighborhood and onto a main drag.

The blocks slid by as we drove down West 73rd. Anxiety weighed on me like a lead jacket. I wanted to get out of the car, to run away from Tony, not knowing where we were headed. The inky emptiness of Lake Erie appeared, and I recognized Edgewater Park. Here I was again. "What are we doing here?"

Tony pulled into a spot next to a wooded area and killed the engine. "Nate, you were a great help to me tonight, and I appreciate it. How would you like have another shot of my finest?"

The anticipation made sweat pop out on my forehead, but even through the craving, the violence that surrounded heroin ate at me. The thing that would fix me might cost someone else their life. It all seemed so screwed up. But my need overrode my conscience. And my fear. "Yeah, I would."

"Great. Let's take care of you."

"Shoot up here? Now?"

"Sure, why not?"

My motorcycle was at his house, but I wanted that relief, and now was better than twenty minutes from now. "Sure."

"Okay. We're going to walk into the woods a little ways, away from prying eyes. I have everything in the glove box."

I pushed the button, and the lid came down to reveal three loaded syringes.

"Bring them." Tony retrieved a flashlight from under his seat and got out of the car. "Follow me."

I grabbed the syringes and climbed out of the car.

I handed the needles to Tony. He led the way.

As we got deeper into the woods, I began to shiver. The smell of rotting leaves clogged my sinuses. Tony's unpredictable behavior nagged at me. Anything could happen in these woods, and no one would know. But I wanted the heroin more than anything.

The light from the parking lot dwindled. Tony shined the light on a fallen log. "Have a seat."

The night had grown cooler. I stilled shivered, but now with anticipation. Being here, so close to feeling the drug's relief, I couldn't wait any longer.

Tony took his belt off and wrapped it around my arm. "Make a fist."

He tapped my arm until he found a vein, cleared the bubbles, then slid the needle in and pushed the plunger.

Poof, all my troubles melted. Anxiety, fear, discouragement, disappeared. Here I was again, in the place of ease.

"There you go, my friend. Now, your troubles are over."

"Thasss good," I said. "Yesss, troubles are so, so, over."

I must have nodded off for a minute. When I came to, Tony's belt was tight on my arm again, and he was looking for a vein.

"What you doin'?" I asked. "You already got me high."

Tony didn't say anything. He stuck another needle in and pushed.

"Hey, Tony? Whass that for?"

He was smiling. "Don't fight it, Nate. This shot is even better. You're going to love this. And the third one's so good you won't come back from it."

I started to nod off again, but heard the sound of a window breaking in the parking lot.

"Motherfucker. Better not be my Riviera." Tony grabbed his belt and loped back toward his car.

"Tony, where you goin'? Leave me the other..."

•   •   •   •   •

When I regained consciousness, I threw up all over my shoes. Tony was gone. It was dark. I was alone. I didn't care. I slid off the log where I was sitting, leaned over and passed out again.

•   •   •   •   •

Light shone through the trees. Hadn't I already gotten out of these woods? Then I remembered these were different woods. This time I would know better than to run out expecting help.

I was still high from the dope. I remembered Tony shooting me up twice and wondered what that was all about. The sound of rustling leaves and cracking twigs made me duck down behind the log. I knew I couldn't take another beating. The stench from my vomit burned my nose. But I lay as still as my aching back allowed.

A female voice came through the trees. "Do you remember any of this?"

That sounded like Evvie.

"Naw, shit, not really."

I knew that voice for sure. It was Spider. Or, at least I thought so, but memories of being beaten with a chain kept me from calling out.

The sound of their footsteps approached the log I lay behind.

"I can't be sure. But I think this is where Wendell found me. I don't like to think about it. I was so sick."

It *was* them. "Spider!" My voice cracked.

They kept walking.

The woman said, "This is a good way to honor Wendell on his birthday. He saved your life, and you need to remember it."

There was no answer, but the footsteps stopped.

"Evvie!" I wanted to call out, but all I heard was a whisper.

"Well, I ain't gonna make a prayer or anything. You know I don't b'lieve in that shit. And even if I did, Wendell didn't like formal stuff. So, whatta we do now?"

"Spider! Spider, it's me!" I thought I was yelling at the top of my lungs. How could they not hear me?

"Just stand there for a minute and feel grateful. Maybe that'll get you to straighten up. I need you to be my friend. I need to know you're here for me and Norma. You gotta get yourself away from the drugs and the stupid violence. You're better than that."

I was worn out from calling their names. I tried pulling myself up onto the log, but my arms weren't taking orders from my brain. I tried twice and then a third time, only to sink back to the leafy floor of the woods. Fatigue descended, then oblivion.

•   •   •   •   •

"I'm gonna try ta lift 'im up." It was Spider. "You got anything you can lay on your back seat?"

"Whad're you doin' here? Wher're you takin' me? Don' use chains. Jus' leave me be."

Spider tapped my face. "What are you mumbling, dumbass?"

My head hung upside down as he carried me out of the woods. In the parking lot, Evvie, stood by her old red car. "Ooo-wee! He stinks. Why'd he have to show up again?"

Spider said, "Open the door. We need to get him someplace we can watch 'im til the dope washes out."

Evvie opened the rear door and stepped aside. "He's like every guy I ever met. They ruin everything."

"I wouldn't ever ruin anythin' for you, Evvie," I said.

"Shut up, dumbass. Nobody kin understand a thing your sayin' anyway." Spider half-threw and half-laid me onto the seat. "You're outta your head. Better keep yer mouth shut."

Evvie got into the driver's seat and started the car.

Spider sat sideways in the passenger seat keeping an eye on me as we pulled out of Edgewater Park. "Well, he should make it. Looks like he mighta almost OD'd, but I suspect he'll survive."

Every bump in the road sent daggers into my forehead. My skull felt like it might explode.

"I can't take him home," Evvie said. "Norma'd have a shit fit if she saw Nate like this. She thinks he's the best thing ever. Maybe I *oughta* take him over there so she can see what a goddam loser he is. Ohh! I'm so mad I could strangle him."

Evvie's words were like blows from a hammer.

"He's already ruined my car. I'll never get this stink out."

Now, I wanted to die.

"Okay," Spider said. "He's acted stupid, and he's payin' for it. Don't add to it, okay? One thing about Wendell, he was one non-judgmental son of a bitch. That's what I remember. He came and got me and didn't preach and didn't accuse me o' nothin'. Just helped me get well and then showed me how to do better."

"I told you, I'm not Wendell." Evvie's voice was hard as ice. "He loved people. I'm not like him. I'm only doin' this 'cause it was his birthday, and I know he'd a wanted me to."

"Okay, Evvie. We're takin' him to the Hellhouse. There ain't nowhere else. Then you're off the hook."

Evvie shook her head, then pulled out.

I couldn't keep my eyes open, partly because of fatigue and partly because the light hurt so bad. Even with the pain, I passed out again.

Chapter 20

"Hey. Wake up."

The voice came from some place far above. I seemed to be in a dark, grave-like pit with my head protruding. I opened my eyes to see if it was a devil or an angel talking to me.

"Nate."

A pasty white face and stringy brown hair hovered over me. The face was neither demonic nor angelic. It was there, though. Real. Not a vision. Not a dream.

"Wake up, man. You gotta move pretty soon. Horse is pissed. Spider's on his shit list for sneakin' you in."

The voice. I knew the voice.

"Here. Take these. You need ta wake up, Nate."

The Voice grabbed my hand and placed some tablets in it.

"Take 'em. I got three. That'll get you goin' enough to get outta here."

"You're Annette," I said.

"Yeah, sweetie. I'm Annette, and you're outta luck. Take the goddam pills. You don't want to be around with Horse as pissed as he is."

I felt the pills in my hand. I remembered pills making things all right. I aimed them toward my mouth. My hand crashed into the side of my face, and the pills fell somewhere.

Annette picked up the pills. "Shit, man. You are one stoned motherfucker." She put one on my lower lip. "Suck that in... go on."

I raked the pill into my mouth with my upper teeth and swallowed. I was so dry. "Got any water?"

The mattress shifted as she got up. I heard water run. In a moment she was back. "Sit up."

I struggled to free myself from the tangle of blankets that covered me.

Annette handed me the other two pills and a glass of water. "Wake up and get gone, Nate. Horse knows you were shootin' up. He ain't gonna let that slide. Not after what happened with Spider."

I wasn't even sure yet where I was. Or why Annette wanted me gone. But, I washed the last two pills down with the tepid water, then laid back down.

"Oh no. Uh-uh. Get up." Annette pulled on my arm. "Let's go. I'll help ya."

I realized I was in the upstairs room at the Hellhouse. The pills weren't kicking in yet. My head ached. I felt like I had the flu. But maybe it *was* time to get up.

"I can do it myself." I jerked my arm free of Annette's grasp and swung my legs over the edge of the mattress, pushing myself up, but collapsed back onto the bed.

"Don't be such a macho prick. Gimme your hand."

I lifted my hand in her direction.

She took it and tugged on my arm until I was standing, then wrapped her arm around my waist and led me to the hallway.

"Hold up, hold up," I said

Annette let go of me, and I teetered against the wall.

"You gotta get goin', man! I keep tellin' ya."

"Okay, okay. But how did I get here? What day is it?"

"It's Monday, if that matters. You've been sleepin' most of two days. Spider and some straight-lookin' chick brought you. I can't believe you slept through everything. We even stuck you in the shower, and you never woke up. The Reaper was watchin' you, waitin'.'"

My tennies were missing, and my jeans were still damp and sticking to me. "Where're my shoes?'"

"Goddam it! It don't matter. You need to get gone."

"I can't leave barefoot. I need my shoes."

Annette slapped her thigh and said, "Okay, Nate. It's your ass that'll get whipped. Stay here, and I'll find your goddam shoes."

As soon as she walked away, I slid down to the floor and hung my head between my knees. I could smell vomit and sweat on me. Getting out of the bed was hard enough. Leaving the house and finding my way somewhere else seemed beyond possible.

"Here." Annette stood over me, holding a pair of boots.

"Those aren't mine."

She dropped them in front of me. "They are now. Dieter won't miss 'em until you're long gone. That is if you get your ass up and get out of here. I'm tellin' you again, you don't wanna run into Horse right now."

I pulled the boots onto my bare feet and tried to stand. When I started to fall over, Annette threw my arm around her shoulders and held me up.

"That's it, cowboy. Annette is gonna save you."

I stumbled down the stairs, but managed to stay on my feet. The house seemed deserted, unusual for a late afternoon. "Where is everybody?"

"They took off to some titty bar that has half-price drinks on Mondays." Annette's face scrunched into a scowl. "They're so dumb. Half price drinks just means more money for the dancers. The drunker those assholes get, the more they'll think them young girls dig 'em. That's the system, ya know. It's stupid."

I didn't like her bitching about guys and strippers. I'd only been once, but I remember how special I felt when the dancers looked at me and licked their lips. "You go to titty bars much? You sound like an expert."

"Where did you come from, bumpkin?" She slapped me on the arm. "I was strippin' since I was fourteen. I know how it goes."

She shoved me toward the front door. "Go. Git. Leave. And if you know what's good for you, don't come back."

"What'd I do? Why am I all of a sudden in trouble here?"

Annette sighed. "If you still have to ask, I can't explain it to you. Hells Angels don't play, Nate. These guys are real. You went and got fucked up on H. They don't allow no needles. Horse made a big exception for Spider and took a lotta shit. He won't do it for you. You're nobody, sweetie. Save yourself. Go."

I walked out into the fading afternoon sun. My clothes stuck to my skin in the humid air. This was the second time I'd seen this street in daylight. It was a pretty nice street. The neighbors must have loved having a house full of bikers on the block.

I turned left and started walking. The amphetamines were clearing up the mud pit that was my mind. I could walk pretty good, and my balance was better. I turned around. Annette was leaning in the doorway. I waved.

She shook her head and walked inside.

I didn't like being rejected. I'd had plenty of practice, but it still stung.

A mailbox was bolted to the cement at the corner. I shuffled over to it and slid down, resting against it. The air was liquid heat. Sundown couldn't come soon enough. A circus parade looped non-stop through my brain. I'd killed Brian, I'd helped a heroin dealer kill another guy, I'd almost died from an overdose, I was broke and had no place to go. The bennies had me awake and aware of how sick I felt. Sundown didn't matter anymore. I just wanted to die.

My head hung between my knees. Could I make myself stop breathing? I tried. But soon enough, I was gasping for air, angry and frustrated.

The growl of a motorcycle broke the late afternoon stillness. I wondered if I should run, but I didn't care what they would do to me. If I was lucky, they would kill me fast.

The bike rounded the corner. It was Spider. He pulled to the curb and stared at me.

I stared back. No words came to mind. He had saved my life, but I didn't know what he thought of me now, what he might do to me.

"Where's the Police Special?" he asked in an even tone.

I threw up my hands and shook my head, frustrated I couldn't remember.

"Okay. We'll find it," he said.

Tears welled up in my eyes, but I still couldn't speak. Too many things to say, to feel.

"C'mon, let's go."

I looked up at him. "Where?"

"Just ride with me, Nate. C'mon." His voice was gentle, calm even.

I pulled myself up. I wanted to hug him for his kindness. I swung my leg over the rear fender and onto the bitch seat. I grabbed onto Spider and hung on. I needed him, and he showed up just in time.

He pulled away from the curb, away from the Hellhouse. That made me happy. We rode to the same coffee shop where I had been beaten. "Why are we here?" I mumbled. Fear of seeing the people from the woods, or the Outlaws, made me tremble.

"Sit tight, Nate. You need food. I'm gonna get something to take with us."

Bewilderment overcame me. No 'dumbass' or 'shithead' from him. He was speaking in low tones. What had happened to him?

The parking lot was filling up in the late afternoon. The people walking in all looked so normal, with clean clothes and easy smiles. I had been a member of their tribe not long ago. Now, standing a few feet from them, I sensed a gulf too wide to cross. Murderers didn't just walk into a diner. Dope dealers didn't bring their kids along, carrying them on their shoulders and promising them ice cream if they ate their peas. Life as I knew it ended when I woke up in that car in Warren, PA.

Spider brought back a sack of food and a couple of paper cups. He handed a cup to me and set the bag on the seat of his bike. "Burgers. I had 'em leave off the ketchup on yours."

I reached into the bag and found the plain burger, then handed the other to Spider. "Thanks, man. I need food."

"Hmph," was all he said.

"Annette gave me a few bennies to help me wake up enough to leave the Hellhouse. Thanks for taking me there and cleaning me up."

Spider chewed his burger and nodded. "Well, fer sure you can't go back. That bridge burned when me and Evvie snuck you in."

"You're out of the Hells Angels again?"

"Aw, no. I just ain't welcome at the house. Horse's got his rules, and I broke a big one when I brought you in all strung out on H."

"Why were you riding back that way, then?"

"I knew I had to get you out. Annette did you a huge favor. I called to see if anyone else was there and told her I was on my way."

I started to thank Spider when a familiar figure walked across the parking lot toward the cafe door. I elbowed Spider. "Hey, turn slow, but take a look at who's here."

Spider turned and froze. "Holy shit. That fucking prick."

Tommy Boyle's nephew, Sean ambled into the restaurant. He'd been in the car when Spider and I were drugged and stranded. Retribution was screaming for its day.

"Well, this calls for a change of plans." Spider threw the rest of his burger into the bag and tossed it. Paper and meat and tomatoes flew everywhere as it slammed into the pavement a foot short of a trash can. "Get on," he said as he swung his leg over the bike. "We need to be out of sight when that guy walks back out that door."

This could only end badly. "What are you thinking? I mean, he's got it coming, but two people have already died over this."

"Get on, dumbass. We got no time to argue."

I climbed on the bike as Spider kicked it to life. He eased out the clutch and idled the bike along the lot until we came to an opening in the woods, then backed the bike in several feet and killed the motor.

"What now?" I got off the bike. The woods were freaking me out.

Spider sat on the Sportster staring at the restaurant door, his jaw working.

"What—?"

"Quiet. I don' know. I just know I can't let this peckerwood get away. He walked right past us. I'm not gonna miss the chance."

"Remember what you told me about his uncle being a big mobster?" I shivered in the heat. "Well, when I was riding with the heroin dealer, we had a run-in with a couple of guys who worked for Boyle. These guys were spooky. Ice cold."

Spider took a long breath. "Look, *we* don't need to do nothin'. *I* do."

I slid to the ground and rested against a tree. Spider had saved my life. Didn't I owe him? Didn't I need to back him up? "Look man, as bad as I feel, dying can't be that much worse. Make a plan, and I'll back you up."

Spider nodded, never taking his eyes off the restaurant. "Okay."

A few minutes later, Spider whispered, "Get on. Sean's walkin' to his car."

I climbed on behind Spider. "What's the plan?"

"Huh? No plan. We're going to follow him and see what comes up. If we stay back far enough, he shouldn't notice us."

Sean threw the bag he carried into a late model Dodge Charger and climbed in. The 440 Magnum engine shook the parking lot as Sean revved it. He released the clutch and smoked the tires as he pulled out.

Spider followed half a block back as Sean drove on, unaware he was being followed.

The car traveled for a couple miles before making a left onto a street lined with storefronts. Sean parked in front of one. A small table with two chairs sat out front. One of the chairs was occupied by a man with an acne-scarred face. He wore a black leather waist-length coat and a driver's hat pulled low and to one side.

Sean nodded as he walked by the man and through the door. The man nodded back and took a drag on his cigarette.

Spider went a little slower than normal traffic might have, and stared at the door Sean went through. The man in the chair watched us as we rolled down the street, his eyes tracing our path.

Spider stared back.

"Stop staring," I whispered into his back.

Spider held the man's gaze until we were well past, then gunned the Sportster and roared down the road and around a corner, then slowed to the speed limit.

"What the hell were you doing?" I shouted. "Why would you give that guy a clear look at us?"

Spider laughed. "Told you I didn't have no plan. I just did what comes natural. Ain't afraid o' that guy, or his boss, or the king o' the Irish Mafia."

"Well, guess what, man. They aren't afraid of you either. And now they know something's up."

"How'd they know? You tell 'em?"

Chapter 21

Spider acted like he was buzzing on bennies, twitching with energy.

"You just taunted a soldier in the Irish mafia," I said. "That puts us in a bad spot. He doesn't know who we are, but now he's seen us. That guy will remember the bike. I'll bet he's spent his life remembering stuff like that."

"Yeah, but that might give us a leg up. We just have to look like someone else next time."

"This isn't funny! He sniffs out trouble every day. He'll smell us coming."

"Oh, for chrissake, leave it, man. Shut up!" Spider cranked the throttle again, and we flew down the two-lane street.

His anger came out of nowhere. He went from hinky-excited to pissed in an instant. Some school guidance counselor had told our class once that anger is just the outward face of fear. Maybe Spider wasn't mad at me. Maybe he was scared.

"Okay, man," I said. "We'll figure something out. I mean, we have a good reason to be after this guy. But honest, I'm tired of violence. Part of me wants to walk away."

The bike kept rolling. I had no idea where Spider was taking us, and it didn't matter. I had nowhere to be.

Sundown. Another night approaching with no place to go. The bitch seat offered no cushion from the road bumps and potholes. I wanted off it. "Wanna go get the Police Special?"

"Thought you said you didn't know where it was."

"Not exactly. But I know about where it is."

"Well, let's go, then."

I told Spider to go the park on the lake. I thought I could find my way from there, but my memory was spotty, and I felt worn out again. It didn't take long for us to reach the place where I had met Doreen and started my descent into heroin hell. I remembered Tony offering me the last free ride, him walking me into the woods. I felt stupid now, having offered my arm up to get that shot of dope. How had I not seen he was trying to kill me?

"Take The Shoreway east." I didn't know the names of the streets I had taken when I first went to the dope house, but hoped I would remember. We ended up in a neighborhood that felt right. A few streetlights worked, but most were out, leaving whole blocks in darkness. I studied the houses, trying to remember where I had parked the bike.

"It won't even be here, man," Spider said as we motored up and down the streets. "You left it here a week ago. Somebody's figured out they don't need no key."

"Yeah, probably," was all I could say. I was ready to give up when a woman stepped out of the darkness and into the street.

"Hey, you guys," she hollered and waved us over. Doreen, AKA Jane Doe, stood under the light, dressed in a halter top and hot pants.

"Doreen!" I called. At last, a break. "She'll know where the bike is."

Her arm dropped when she saw me and took off the other way.

We idled along next to her. "Doreen, wait," I said.

"Oh no. Not you, again. Nothin's been the same since whatever happened with you and Tony."

"What *did* happen?" I asked. "Stop, Doreen. Talk to me."

She stopped under a bright streetlamp. Both her eyes were blackened, and she had a split lip.

"What happened to you?" I asked.

She crossed her arms across her chest, hugging herself. "Hmph. What do you care? You ripped Tony off. He blamed me because I brought you. Get your ass out of here. I'm still hustling. I gotta go. Can't be seen with you. He'll kill me. Besides, I need a fix pretty bad. I don't have time to mess with you."

"Ripped off Tony? What?"

Spider shut off the bike and walked to Doreen. "Look, maybe we can help. You need a fix, and I need to find Nate's bike. Can ya help me?"

"Why should I?"

"Do you know where it's at?"

Doreen looked Spider up and down. "Maybe. Give me ten dollars."

Spider chuckled. "Where's the bike?"

"Show me the money."

"Lookit, sister, I've been where yer at." Spider pulled a five spot out of his wallet. "Five bucks, right now, if you tell me where the bike's at."

"I need ten," Doreen whined. "I don't have time for this. Give me the money." She took a step back, straightened up, and said, "I'll do you both for fifteen."

Spider put the five back in his wallet and got on the bike. "C'mon, Nate. This junkie's not smart enough to know who's tryin' to help."

"Wait, wait, wait. I do know where your bike's at. Gimme the ten, mister. I'll lead you there."

"Lead away," Spider said. "How far is it?"

Doreen led on while Spider walked the bike, propelling it with his feet.

She took the first right, walked half a block and pointed down an alley. "Tony had a guy push it around back. It's inside the fence. Gimme the ten."

We had only been a block over from Tony's dope house with the backyard where he kept his fancy car.

Spider got off his bike. "Show me."

"Are you trying to get me killed?" Doreen pleaded. "Tony sees me with you, especially pointing out that bike, he'll beat me to death."

"Nate, go see."

I did not want to go down the alley. Tony had already tried to kill me once. I didn't want to give him another chance, but I didn't see an alternative.

I walked down the dark alley. A large dog rushed the fence of the yard next to Tony's house, barking in an odd, muffled manner. I jumped back, terrified, then hurried to the fence at the rear of the dope house.

I didn't remember unlocking the gate when Tony and I took his car that night. I gave the gate a gentle tug, and it swung open. Tony's Cutlass was in its spot. The Police Special leaned against the back of the house. Excitement pulsed through me. I'd have to get the bike past the car, but it looked like there was enough room. Just as I stepped into the yard, the light above the stairs came on. I dropped to the ground and rolled into the shadows.

Tony walked down the stairs, car keys in his hand. He looked toward the open gate, reached behind his back and pulled a pistol from his waistband. "You little fuckers keep coming in here and messing with my stuff. I'll hunt you down and shoot you dead." He waved the pistol around a couple times, then pushed the gate all of the way open, got in the Riviera and pulled out.

He stopped the car in the alley and closed the gate. I felt elated. Now it would be easy to push the bike out. Then, I heard a metallic "click." "Now you're locked in, you little bastards. I'll deal with you when I get back."

Oh, shit.

Spider had to have heard Tony yelling. At least I hoped he did. The sound of Tony's Riviera faded.

"Spider!" My voice rasped as I tried to whisper loud enough to carry down the alley. No answer. "Spider!"

The dog next door rushed the fence, barking in that same odd manner. I hoped the fence was strong enough to keep it away from me. I looked around until I found a 2x4 to use as a club. "Quiet doggie," I whispered.

The barking and fence-rattling stopped. "Good doggie."

The dog lunged again.

Fear took over. "Spider!" I yelled. "I'm locked in."

The dog charged the fence again and again.

I grabbed at the top of the gate trying to pull myself over, but I was too weak. The beatings, the uppers and downers had left me on empty. Where was Spider? Had Doreen signaled Tony when he drove by? Where the fuck was he?

"Nate, where are you?" Spider whispered.

"Goddam. About time. I'm locked in. Help me get out of here." I rattled the gate. "Bastard locked me in."

"Jesus, hold on a minute."

"You hold on, man. I've got a dog tryin' to eat my leg and a dope dealer with a gun who'll be back here any minute." I leaned on the gate in exhaustion, then almost fell over as the gate swung open. "Whoa, what'd you do?"

"This's what he shut it with." Spider held up a length of stiff wire. "Get your ride and let's go."

The bike looked to be in the same condition I'd left it in. I twisted the wires together and jumped on the starter. The engine turned, but didn't fire. I kicked the starter again. No good.

"Spark advance, dumbass," Spider said. "And choke it. It's been sitting for a while."

The bike roared to life. I swung my leg over the pulsating machine and pushed it toward the street. "Where's Doreen?"

Spider jogged toward the end of the alley. "I gave her the ten, and she took off."

"That's odd."

"How come?"

"'Cause her dope house is right here."

"So? Maybe she already had a bag." Spider started the Sportster.

"Did she leave before Tony drove off?"

"Yeah. So?"

"She probably flagged him down and is telling him all about us."

Spider pulled out, and I followed. I had no clue where we were headed. If there was a plan, it was Spider's alone. I hoped he had one.

We made our way back to Lake Erie and headed north along the lake shore. We left Cleveland behind. The temperature dropped, my head cleared. We rode in silence for half an hour until curiosity got the better of me. "Where're we headed?" I hollered over the engine noise.

Spider shrugged.

"No, I mean, w*here*?"

"I heard ya." He shrugged again. "But, I can't tell ya."

"Why?"

"'Cause I don't know."

Oh brother. Another losing deal brought to me by Spider Kowalski. My alternatives were non-existent. Most everyone I knew in Cleveland was out to get me. Being broke and feeling beat up and sick, having no one else to turn to made Spider my best bet. My only bet. So I rode on in silence for another half hour.

We came to a spot where the road hugged the shoreline of Lake Erie. The moon shone brightly enough to reveal a narrow strip of sandy beach.

Spider pulled his Sportster across the road to the opposite shoulder, and I followed. "We kin stop here for the night. Sleepin' on sand beats sleepin' on rocks." He released the clutch and idled down the slight embankment to the beach.

The Police Special was larger and more top-heavy than his Sportster, but I managed to get the bike onto the beach without dumping it. It wouldn't stay up on its kickstand, so I leaned it against the ledge that separated the beach from the road.

I was exhausted. The bennies had worn off. I felt achy and nauseous, and now that we weren't in motion, my arms itched, and I felt a chill. A shot of dope would fix everything.

Spider sat on the sand and leaned back onto a boulder. "Bet you feel like shit."

I sat next to him and nodded. "I do."

"Well, the worst is likely over for ya. All 'cept the 'I'd sell my left nut for a shot o' dope.' feeling."

He'd read my mind. Though I still felt like shit, it wasn't as bad as earlier. But man, I craved a shot. It was all I could think about. I didn't know how to say what I felt, so I just nodded again.

"You'll get through it." Spider slid down until he was lying flat. "Try ta sleep. We'll figure somethin' out in the mornin'." He turned onto his side and laid his head on his colors.

Sleep would've been welcome, but my thoughts whirled and pulsed and stabbed at me. I wanted the release heroin would bring, the dulling of the guilt and shame and fear. I squirmed on the sand, trying to find a way to make my mind stop running.

"Spider."

No response.

"Spider!"

"Oh my God. Don't tell me you feel like talkin'. I'm too tired, man. Go to sleep."

I rolled onto my side and let the thoughts spin. Nothing would stop them. It was an hour or two before I fell asleep.

●   ●   ●   ●   ●

I woke up in a panic, not knowing where I was. Wind-whipped waves rolled higher on the beach than they had last night. It was chilly with just a t-shirt. My head throbbed as I sat up. Spider stood at the waterline thirty feet away, staring into the empty sky.

"Hey!" I called."

He raised his right hand and waved without turning around. I leaned back against the berm and tried to settle my pounding head. I fell right back to sleep.

•   •   •   •   •

Something tapped my shoulder. "Wake up, man."

I sat up again. The pounding in my head had stopped. The wind was calmer, and the sun rose higher. "What now?"

"Well, I done some thinkin'. Maybe I shouldn'ta egged that Mick on, but what's done is done. I figure we need to stand up to 'em, else we'll be lookin' over our shoulder forever." Spider sat on a flat rock. "I won't do that. Them bastards ripped me off, pure and simple. I don't care who his family is. Why should I just let it go?"

"Well, maybe to keep on living? This is bigger than you and Sean. His uncle is a gangster."

Spider shrugged. "So? Everybody's got something goin' for 'em. He's a gangster, I'm a Hells Angel."

"I'm not exactly qualified to give advice, but the comparison doesn't seem valid. Besides, you're kinda on the outs right now, aren't you?"

"Yeah, but it's a brotherhood. Brothers get into fights with each other, right? But in the end, they always get over it. My Hells Angel brothers? They'll get over it, too." Spider stood up. "C'mon. We need to make peace with the brotherhood, then go after the bastard who started this whole thing."

Chapter 22

Our engines roared and popped as we rode back to Cleveland, but we didn't say much. The whole idea of revenge was stupid, and the risks were huge. Spider was stubborn, though. Stubborn enough to be blind to the danger.

He slowed down as we neared the Hellhouse. His anger may have blocked his senses about Sean and Tommy Boyle, but fear seemed to be getting through about his relations with "the brotherhood." His shoulders drooped, and he shifted in the seat of his bike. We were barely moving as we pulled into the yard in front of the house.

"Stay here." Spider dropped the kickstand on his Sportster and ambled toward the front door. Before he got there, the screen door slammed open. Horse's fists were clenched as he took two long strides toward Spider.

"You goddam two-time loser." Horse's fist connected with the side of Spider's head.

Spider put his hands up to protect himself, but he didn't swing at Horse. "Hold on, man."

"No, you hold on." Horse threw a roundhouse left which Spider dodged. "And you brought back that worthless hang-around."

Spider backpedaled. "This whole thing's a mess, fer sure. But it's over. Let it go."

Horse swung with his right arm, but it went wide. He bent over at the waist and put his hands on his knees. "You ain't fightin' back."

"No, I ain't gonna fight you, man. I get why your pissed, and I don't blame ya. But I had to help out Nate. That dealer was gonna kill him."

Horse nodded toward me. "That kid there, he's not Angel material. Why you care about him?"

Spider hung his head for a moment, then looked up. "Everybody oughta get a second chance. You gave me one a few years ago after Wendell cleaned me up. So, I guess this's me payin' it back."

"I was ready to rip that patch right off yer back." Horse straightened up. "After lettin' you back in last time an' all. An' now you bring that strung-out piece of shit to the house? It's too much, man."

Spider stepped toward Horse. "I ignored the rules back then. Don't think I don't know it. You let me slide, and I always appreciate that. But this kid, man, he'd a died. He didn' deserve that."

Horse turned to me. "What do you got to say for yourself, you sorry-ass junkie?"

I glanced at Horse, then looked toward Spider. I didn't want to say the wrong thing and mess up Spider's chance at getting back with Horse and them. "I've got no excuse."

Horse snorted. "That's a fact." He pointed his finger at me, his lips curled in a sneer. "This's it, man. You straighten up and fly right, or I'll stick the Police Special right up your ass." He turned to Spider. "This joker is your responsibility. If he fucks up, you own it. Clear?"

Spider nodded. "Clear."

Horse took a step toward the door.

Spider said, "Wait."

Horse stopped.

"There's somethin' we need to talk about," Spider said.

Horse shrugged. "So talk."

"We found the second guy who was in the car when they ripped me off and started this whole thing."

"So, go git him."

"That's what I aim to do. Trouble is, he's Tommy Boyle's nephew."

"Oh." Horse rubbed his chin. "That's pokin' at a tiger for sure. Whaddya want me to do?"

"If I go for this guy, every Mick with a gun'll be looking for Hells Angels. I'm just warnin' ya."

Horse shrugged. "Well, c'mon in and we'll talk about it. But don't expect yer troubles are over. There were a couple of guys who wanted to cut yer arm off for fucking with heroin again."

Horse made it sound like Spider had started back on the drug. He had risked a lot to help me.

The house was quiet. The pool room was empty, too early for the Angels with jobs.

"Dieter here?" Spider asked. "I saw his bike out front."

"He's sleepin' I think. I don't want no trouble between you two, so I'd avoid him as much as you can."

"Why?"

Horse squinted his eyes and rubbed his jaw again. "Well, I shouldn't tell ya this. Dieter was the one offered to cut off your arm. Said it fit the crime."

Spider balled his fists and tightened his jaw. "That pervert motherfucker—"

"Hold on, dammit. I told you so's you could avoid trouble. Don't go lookin' for it, Kowalski." Horse punched Spider's arm. "He was drunk. We were all pissed. Well, most of us. Just let it go. I only told ya so's you could stay out of his way for a while."

Spider glared at Horse. "I won't go lookin' fer trouble. But I'll run a knife up that guy's armpit before I avoid 'im. I don' live that way."

Horse rolled his eyes, then glared back at Spider. "You came here lookin' fer help. I'm the goddam president of this chapter. You will do what the fuck I say, or I will *help* Dieter cut off yer fuckin' arm."

"What is all this fuss about, so early in the day?" Dieter leaned on the wall next to the stairs. "I see our resident nursemaid is back with his little patient."

Horse jabbed a finger toward Dieter. "Don't need yer bullshit right now." Horse spun and faced Spider. "And you, git along or git the fuck outta this house." He looked from Spider to Dieter and back. "Got it?"

No one moved.

"Do you got it!" Horse hollered.

Spider folded his arms across his chest. He stared at Dieter but spoke to Horse. "You're president, man. I'm loyal to this chapter and the greater club."

Dieter pushed himself up from the wall and returned Spider's stare. "Of course, of course. We are all loyal. We pledge to follow the rules. And some of us do."

Horse stepped between Dieter and Spider. "It's over. You both shut up. We got bigger problems. You guys need a beer." He stepped toward the kitchen. "Hang-around, get us all a beer and make sure there's plenty more in the fridge."

Spider sat across from Dieter at the beat-up table. Horse sat at the end. I brought them beers and moved toward the last chair.

"Oh no," Horse said. "You go sit on the back porch. If we need somethin', we'll call for ya."

This sounded great to me. I didn't want to be around when the shit blew up with Dieter and Spider. Horse's name-calling didn't bother me a lot. I had it coming for one thing, but people's opinions didn't matter much any more. Seems like every time someone was saying something nice about me, they just wanted something. At least when they called me a sorry-ass junkie, I knew it was true.

Metal lawn chairs lined the back porch. I picked the least rusty one and sat. The chair bounced under my weight. It felt good to sit with the sun shining onto my face. My thoughts slowed, and my eyelids got heavy. My head leaned back, and—

"Get your ass in here and get us more beer."

I jumped up and fetched the beers. Spider and Dieter seemed to have relaxed some, but Horse seemed tense as ever.

"How's it going?" I asked.

"Did you hear something?" Horse said, looking at Spider, then at Dieter. They both shook their head. He looked at me. "Put down them beers and get your sorry ass outta here."

I fled back to the porch and the warm sun. Kicking me out was their loss, or so I told myself.

Horse called for beer a couple more times. The talk around the table had been quiet enough I could hear the chatter but couldn't make out the words. But with each round, the volume increased. I knew I would be able to hear them loud and clear by the time they'd drained these bottles.

Dieter's drunken voice came through. "I'd fight to the death for my brothers."

Spider said something back, but I didn't catch it.

Horse said, "We just needta make sure we have a plan and stick to it."

"Whatever you say, mein leader." Dieter was sounding unlike what I was used to hearing. He sounded sincere and respectful. Until now, even when he spoke of Hells Angels business, it was with a dismissive, superior attitude.

Chairs scraped, and Spider stepped onto the porch.

"Can I ask how it went?" I was curious if they'd actually made a plan, other than to roar down there and shoot 'em up.

"You kin ask," Spider replied. "Eventually you'll know. But for now, it's early. Things 'r subject to change."

Horse gave me ten bucks and sent me out to get some burgers. When I got back, we ate around the kitchen table. Talk was loud and full of verbal jabs, but everyone seemed to be on the same Hells Angel page. Life was meant for drinking and riding and fucking.

Horse left the table first. "Annette! Where are you?"

She walked into the kitchen in a bra and panties, with glassy eyes and a slack smile. "Do fer you, baby?" she mumbled.

Horse turned her around, so she was headed upstairs, then swatted her butt. "Git up there woman." Then he turned toward us and made a show of licking his lips and grabbing his crotch. "Yeow!" He followed Annette as she stumbled up the stairs.

After he was out of earshot, Dieter said, "I like to go second, even third." He leered at Spider. "Of course going after you won't add to the pleasure. Your little dick won't stretch her out at all."

Spider's cheeks turned red. He placed his hands palm-down on the table and stared straight ahead, avoiding Dieter's line of sight. "Nate, let's go." He rose from his chair, stiff, like he was hurting.

"You all right?" I asked.

"He'll be fine, schwein. He's just being a good club member and obeying his president, aren't you, my brother?"

Spider walked past Dieter and out the back door with his gaze fixed straight ahead. I followed. I didn't understand what just happened, but I knew better than to ask. Spider mounted up, and I followed suit. We tore out of the Hellhouse yard and headed toward town.

Twenty minutes of riding took us to the same tavern Spider and I had visited when I first got to town. The last time we were here I remember the folks weren't all that happy to see Spider. That'd been the middle of the day and the place had been empty. Now, the lot was mostly full.

Spider pulled up right next to the door and backed his bike into a space by the walkway. I backed the Police Special in next to his bike. "Why're we here?"

"I'm hopin' to hear what's going on with Sean's uncle."

"This place isn't exactly O'Flannery's Bar."

Spider glared at me. "I had no idea you was so prejudiced." Then he laughed loudly. "Yer right shithead. You started payin' attention."

I smiled, in spite of not knowing if he'd paid me a compliment or was fucking with me. Had to be the latter. It was always the latter.

"Look, Nate, These guys are a bunch of Polacks, fer sure, but there's always scuttlebutt. People can't keep their mouth shut, and a lot o' these guys work at the same factories as the Micks. Keep yer goddam face shut, no matter what. I'm here ta see if anybody's been runnin' on about Hells Angels and trouble brewin'."

When Spider opened the door a wall of country music, cigarette smoke and loud conversation slapped me in the face. The bar was full of men in work clothes and a few women in t-shirts and shorts. Nobody paid much attention to us as we made our way to a table in the rear.

Ted, the bartender was working as fast as he could to replace empty beer bottles and slide whiskey shots in front of his thirsty clients. A weary waitress came by. Without looking at us she said, "What'll it be?"

"Two Black Labels, Cherie."

The woman looked up. "Oh, it's you, lover boy. How you been?"

"Been better. You?"

"Aw, hon, you know how this gig goes. Everybody gets drunk but me."

Spider laughed. "Same ol' Cherie. I always did like you."

Cherie rolled her eyes. "I'll get yer beers. Wanna run a tab?"

"Sure, as long as yer taking care of us." Spider smiled at her. I didn't remember ever having seen him look so happy to see someone.

Cherie nodded and started pushing her way toward the bar.

"Damn, man. What was that all about?" I asked, grinning at Spider.

He was still smiling. "I need info. That sweet young lady is like a bank. She keeps her mouth mostly shut, but hears everything goes on in here. Everybody likes her. They all talk to her like she's their sister. I'm just hopin' she feels like sharin', cause if anyone knows what's up with the Micks, it's her."

"Why? What's her connection?"

"Well, her name's Cherie Dubanowski. She was married to a guy from around here, but he disappeared six or seven years ago. Anyway, her name used to be Cherie O'Dowd. She's got kin all over Irish town. Nobody'll know more'n Cherie. That's fer sure.

Cherie made her way through the crowd and set our beers on the table.

"How's yer family?" Spider asked.

Cherie shrugged. "Drunk as usual, I s'pose. Don't get to see 'em as often as I used to."

Spider took a long pull on his beer. "Why's that? I thought you was pretty close to each other."

Cherie was holding a small, round drinks tray. She put it to her chest and crossed her arms over it. Her lips became a thin line as she looked at Spider. "I'll be right back," she said, and headed toward the rear of the bar.

"What's up with her?" I asked.

"Dunno. Looked like she was about to cry, though, and she went to the ladies room." Spider took another drink of his beer. "Hope she comes back. Somethin's cookin'. Maybe we can help her, and maybe she'll pass on some info. 'Sides, I need another beer."

Cherie reappeared in the crowd and made her way to us.

"You all right?" Spider asked.

"Oh, Spider, things are *not* all right, but I can't talk about it now. Ted's been givin' me the evil eye already for not bein' faster. Can I get you guys another beer?"

Spider ordered another round. When Cherie brought the beers, Spider took out a five dollar bill and shoved it into Cherie's apron. "I don't know what yer families trouble is, but I wanna help. We'll be back at closin' time. S'pose you'd have time to talk then?"

Cherie studied Spider's face for a moment. "Why would you want to help, Kowalski? We've had a few laughs, but why're my problems so important to you?"

Spider's smile covered his face. "'Cuz that's who I am, pretty lady. I'm a helper. Besides, I'd like to catch up on old times." Spider pulled out another five spot and shoved it into her apron. "See ya at closin' time?"

Cherie smiled a lopsided smile. "Sure, I'll be here. And the beers are on the house. Now get outta here so I can get somebody decent to sit at this table."

We made our way through the crowd and out to the parking lot. Spider climbed on his Sportster and said, "Let's ride."

We rode through the darkened streets, heading first west and then south towards Parma where Evvie lived. "We're not going to Evvie's," I said.

"Oh hell no," Spider said. "We're just ridin'. But I like to ride past places I know, just to keep in touch, sorta."

We passed the darkened house just faster than idle to keep the noise down. Evvie's warmth flooded my thoughts. I supposed I had blown that forever, just to learn drugs made me *feel* better, but they didn't make me *better*.

After we were past Evvie's place, Spider gunned his bike, and we took off west again until we were out of town. We found some two-lane blacktop roads and rode in circles, enjoying the night air and the power of the bikes.

•   •   •   •   •

At two-thirty we were back at Ted's bar. The parking lot was almost empty, though a few satisfied customers weaved their way to their cars. Cherie sat on the steps.

"Hoped you weren't bullshitting me," she said.

"Glad you waited, Cherie. C'mon, let's go get some coffee."

Cherie rode on Spider's bike, leaning into his back like she'd ridden with him forever. A pang of jealousy hit me. I would have loved to have a girl embrace me like that.

At the restaurant, we took a booth and ordered. Spider was the first to speak.

"So, what's up with yer family?"

Cherie shook her head and looked down. "This is hard to talk about. 'Specially to you, because of your past troubles. But then maybe you'll get it."

"Get what?"

"My brother is runnin' with Tommy Boyle and them. He thinks he's gonna live high on the hog. But I know he'll end up dead. They'll use him up and spit him out. Anyway, my mom thinks it's part my fault, cause I hang around with you guys sometimes. I dunno, maybe it is."

Spider put his arm around her. "This ain't yer fault. And, fact is, we may be able to help."

Chapter 23

Cherie pushed her pancakes around her plate as Spider asked easy questions, trying to get her to talk. "So, yer brother's Francis, right?"

Cherie nodded, never looking up.

"How old is he?"

"He's almost twenty. But he dropped out when he was sixteen. Doesn't work. Hangs around with kids who steal cars and get high."

Spider laughed. "Sounds familiar."

"It ain't funny, McGee. He's my brother, and he's headed to the feckin' penitentiary. And that's if he doesn't die first." Cherie stabbed the air with her fork. "I thought you were here to help." She stabbed the fork toward Spider. "Well, this ain't helpin'."

Spider sat on the outside of the booth. He slipped his arm around Cherie's shoulder and pulled her to him. "I didn't mean to upset ya. I am here to help. Look, if anyone can get to Francis it'd be someone like me." He pulled his arm back and turned to face her. "He thinks his chances at the straight life suck. His friends seem to have a lot of fun and don't have to work. Someone comes along and tells him there's an easy way to be somebody, well, every nineteen-year-old is gonna take notice o' that."

Cherie set down her fork. "So what can we do? Mom's been beggin' him to come back home, even lined up a job for him. He told her to bugger off; that he was a grown man and could make his own way."

"How far into the gang is he?" Spider asked.

Cherie shrugged. "Don't know."

"Has he bragged about knowin' Tommy Boyle, or bein' sent on special jobs? That's how they suck young guys in. Make 'em feel like they're special, then send 'em on some dicey jobs. He might be one of the soldiers sent to deal with us."

Cherie's head jerked up. "What? Deal with you? What are you talking about?"

Spider sighed. "Me and my big mouth. I didn't mean to talk about that, but, yeah, we're about to cause a big beef with Boyle's goons. I hoped your brother might help us out a little, and in the process, we could persuade him to go a different direction."

Cherie shook her head. "No, no, no. You'll get him killed."

"Boyle will get him killed, Cherie. We're his best shot at gettin' out alive. You said it yourself."

Cherie clenched her fists. "Uhhnnn!" She took a deep breath. "Talk to me Kowalski, but you better have a plan. If Francis gets hurt, I'll never forgive you. Or myself."

I was all ears. I had no idea what Spider might come up with to rescue Cherie's brother and use him as an entryway into the Boyle mob.

"Well, first, you gotta call him. Find out what they have him doin'. Ask if he's heard anything about someone coming after Sean, Tommy's nephew or if there're rumors of anyone else missin'."

Cherie was still shaking her head. "I don't know these people."

"You don't have to. Francis does."

"Oh, I see. So I pump my brother for info, and then you use it how?"

"I'm not gonna tell ya the whole story. But, let's just say Boyle's nephew stole something from me and left me in bum-fuck-Egypt with nothin'. I owe him. But he is Boyle's nephew, and I don't want a war. So, if Francis kin get me a little info, I can get my revenge on the little bastard and not kill him. Then I'll owe Francis and get him a job in the real world."

"Doin' what? Slingin' your drugs? Oh, that's a high-class solution."

"No, not sellin' drugs. I'll get him in as a mechanic at the garage I used to run. He'll be able to make a few bucks if he hustles, and it'll keep him off the streets and out of Irish town."

Cherie looked down and shook her head. "Feckin' church-going, Mackeral-snappin' stupid ass Irish! Dammit!" Tears sprung from her eyes and rolled down her cheeks. "How can they be so feckin' stupid?"

Spider sat back again. Cherie's outburst had him backing off. "I'm sorry. I know ya love yer brother. So does your family, prob'ly. Everyone wants the same thing, Cherie. We all want to help Francis."

Cherie's head moved slowly from left to right to left to right, picking up speed as her face turned red and then crimson. She flung her fork at Spider and grabbed at her plate as if to throw that at him also. "Find yourself another fool to save your sorry ass. You don't care a rat's ass about my brother, you wasted, motherfecking prick! You dragged me here to use me. I am done with that!" She tried to push Spider out of her way, but his bulk proved too much. "Move, you selfish prick! Get out of my way before I bite yer feckin' ear off!"

Spider wrapped his arms around her shoulders. He pulled her into him and stroked her hair. "Oh, sweetie, please. Take a few breaths n' hear me out. I want nothin' but the best for Francis. I want nothin' but the best for your family. Can't you see yer mom and sisters and cousins all sittin' around the dinin' room table with Francis, liftin' a glass and toastin' the dear departed." Spider hugged her tighter. "That's all I'm tryin' to do, sweetie. That's all I want fer Francis and for you."

Cherie melted into Spider's embrace. It was a tender moment in a rough night. I even thought I could see the embers of a romance there, but wondered if Cherie would go along with his plan. If she walked out of this restaurant without agreeing to help, we were back at the beginning.

Cherie sat back and wiped tears and snot from her face with a lacy handkerchief she'd pulled from her waistband. "I've been screwed so many times I feel like a hooker. And now you come back around askin' for somethin' that seems like there's nothin' in it for Francis. I wanna help my brother, but I'm not that smart. You tell me you can help. You're gonna hafta tell me how."

Spider's shoulders sagged. "I don't like you knowin' too much about my plan, but I'll tell you this. Francis is prob'ly bein' brought along, doin' low-level stuff. If he lives through it, he'll move up. My point bein', Francis is already in danger, and it'll never get better. What I'm gonna try to do is move him away from that. Get him to join the straight world."

"Ha! That's a laugh, Kowalski. You wouldn't know the straight world if a helicopter dropped you right in the middle of it."

"I do know people who'll help. Like I told ya, that garage I used to manage."

"Yeah, whatever happened to that?"

Spider squirmed. "I blew my chance. Don't matter how. But I didn't burn all my bridges. If I tell the owner Francis's situation, I'm pretty sure he'll give him a job."

"What about your remodeling company?" Cherie asked. "You were hot on that a while ago."

"Look, this ain't no job interview for me. I know how many times I've screwed up. I was born into a family that didn't know no other way. But dammit, I'm tryin' to do somethin' good here." Spider's face was red, and he was breathing heavy.

"Hey man," I said, "you gonna be all right?"

Spider ran his fingers through his hair, first one hand, then another. His lips were clamped shut, and his nostrils flared each time he exhaled. "I'm fine. I just get tired of havin' my failures dug up." He turned to Cherie. "I get why you feel like ya do, but I'm askin' ya to trust me this one time. This is gonna turn out good."

Where had I heard that before? I didn't want to piss Spider off even more, but he was not good at making plans. He hadn't said how he was going to rescue Francis from the mob life, get his revenge on Sean and avoid bringing the wrath of the Irish Mob down on the Hells Angels.

Cherie's shoulders were hunched, and her head hung down.

Spider drew a deep breath. "I need for Francis to find out where Sean lives."

Cherie's head shot up. "That's all?" She shifted around to face Spider in the booth. "That's all you need?"

Spider nodded. "For now."

"Hah! I can get ya that!"

"How?"

"Right off the parish register. Ma still does some volunteer work. She can get the address. We don't even need to involve Francis."

Spider pulled on his beard. "Well, okay."

"You still gotta try to help out Francis, though. Get him a job, convince him to go straight."

"I will, sweetie. I will."

Spider left to take Cherie home. He said I should watch myself when I went back to Hellhouse. Well, what he really said was, "Keep yer damn mouth shut unless somebody asks you somethin'."

By the time I got there, few stragglers were left. I crept upstairs as quietly as I could, and fell asleep.

•   •   •   •   •

"Hey, Nate."

My eyes shot open. In the darkness, I could see an outline against the moonlight from the hallway.

"Evvie?" I mumbled.

She slid into bed beside me. "What, sweetie?"

It was Annette.

She leaned her head on my chest and rubbed my cock through my undershorts. "Mmm. It's so nice to be with somebody who's all innocent and nice. In all my life I've only known a few boys like you." She pulled down the waistband of my shorts and took me in her hand, then raised her head and kissed my mouth. "Don't let them run you down, sweetie. They're all takers. They might act like they're helpin'. Believe me, they're not."

Her hand worked up and down on my penis. "Uh, uh, uh." I felt the end coming. "Oh, shit."

Annette clamped her other hand across my mouth. "Keep it down, baby. I know you like it." A few more strokes made me bust all over the place. Annette kissed me again, then got a washcloth and cleaned me up. "Stay nice, Nate. You're not like these knuckleheads."

I patted the bed beside me.

She sat on the edge.

"Why'd you do that for me? You know it's not right for Horse to say they own you."

She shook her head. "My uncle taught me how to give him a hand job when I was six. I didn't tell anybody. I didn't know no other way. Like I told ya, I was strippin' at fourteen to make enough to get away from them. Bein' here seemed like an improvement. Sex is all I got, Nate."

I felt sick. She was trapped, and it wasn't her fault. I needed someplace to belong, but I could never sell my soul like that. At least I didn't think I could.

"Is there anything I can do to help you?"

"Figure out how to get away. And, when you do, take me with you." She blew me a kiss and walked out as silently as she had entered.

It was light when I woke again. I stumbled down to the kitchen. No one else was awake in the house. The clock on the stove read 9:22. The four hours of sleep didn't feel like enough, but I was up now.

I made coffee and sat out on the back porch. Between sips, I dozed in the sun. I set the cup down and let sleep overtake me. The roar of a Harley soon woke me up.

A minute later Spider joined me on the back porch. "Fetch me a cup o' that coffee."

I rolled my eyes, but went to the kitchen and came back with a steaming mug. "Where you been?"

"Ha. Where ya think?"

"You figure out how to talk Francis out of a life of crime?"

Spider shook his head.

"You and Cherie must have had something together," I said. "She was pretty warm toward you last night. That is, when she wasn't throwing stuff at you."

He smiled. "Yeah, we had something. Maybe still do."

"So, her ma's going to get the address?"

Spider sipped his coffee. "I've been thinkin' about that all morning. I figure I need to get that little bastard alone and make sure he knows who I am."

"Remember the guy outside their club? Even you said showing ourselves wasn't a good idea."

"This is different. He needs ta know it's me, otherwise, what's the point?"

I nodded. "I guess."

"Anyway, I plan to do somethin' to him. Break a finger, I think, then tell 'im if he tells his uncle it was me, I'll come back and cut off his balls." He laughed.

This didn't seem like much of a plan to me, but I didn't know gangsters. "It might work, but what are you laughin' at?"

"I wasn't laughin' at that. I was laughin' because I don't even wanna do this anymore. It's all so goddam stupid."

I picked up my coffee and took a long drink. It was cold, but that didn't matter. This must be The Twilight Zone. Spider was calling his whole life stupid. At least it sounded like that's what he meant.

"But," Spider continued, "it ain't just about me. If I let this pass, it makes Hells Angels look stupid. They saved my ass as a kid then took me back when I messed up. I can't just let it go."

Things thudded back to normal. Spider was a loyal, true badass. For the gang, he would walk away from anything, even love. His own life mattered less than the group. There was a nobility about it, but I'd seen enough to know most of the bikers wouldn't do the same for him. Horse maybe. But the others seemed like they cared about nothing but beer and fucking.

"When will Cherie's mom have the address?"

"Prob'ly take a few days."

A phone rang inside the house. "Yeah? Oh, hi Cherie. How you been?" Annette had answered. "A course he's here. That loser ain't got nowhere else to go. Hold on." She walked to the back door. "It's your chickie, Spider. I don't know how you keep gettin' her back."

Spider slipped past Annette and picked up the phone. "Hello?" He passed the receiver to his other hand. "Oh, that's great. Let me get a pencil." He put the phone to his chest. "Nate! Get me a goddam pencil and paper."

I stumbled into the kitchen with no idea where to look. Annette pulled open a drawer and rummaged around until she found a pencil and an old receipt, which she handed to me, and I gave to Spider.

He cradled the phone on his shoulder and wrote. "1111 Pine Bluff Circle. How'd your ma get this so fast?"

Spider smiled as he put the paper down and held the phone to his ear. His smile faded, then his face reddened. "Oh Cherie, tell me your ma did not do that." He shook his head. His shoulders slumped. He took the receiver from his ear and bent over for a moment. When he straightened up, he said, "This is not good, Cherie. You know that priest is gonna tell Tommy Boyle."

Annette had disappeared. I slouched in a kitchen chair.

Spider leaned against a wall, holding the phone with one hand and rubbing his face with the other. "I gotta go. We'll talk later." Spider pushed away from the wall. "I know you tried." Spider nodded. "Yes, sweetie, I will still try to help Francis. It's just gonna be a lot tougher now. Bye." He hung the phone up and grabbed a beer from the fridge. "Goddamit!"

"What happened?"

Spider gulped half the beer. "Cherie told her ma I was going to try to get Francis on the straight and narrow, so she got all excited and went to see the priest about the address. So the priest asks her why she needs it and the old lady tells him. Fucking tells him I'm going to try to help Francis and I need the address to talk to Sean. Jesus! Talk about sinkin' a damn good plan! What the fuck do I do now? Jeezus."

"Why's all this so terrible? Why would the priest tell Tommy Boyle?"

"The mob puts up a lot o' money. That priest knows who butters his bread.

"What now?" I asked.

Spider took another long swig of beer and slumped in the chair. He sat motionless for a few minutes, then straightened up. "C'mon. We gotta go."

"Where?"

"We need to get to Sean before the priest tells his uncle."

"What? Are you nuts?"

"Yup. Let's ride.

Chapter 24

Spider rattled off a list of reasons we needed to get to Sean first and fast.

Traffic was light in the mid-morning and we made good time as we rode side-by-side to the address Cherie's mom gave us. It was to an upscale complex overlooking Lake Erie. Spider and I rolled past, scanning for a lookout. A few blocks later we turned and rode past again, then headed to Edgewater Park.

My stomach knotted as I pulled into the parking lot. My life in Cleveland was stitched together with frightening visits to this place. I came close to losing my life here, both figuratively and literally. I didn't want to be back.

"This place freakin' you out?" Spider asked.

I didn't want to look scared and weak, but I nodded, afraid I would choke up if I spoke.

"Well, good on you for admittin' it." Spider walked onto the boulders that lined the shore and sat.

His words made me feel a little better. I scrambled out to where he was and sat. "So, now that you've seen Sean's place, what's the plan?"

He stared into the distance, silent for a while. "Well, we know where he lives, but we don't have time to waste spyin' on 'im. I figure we go back, wait for him to show and grab him. I got a Vise-Grip in my saddle bag. You hold 'im from behind, I'll grab a knuckle and twist."

"Great. And then what?"

"I'll remind 'im of who I am and he better not send his uncle after us, 'cause I'll cut his nuts off if he does."

"He's going to scream, man. That'll bring attention."

"So, what's yer plan, then?"

"I don't know. Never tried anything like it before."

I sat on my hands so Spider wouldn't see them shaking. "I'll do my part. But I have no ideas."

"Hmph. Well then, we'll go with my plan."

Spider talked through the order of things a few times, adding details, like I should wrap Sean up with a tow strap he had. Every time he added a new twist, he sounded more confident, and I felt a little more like I might survive.

We rode to Sean's place and parked the bikes a block away. Spider grabbed the tow strap and the Vise-Grip, and we walked to the complex.

The parking lot was almost empty, making Sean's Dodge Charger easy to spot. It was backed up in front of the entry to a first-floor unit.

"That wasn't there earlier," I said.

Before Spider could respond, the apartment door opened and Sean walked out reading a folded-up paper and twirling his key ring on his finger.

Spider ran towards him, swinging the tow strap above his head.

Sean never looked up from the paper.

As Spider closed in, he lowered the strap. It swung around Sean's midsection, pinning his arms. Keys and paper flew from his hands.

"Unlock the car," Spider hollered.

Sean struggled to free his arms. "Who are you? You're making a mistake!"

Spider got him in a bear hug. "Shut up, asshole."

I lunged at the keys, almost knocking them away. My hands shook as I opened the driver's door and pulled the lock on the rear. Spider flung it open and shoved Sean onto the seat, throwing himself on top of him. "Drive, dammit, drive!"

"You're making a big fucking mistake," Sean hollered again. He struggled to free himself from Spider's grasp.

Bone smacked bone as Spider punched the side of Sean's head. "Shut up, you low-life maggot."

"Goddamit, stop! You are in real deep shit. My uncle's Tommy Boyle, you morons."

Spider slugged him again. "Oh we know, Sean. That's why we're going to have a private visit and set a few things straight."

The back seat became quieter as Sean stopped struggling, though he gasped for air in great, rapid gulps.

"Where should I go?" I asked.

"Well, I don' know," Spider said. "This didn't quite go accordin' to plan."

"You can still get yourself out of this mess," Sean said. "Pull over and get out. Just walk away."

"You don't know who I am, do ya?" Spider asked.

Sean didn't answer, but I heard him thrashing again, trying to get Spider off him. "Don't know, don't give a fuck."

"Well, I remember you, and yer buddy, and bein' left in the middle of BFE without my case a' dope."

Sean started kicking the back of my seat. "You're the stupid-ass hippies we ripped off in Pennsylvania! Oh, shit! Don't tell me you losers got the jump on me. Jesus!"

"I ain't no fuckin' hippie, shithead. I'm a Hells Angel. You fucked up when you messed with me." Spider thumped his fist into Sean's head.

Sean quit thrashing, again. "Stop, stop, stop. This is not the way to handle this."

I kept driving straight. We were heading to the Lake again. I swear, Lake Erie was a magnet. I could not seem to get away.

Spider's head appeared in the rearview as he surveyed our surroundings. "Go to the park again. Maybe we can make something good come out of that place."

I drove into the parking lot of Edgewater Park, my stomach in knots, this time because of what we planned to do.

"Park over by them trees." Spider sounded confident, like he might have a real plan.

I pulled into a spot right next to the wooded area.

"Open the back door and be ready to clock this son of a bitch if he tries runnin'." Spider held the tow strap tight around Sean as he shimmied out of the rear seat. When they were standing, Spider kneed Sean in the ass. "Move, dipshit. And keep yer mouth shut or I'll just shoot ya and end this. Got it?"

Sean sneered, his face shaded with defiance.

Spider marched him into the woods, and I followed. This was the same place Tony had OD'd me only a few weeks ago, the same place Spider and Evvie had saved my life. And I knew this was also where Spider almost died from exposure. It was Lake Erie's Bermuda Triangle.

Spider turned Sean around and pushed him to the ground. His head hit a log on the way down. "Dammit! Stop! You don't know what you're doing!"

Spider pulled a pistol from the back of his waistband. It was bigger than the gun that had killed Chad. He waved the gun in my direction. "Tighten the strap 'round his arms, but get his right hand free." He knelt facing Sean. "I do know what I'm doin'. I'm teachin' you and every other wannabe badass that I'm not your chump. You stole from me, which means you ripped off the Hells Angels, and now yer gonna pay for it."

"I didn't know that! Anyway, those drugs were stolen from me, too. Or at least I think they were. All I know is, I asked someone to peddle them, and they disappeared. So, you can't expect me to pay. I didn't even profit from it."

I listened with utter amazement. What kind of fool thought *he* got a pass if things didn't work out for him? He stole the drugs. He was guilty. How could he not see that?

Spider spat on Sean's shirt. "I'd laugh, but what you just said ain't funny. It just shows how you rich pricks think. Somehow everybody owes you. Not me, dipshit. You ripped me off. There's no way around it." He put his pistol into his pocket and pulled out the Vise-Grips and a bandanna. He tossed the bandanna to me. "Gag 'im."

I tied the red cloth over Sean's mouth and pulled it tight.

Sean tried talking through the gag. "Lemme go. Dohn do 'his."

Spider kicked Sean's thigh. "Shut up." He waved the Vise-Grips in front of Sean. "You can't seem to keep yer fingers out of other people's stuff, so I'm gonna give you somethin' to remind you ta keep yer hands to yerself."

Sean's eyes were wide open as he stared at the pliers Spider held. "Dohn! Dohn, please." He scrambled into a sitting position and clasped his hands in front of him.

Spider grabbed the middle finger of Sean's right hand and bent it back.

"Ahhh, sop! Gohamit, sop." Sean's yelling became a whimper. "Please."

Spider clamped the Vise-grip onto Sean's finger just above the middle knuckle.

"AAHHH!" Even through the gag, Sean's scream made birds take flight.

I looked to see if anyone was coming from the park.

Spider twisted the pliers. Sean's finger snapped with an audible 'crack'.

"AAHHH! AAHHH!" Tears rolled down Sean's cheeks. His cries became whimpers.

Spider sat on his haunches and got his face level with Sean. "Now, when ya see that crooked finger, ya might remember to leave other people's property alone."

Spider swatted my shoulder. "Take that gag offa' him."

I unknotted the bandanna and took a step back.

Sean spit at Spider. "You're dead-"

"Naw. You're just lucky you're not dead. I'da cut that motherfucker off, but I don't want to start a war. So, we're even now. If yer ever dumb enough to try to rip me off again, or any of my Hells Angels brothers, You'll lose that finger. Understand?"

Sean glared at Spider. His eyes were wet with tears, but there was no fear, or remorse in his expression. His sneer showed defiance.

His scorn was a mystery to me. He had to be in pain. He had no defense against more to come, yet he scowled at Spider, narrowing his eyes. I was scared just watching this violence. I'd have been out of my mind with fear if I had been him.

Spider stood up. "Man, I see you don't take to lessons very well. That's okay. I was a slow learner, too. But I'm gonna make you a promise." He poked him in the chest. "Just like we found you this time, if you go runnin' to yer uncle whinin' about yer finger, we'll find you again and—"

"And what? Kill me?"

"No, smartass. I will cut off yer nuts and feed 'em to you. You'll be able to sing soprano in the choir."

Sweat dripped off Sean. Maybe Spider *had* gotten to him. His jaw relaxed, and his eyes lowered. He cradled his broken finger in his left hand. "So, what now?"

I looked at Spider, eager to hear his reply. I hadn't thought that far ahead. I doubted he had either.

"Well, you get ta rest here a while, think about how crime don't pay, or somethin'. Don't get up 'til we're out of the parking lot. Then do whatever comes natural, 'cept for two things; don't say nothin' about who broke yer finger, and don't ever rip off a Hells Angel again." Spider took a step back. "C'mon. Let's go get our bikes."

We walked out of the woods, leaving Sean sitting on the ground, his back leaning on a log. The Charger started with a roar, and we headed back to Sean's apartment. Spider's leg bounced a hundred times a minute. He pounded a fist into his thigh.

I turned to Spider. "What's up, man? You look like you had a bad bunch of bennies."

"Naw, I'm alright. I just got a queasy feeling about this. I know I had to do that back there, but that little psycho won't keep his mouth shut. Trouble's comin'."

Oh shit. If Spider thought trouble was coming, then it most surely was. "What do we do?"

"Let's get the scooters and take it from there. We'll leave the car on the street with the keys. Maybe it'll get stolen."

I took some comfort in thinking some schmuck might take off in Sean's car. Then Tommy Boyle's guys could take their wrath out on the car thief. By the time we were on Pine Bluff Road I felt our chances of getting away with Sean's abduction were pretty good.

As we drove by Sean's apartment a guy in a waist-length jacket stood on the sidewalk, pointing at us and hollering, "Hey! There it is!"

"Oh shit," Spider said. "They know about us. Hit the gas!"

I looked in the rearview and saw two men running after us, pistols drawn. Gunshots blasted.

"They're shooting at us!" I cried.

"Get to the bikes."

I pushed on the accelerator and the Dodge fishtailed. I controlled it, but had to let off to take a corner. We were out of sight of the gunmen when we reached the bikes. I jammed the transmission into park.

We jumped out of the car. I threw my leg over the Police Special and wound the wires. Spark advance, throttle, kick. The Harley roared to life. The engine must have drowned out the sound of the pistol shot, but I felt the bullet pierce the tank, going clear through. Gas spilled from the holes spewing over the running engine.

Spider hollered, "Get off! Get off! The gas'll flame. C'mon!"

I jumped off the Police Special just before it erupted in flames. I leapt on Spider's bitch seat and grabbed his jacket. The gunmen seemed frozen by the sight of the burning motorcycle, but only for a heartbeat. They aimed their pistols at us as we sped at them.

"Turn Spider, get out of here!" I yelled.

He kept the throttle open. We were ten feet from them. Spider pulled his pistol and fired three shots. Their pistols fired. We didn't seem to be hit. Spider fired again. One gunman fell, the other jumped out of the way of the bike.

Spider wheeled around. Headed straight for him. Fired his pistol again.

The gunman fired back.

Spider fired yet again.

The gangster dropped his gun and grabbed at his shoulder.

We roared past him and down the road out of the neighborhood. We seemed to be in the clear. The Sportster slowed. I figured Spider felt like we were out of danger, but we kept slowing to where it was difficult to maintain balance.

"Spider, what's up?"

No reply.

I didn't see the blood until we fell over. Spider's chest was covered with it.

"Spider! Get up, man."

He didn't answer.

I looked back and saw one the gunmen limping towards us.

"Get up. Get up! He's coming. Get up, Spider. We gotta move."

Spider's mouth was moving, but I couldn't understand the words. I leaned close to hear what he was saying.

"In my boot." His voice was phlegmy. His chest rattled as he gasped for air.

"What?"

"The other gun. Shoot that guy."

I reached into Spider's boot and grabbed the gun. It slid out of the ankle holster. I hated how it felt in my hand. "Spider, I can't shoot that guy. I'm not made for this. You gotta do something."

What sounded like a laugh gurgled out of Spider. "Nobody was made fer this. Ya do what ya gotta. Shoot him, or die." Each breath became shallower and closer together, his chest rattling with each one. "Do what you got to, man. Nobody can do it for ya." The wet sound of his breathing slowed. His eyes grew wide and looked into mine. Then his head fell sideways and the rattling breath stopped.

Tears ran down my cheeks. Spider was dead. I was in deep shit and no one was coming to the rescue.

The gunman was a block away, blood-soaked, yet limping towards me. I aimed the pistol at him, "Stop there and I won't shoot."

He ducked behind a car and rested his pistol on the trunk lid. His hands shook. He could barely hold his head up.

I pointed Spider's pistol at him.

He struggled to stand, then hobbled toward me, ducking behind parked cars. He stopped a car length away and tried pointing his pistol, resting it on the hood of a Ford LTD to steady his hands.

"Stop, mister. Please. I don't wanna shoot."

The silence was eerie. Nothing moved except the pistol he was aiming at me. The gun shook in his hands still. Blood smeared the car hood. His face gritted in determination. His finger tensed on the trigger.

My feet wouldn't move. I was frozen in place.

A pistol shot cracked the silence. The man dropped his gun and fell behind the car. I turned to see who had shot him. It wasn't until my hand started throbbing that I realized I was still squeezing the trigger of the gun in my hand. The shooter was me.

Chapter 25

He reached for the gun laying in the street. I kicked the weapon away.

Anger raged in me. Just a minute before, even with his gun aimed at me, I blacked out before I could pull the trigger. That hesitation was gone. "Stop trying to kill me and just lay there 'til I'm gone, or I swear, I will shoot you in the fucking head."

The bloodied man stared at me, then shrugged and lay motionless.

Sirens wailed in the distance. I didn't want them bastards to get Spider. The Police Special was in ashes, and the Sportster was banged up. I shoved the gun in my pocket and ran back to Sean's car. The guy Spider shot lay dead in the street. I started the car and peeled out to get back to Spider's body. I tugged and pushed his body into the back seat, slammed the door and headed out of the neighborhood. Instinctively, I observed the speed limit. A few minutes later I no longer heard sirens.

I turned left onto the Shoreway, heading toward Hellhouse. After a couple of miles, I realized taking him there would draw Boyle right to the Angels. I didn't want that. Dropping him at a hospital was out. Gunshot wounds would bring an investigation. No matter how Spider had lived, he died saving my life. He deserved respect even in death, not some detective with a beer-gut trying to hang a shooting on him.

The only other place I knew in Cleveland was Evvie's. I shuddered at the thought. I had disrespected and hurt her. But there was no other choice, so I worked my way toward Parma, hoping the Charger hadn't been reported stolen.

It took me a while to find Evvie's place. By the time I did, my stomach churned, and my hands shook. The prospect of seeing her terrified me. I didn't know how she would react to Spider's death. I felt guilty involving her. Would she help me? What could she even do?

Driving down her block I felt like throwing up. When I reached her house, the driveway was empty. I parked on the street then looked through the window in the garage door to see if her car was there. Nope. As I walked back to the

Charger, the front door of the house opened. Norma looked through the screen door.

"Am I having a vision, or is that you, Nate?"

Her voice startled me. I hadn't planned on dealing with Norma. I turned to face her, but didn't speak.

"It's okay, Nate. Evvie's mad at you, with good reason. But I'm glad to see you. Why're you here?"

Words tumbled out unfiltered. "Spider is dead in the back seat, and I need to find someone to take care of the body, and I didn't know anyone but you and Evvie, besides the Hells Angels. Do you know any relatives of Spider's I might contact?"

Norma pushed the screen door open and walked onto the stoop. "Spider's dead? His body's in the back of the car?" She walked over and looked in. "Oh, my God. What happened? Oh, Spider! Oh..." She buried her face in her hands and sobbed. "What happened, Nate? Who did this to him?"

A hot breeze hit my face. "We got into a gunfight."

"A gunfight? We need to call the police."

"No!" I walked to where Norma stood. "No police. Besides Spider, there's another guy dead. And the guy I shot might be dead. No police! You need to help me, but no police."

"All right, all right. No police." Norma stepped back from the car and looked around. "I can't believe Spider's dead." She wiped her eyes and looked at me. "Pull the car into the garage."

I drove the car in and pulled down the overhead door.

Norma held out an arm and ushered me to the back door. "Come in. We'll figure something out."

She sat in the easy chair, I perched on the edge of the couch. "Where's Evvie?" I asked.

"Evvie's at work. I'm glad she's not here."

Norma looked calm in the midst of this crazy situation. Last time I'd seen her, she was delusional, suffering the loss of her son. "Why're you glad Evvie's not here? What with Wendells' death and all you don't need my problems."

Norma sat back and took a deep breath. "I finally saw that I was hurting Evvie with my crazy behavior and went to a counselor. Made a huge difference. Wendell's gone, and I'll never get over it. But I can't let his death be the end of me, too. Somehow, I thought if I went on with life, I was forgetting him. At last, I realized I'll never forget him. Now is my chance to live up to his ideals." She rested her elbows on her legs. "Wendell was the most upright person I knew, but he stood by his friends no matter what, and that caused him to get into trouble once in a while. You're in a jam, and I'm going to help you. I just don't know how, yet."

My arms and legs twitched as the adrenaline drained from me. Fear replaced the energy that had allowed me to function. I went from mindless, reactionary survival, to imagining life in prison. "I shouldn't have come here. I'm dead anyway."

"What are you talking about, Nate? You've got nowhere else to go. I hate that you're in such a bind, and I'm going to do my damnedest to figure something out."

"Why should you do anything? It'll just bring problems you don't deserve."

"Stop talking." Norma leaned forward. "The first time I met you, my chest tightened up. You don't look much like Wendell, but you have a good aura. I think your intentions are pure. You reminded me of Wendell's determination to help people."

My face heated up. Her talking about me like that embarrassed me. Seems everyone thought I was innocent, but I had lost that. I knew a lot more about the evils in the world, but I didn't feel any wiser. Experience doesn't always breed understanding.

"I always thought I was a good guy." My hands still shook. "But I've blown it. I shot a guy... well... now two guys. One I know is dead, the other I left lying in the street, bleeding. I'm not a good person. I'm not like your Wendell. I don't rescue people. I can't even rescue myself."

Norma slapped my knee, then snapped at me, "Stop feeling sorry for yourself. You're wasting energy that you need to make some tough decisions. I'll help, but you need to focus."

Focus? What did she mean? I could only think about Spider dead in the car, the gangsters lying in the street, and Brian buried somewhere he'd never be found. I was responsible, at least in part, for all of that destruction. Fear overrode everything. And where was Norma getting this determination? Last time I saw her, she was a nutcase.

She leaned back in the chair and stared at me. "What are you thinking?"

"Nothing."

"Don't bullshit me, buster." She pointed her finger at me. "You were thinking 'who the hell is this little old lady to be telling me what to do'? You were thinking I don't get what a mess you're in. Well, I get it! People have been getting killed around me since I was old enough to understand complete sentences." She jabbed the air in front of me. "Didn't Evvie tell you where we came from? She's the one who kicked me in the ass to stop thinking of myself as a victim. We're out of the slums because she was relentless. You should be so lucky as to get back in her good graces." Norma dropped her arm. "I've dealt with problems before. We're going to work this out."

"How? That's great that you know about things. I'll admit I don't. Before I came to this hell-hole that is Cleveland I'd never been high, sold drugs, handled a gun, fought back in a fight, killed anyone." I stopped at that because *that* was the thing that tore at my heart. I had killed a man, probably two. My hands flew to my face as tears burst forth. Goddammit, crying again.

Norma sat quietly for a moment, then put her hand on my knee. "Are you done, son? 'Cause we have work to do."

I drew in a few deep breaths, then wiped my nose with my t-shirt. Norma was silent, apparently waiting for me to do something, though I didn't know what. I was good at getting into trouble, less so at getting out of it. "What? What can I do? Like I said, I only know you, Evvie and the Hells Angels. And the Angels don't want anything to do with me. Besides, if I go to them for help, it'll be war. Those gangsters'll be gunning for revenge. As of now, they don't know who kidnapped Sean."

Norma's eyes grew round and her eyebrows arched. "Wait, who's Sean?"

"I don't know. That's what this whole mess is about. Sean and his buddy stole a load of drugs from Spider, and we were trying to settle it. But somehow Boyle's guys—"

"Boyle's guys?"

I nodded.

"Oh God. What else haven't you told me?"

How could she not know what I had been talking about? "Nothing! Spider and I broke the finger of Boyle's nephew and killed one of their soldiers. I'm not trying to hold back stuff. There's just so much shit it takes a while to get it all out." My head felt like it was about to explode.

Norma studied me for a minute, then sat back in the chair. She drew a big breath and exhaled through pursed lips. "The good news is, I know one of Boyle's guys. At least I used to."

"Do you think he'll put in a good word or something?"

"Hah! That's not likely."

"At least it's something. How do you know him?"

Norma's face reddened. "Back in the old neighborhood, Boyle's guys used to come around and offer little helps to families. You know, if the kids needed shoes for school, something like that, they'd give the mom a tenner compliments of Tommy. Well, Paddy came around a few times and we sort of hit it off. But, like I said, I haven't seen him. So, it's a long shot."

"That seems so weird, them giving presents out. Weren't they also selling numbers and drugs and running women?"

Norma shook her head. "So, what do you think the politicians do? They come around and do a little favor, then carry off a suitcase full of money. It's no different."

I held up my hands. "I'm not judging. I just never thought about them giving gifts is all. But I need to figure out what to do with Spider. I need to get rid of Sean's car. I need to disappear. I'm not ready to die, and I don't want to live like this anymore. I need your help. Tell me what to do, and I'll do it."

Norma got up and walked to the kitchen. The rotary phone ground down each number she dialed. The long silence that followed made me think there would be no answer.

Then, "Yeah, hi. Is Paddy there?" Norma's foot tapped on the linoleum. "Tell him it's Norma." Silence, then, "Hello Paddy. It's Norma. Remember me?" Another silence, then she laughed. "Yeah, them were some good times." Her head appeared in the doorway. She smiled and held up her thumb. "You bet, Paddy. I'd like that."

Apparently, Paddy remembered her, and was still a fan. How that was going to help escaped me. I was in deep shit with Boyle. What Norma could get from Paddy escaped me.

"No, really, I'd love to see you this afternoon. Whaddya say? For old time's sake... Okay, then. See you at six. 'Bye."

Norma almost skipped into the room. "It's all set! He's picking me up at six."

"Great. What are you gonna tell him?"

Norma's enthusiasm fell off her like a second skin. "What do you mean? I'm going to tell him I need some help. You have a better plan?"

"Sorry. I didn't mean to question what you're doing. I just don't see how asking the enemy for assistance is a good idea."

Norma put her hands on her hips and scowled. "I don't know what Evvie saw in you other than your good looks and innocence. You are the densest eighteen-year old I have yet to encounter. Where did you grow up?"

Oh, God. I had succeeded in asking for help from yet another person who viewed me as an imbecile. "I grew up in Milwaukee and went to Catholic school. I hung around with a bunch of kids that used dope and stole cars. I never did those things. I was too scared of going to Hell, okay? I was dumb enough to believe in Hell back then. Now I no longer need to believe in Hell, I'm in Hell. I have gotten myself in way the fuck over my head. I'm asking-no, I'm begging you, help me out. I'm not questioning you. It's just that I appear to be the most ignorant eighteen-year-old in existence. Help me out!"

Norma dropped her arms to her side. Her jaw relaxed, and her eyes softened. "Now I get it. Evvie saw your need. She's just like Wendell, though she won't admit it." Norma held her arms out to me. "C'mon, Nate. Let me give you a hug."

At first, the hug felt odd, but after a few seconds, it felt good, like I might come out of this all right. It felt like she was on my side.

Then she pushed me back. "Do you still have the gun?"

I nodded.

"Give it to me."

She took the gun into the kitchen and put it in a drawer.

•   •   •   •   •

Norma had laid out what she intended to tell her friend and that they were meeting at Ted's bar where everyone in Cleveland seemed to go when they needed information to go with their hangover.

"So, you're meeting Paddy at the Polack bar?" I asked.

"Have some respect. What's wrong with you?"

"What? Where I come from, there are only Micks and Kikes and Wops and Spics. Oh, and Negroes. We didn't use that other word in my neighborhood."

Norma shook her head. "The world runs better when there's respect. You can't help how you were raised, but you might oughta start learning how to treat people better."

"I always try to treat people right."

"Well, how you think in your head colors your actions whether you think so or not."

I was in shit up to my armpits. I didn't care what Norma thought of my racial names. "Okay. Whatever you say."

It was almost time for Norma to leave. She and Paddy were going for drinks. She was going to ask him who they used for "funeral services," the idea being that we could get Spider cremated. He had no family that Norma knew of, his mother having died years ago from a lifetime of addiction. Norma aimed to reestablish a spark with Paddy. I would stay at the house.

Norma walked out of her bedroom and struck a pose. She was wearing a knee-length skirt with a white long-sleeved blouse. Her hair was perfect, and the faint aroma of roses surrounded her. "I look okay?"

"Wow. That guy doesn't have a chance." It was hard to imagine this was the same addled woman I had met not too long ago.

A car horn sounded. "Okay, then," Norma said. "I'm off. You can watch TV or whatever 'til Evvie gets home."

Evvie! Oh shit. What was I going to do when Evvie got home? "Thanks for doing this, Norma. I don't know what I'd do if I didn't have your help."

"Don't thank me yet. Paddy may tell me to forget it. After all, his life is in what he does. If he makes Tommy Boyle mad, he may lose more than his job."

The reality of the mess I was in weighed down even harder. People had died and more people were putting themselves out to help me survive. I hugged Norma. "Thank you."

I stepped into the kitchen to make sure Paddy didn't see me through the open door. After I was sure they were gone, I went into the bathroom to rinse off the stink of sweat and fear. I had just soaked my face when I heard the garage door go up and then the back door open.

"Mom? Who's car is in the garage?" Footsteps crossed the kitchen linoleum. "Mom?"

I opened the bathroom door and crept into the living room. The sound of Evvie's voice made my stomach melt, both from the thrill of being near her and the fear of what she might say. I called, "Hi Evvie. Your mom's not here."

Her footsteps stopped. I heard her toss her keys and purse onto the kitchen table. Then she stomped the rest of the way through the kitchen. "You! What are you doin' here? Haven't you caused enough trouble? And where's Norma? Did you hurt her? I swear I'll kill you if you've done anything to hurt her."

My heart was in my throat. "Hurt Norma? No, no. She's fine. She's just left for a couple hours."

"Left? Where?"

"She's out with a friend from your old neighborhood."

"Who?"

"Paddy."

"Paddy? You gotta be shittin' me. And just what the hell are you doin' here, huh? You gotta have bigger balls than I felt 'neath your dick to show up after the way you treated me."

My face heated up in shame. "You're right. I shouldn't have any business here. Believe me, I'd walk away right now if I could. But there's a reason why I have to stay. Sit down a minute and let me tell you... um... some news."

Chapter 26

Evvie stood in the opening, her fists clenched, glaring at me. "You're like that Legionnaire's disease. Everyone that breathes your air gets sick and dies." She flung her arm out, pointing to the front door. "Get out of my house! Leave us alone. Get out!"

"I can't."

"You mean you won't. What do you need now? A place to stay? A place to run your foul, cocaine-fueled mouth? The Hellhouse not good enough? Passin' out in the woods and pukin' all over yourself not workin' out for you?"

Her words stung like bamboo poles tearing into my bare flesh, but I couldn't walk away. Spider's dead body lay in the back seat of Sean's car, the car I had stolen, the one that had been involved in a shootout. I had nowhere else to turn.

"Look—"

"Here it comes," Evvie said, rolling her eyes. "The innocent, 'gosh darn,' spiel."

"Evvie, please, come sit down. There *is* something you need to know. Please."

Her eyes got big, and she pulled in a shuddering breath. "Who died?"

I gestured toward the couch. "Please, sit."

Her shoulders slumped, and her fists unclenched as she sat on the edge of the couch. "Who is it? Who died?"

Her questions didn't make it any easier. My heart skipped a beat. "Spider."

I expected an outburst. But rather than cry out, or bend over in grief, she said, "Hmph. I mighta guessed."

I slumped into the easy chair, exhausted at the effort I had spent worrying about her reaction. "Happened this morning."

"Did he wipe out on his Harley or have a heart attack from all the drugs he used to do?"

My exhaustion solidified into anxiety. "He was shot."

Evvie's head bobbed once. "I guess that's not surprising. He had a lot of enemies."

I stared at her, eyes narrowed. "He died saving my life." I wondered how she could be so casual about this. Then, I realized I wasn't the center of her or anyone else's universe.

Evvie looked at me, lips pursed, jaw protruding. "That doesn't surprise me. For all the mess he was, Spider was real. I think he saw a little of himself in you."

I laughed. "Me? No. He thought I was an idiot."

Evvie stared back.

I stared too, befuddled about what was transpiring. I just told Evvie Spider was dead. She didn't react to the news.

Evvie sighed. "You're lost, aren't you?"

She still thought I was stupid. Trying to change her opinion, I said, "No."

"Spider did think you were an idiot, but he wanted to help you. He knew his own faults pretty well, and I think he saw the same things in you. He struggled with his sense of right and wrong. He got started too late to figure things out. Maybe you'll do better. But I doubt it."

It felt like Evvie had stabbed me and twisted the blade.

"Do you want to know what happened?" I asked.

"You already told me."

"No, I mean about how Spider got shot and all."

"I know what you meant. But, that part doesn't matter."

I thought of Spider's body. "Yeah, it does."

"It's over now," Evvie said, "What else matters?"

"The car in the garage."

Evvie threw up her arms. "What about it?"

"Spider's body is in the back seat."

Evvie buried her face in her hands. She was stone still for a moment, then she started shaking, sobbing. "It's never going to end. We're cursed. I swear, we're cursed."

I went to her and put my hand on her shoulder. "I'm sorry—"

She slapped my face. "Get out! Get out!"

My face stung, but my heart ached. She was crying because of me. I took a step back before I repeated, "I'm sorry."

She buried her face in her hands again, though the sobs stopped.

Humiliation and guilt replaced my fear of being arrested. I needed to leave and take my problems with me. "Move your car. I'm leaving"

Evvie stared at me.

"I'm leaving."

She didn't stir.

"I've caused you and Norma enough pain. My problems are my own. Move your car."

Evvie leaned her head to the side and narrowed her eyes. "What about Norma? She's out with a gangster trying to bail you out, isn't she? She called Paddy to see if he'd help you."

"If I leave now, I'll be long gone before she gets back. So she had a nice date with a good Irish boy. What's the harm?"

"You don't know how anything works, do you?"

"Christ almighty, Evvie! I admit I'm an idiot. I'm trying to leave, trying to make this a little more right for you and Norma. You don't need to rub it in my face."

Evvie started shouting. "Paddy doesn't do anything for free. Sure, he acts sweet on my mom. And, he may decide to do her a favor. But nothing comes without a price."

"Jesus, Evvie. Your mom's an adult. She doesn't have to sleep with the guy unless she wants to."

Evvie laughed. "You think I'm worried about Norma getting laid? Hell, she'd probably love that." She shook her head. "No. Paddy will want some info. He'll want Norma to ask around, to nose into stuff. This shit never ends."

I guess I knew Norma's help would come at a price. I hadn't thought much about what that price might be. "Then let me leave. I'll figure it out. I never should have come here."

Evvie went to the kitchen, grabbed her keys from the table and opened the back door, then jumped back and shut it again. "Oh, shit!"

"What?" I asked.

"They're back. Paddy just pulled in behind me."

"I gotta get outta here."

"Nowhere to go, Nate. They're walking to the front door. There's two cars behind yours. I'd say you better get ready to play like you're my boyfriend."

I heard the front door open. Norma called out, "We're home, honey."

Evvie pulled her blouse out of the waistband of her slacks and messed up her hair. "We're in the kitchen. I didn't think you'd be back so soon." She grabbed the front of my shirt and pulled me into the living room. She looked at Paddy and said, "We were just going to go out when you pulled up." She pushed her hair off her face. "Been a while. How've you been?"

Paddy nodded. "Good ta see ya."

It was beyond awkward.

Norma looked at me. "Paddy and me had a good talk. I told him about your friend's unfortunate 'accident' and how you want to protect his family from his committing suicide. So, we came right back. Paddy thinks he can help."

Paddy looked down. "I got ways."

Norma looked me in the eye and cocked her head in Paddy's direction. "So, what do you think, Nate?"

Paddy stared at me through half-closed eyelids.

His gaze unsettled me. "Man, I would appreciate your help. You know how it is. The guy got in over his head and just couldn't take it any more. His family knows about the drugs he was using. They won't miss him for a while. But they'd be sick if they thought he committed an unforgivable sin, like suicide. I'd like to help them think he made it to heaven."

Paddy shrugged. "Yeah, I get it."

"Thanks, man. So, what do we do?"

Paddy looked at Norma. "How about we have a drink?"

"Oh, sure. I got some Bushmills in the kitchen."

Paddy sat in the easy chair looking relaxed. Just another day at the office.

I sat on the couch as far away from him as I could. I wasn't sure if he could smell fear, but I didn't want to test it out.

Norma came back with two rocks glasses. Each held one ice cube and an inch of amber liquid. "Your favorite, right?" She handed one of the glasses to the gangster.

Paddy held the glass up to the light and swirled it before taking a sip. "Mmm, yeah. This is God's own liquor."

Norma sat on the couch near Paddy and took a sip of her own drink. She seemed to savor it. "Yeah, this brings it back. All the good times. Sorry to call you with this problem, Paddy. But, aside from that, I am *so* glad to see you."

Paddy nodded and took another sip of the whiskey. He surveyed the room, swiveling his head to take in the plain but neat living room with the old couch and easy chair, the lamp on the single end table. He looked at me, then Evvie, then Norma. "I've been knowing ya for too many years, Norma. I was surprised when they said you'd moved out here. Not that I blame ya, but this's a different place, ya know?"

Norma looked at him and smiled. "It's nice not ta have the gunfire and all, outside my door, but I haven't changed."

Norma had fallen into an Irish lilt. It sounded natural, but surprised me.

Paddy nodded and drained his glass. "Got another?" he asked.

Norma got up and took his glass. "Be right back."

Paddy sat, staring into the distance.

Evvie broke the silence. "What's it like, Paddy?"

He shot her a look. "Whaddya mean?"

"You know, watching the neighborhood, helping folks, fixing disputes and stuff."

Norma came back with a fresh drink and handed it to Paddy.

He drained half of it and looked at the ceiling. Then drained the other half and held the glass out to Norma. "Make it a double."

Norma hesitated, then took the glass and went into the kitchen.

"Why're you askin', Evvie? You seen how it was back in the neighborhood. That place woulda burned down years ago if we didn't take care of stuff."

"Geez, sorry man," Evvie said. "I didn't mean anything bad."

Norma came back with Paddy's drink. "Ya sure you want this?"

Paddy took the drink and set it down on the end table without tasting it. Looking at his lap, he furrowed his brow and pursed his lips, then he looked up and smiled at Norma. "Yeah, thanks."

Norma smiled back. "Okay."

"Look, Evvie, I'm sorry if I snapped at ya. It's just sometimes things get tense. Not everybody likes us. But we're just tryin' ta make a livin', you know?" Paddy eyed the drink but didn't pick it up. "And, we help a lot of people. You seen that, right?"

Evvie smiled at Paddy. "Sure."

"But, it's not all nice." He shifted in his seat and eyed the drink again. This time he picked it up, took a big swallow, and stared straight at me. "Sometimes I need to do things that are unpleasant."

My stomach churned, and cold sweat popped out on my forehead.

"I know all about your friend and his *suicide*. What he done really was a form of suicide." He sat back again. "What was he thinkin'? I mean that prick Sean had it comin', but Tommy don't care about fair or right. He cares about money, and he cares about his idiot nephew."

I felt lightheaded. My field of vision narrowed. I was as good as dead.

"When your pal offed one of Tommy's guys, well, he went a little crazy." Paddy shook his head. "You shoulda killed the other guy, too. We happened to go by Sean's place and found him just before the cops came."

"So, he's alive?" I asked.

"Who? Jack? Yeah. He said you didn't want to kill him. Well, that worked out good for him, but not so great for you. When Norma told me the BS story about suicide and all, I wondered if it wasn't actually you."

Why did I not kill him when I had the chance? I've brought this on Evvie and Norma, all because I didn't have the balls to kill that guy. I looked at Paddy. "So, what now?"

Paddy looked relaxed again. He even had a faint smile. "So now, I should kill ya and tell Tommy what I done. There'd be a bonus in it for me."

I was about to piss in my pants.

"No, Paddy! Please," Norma said. "Nate was only doin' what his friend made him. The killing needs to stop."

Evvie stood up. "Please, Paddy. Let it go. Tommy doesn't know you found him. Just walk away. Nate'll be gone tomorrow. You'll never see him again."

"Hold on, hold on." Paddy threw back some more of his drink. "I didn't say I was *gonna* kill him. I said I oughta." He shook his head some more. "I'm gettin' too old for this shit."

Evvie sat back down.

Norma stroked the gangster's arm. "C'mon, Paddy. Let him go."

I wanted to melt into the couch, to disappear.

"Okay," Paddy said. "We got a few problems that need to be handled." He downed the rest of his drink. "If I can avoid it, I'm not gonna kill the kid. Okay? So, relax."

"I swear, this shit never ends." Norma hung her head. "We tried to leave this behind when we moved out of Irish Town. But it followed us here. Like the hippies say, Karma, or whatever."

"Hey, I didn't ask to be involved in this. You called me, remember?" Paddy shifted in his seat and looked at me. "So, I gather from what Norma told me, you have a body to dispose of."

"Yeah," I answered, my voice raspy.

He raised his eyebrows. "So? Where is it?"

I told him.

"Okay." Paddy stood. "Makes it easier. Let's go."

I should have felt like I dodged a bullet, but I was still scared as hell. "What are we going to do?"

"We're gonna take the plates offa Evvie's car and put 'em on Sean's. Then we go see a guy who will dispose of the body. He normally charges one large, but he owes me. I can get him to do it as a favor."

And then, I'll be in debt to you. I was beginning to see how all of this worked. "You know I've got nothing, right?"

Paddy shrugged. "Who knows? Maybe I need to do this to improve my, what'd you call it, Norma? Karma?"

Norma stood and hugged Paddy. "I knew you were a good person at heart."

"Yeah, well... c'mon kid." Paddy turned to go. "Norma, get the boy a screwdriver. He needs to change the plates."

She walked with me into the kitchen while Paddy used the bathroom.

"Where's the gun?" I whispered.

"In the drawer. And it stays there." She handed me a screwdriver. "Be careful."

•   •   •   •   •

After we changed the plates, I backed the Charger out and followed Paddy's car. We ended up at place near the river, not far from where the original drug deal went down; the one that started me into the hell of addiction and crime. I felt sick with fear and loathing.

Paddy banged on the door of a brick storefront. A light went on upstairs. A man leaned out of a window. "Yeah?"

Paddy stepped back so the man could see him.

The man grunted, and the window slammed shut. A minute later a deadbolt clicked, and the door opened. "Go around back to overhead door."

Paddy tossed his head toward an alley. "Go."

I pulled the car into a large, lighted space. Paddy and the man stood just inside the overhead door, which rolled shut behind me. I expected a huge furnace-like thing but saw a walk-in freezer.

The man pulled on a rubber apron and gloves with cuffs that covered his arms up the elbows. He opened the rear door of the Charger and pulled on Spider's body until it fell to the concrete floor with a thump. He dragged it into the freezer. When he came out, and the freezer door slammed shut behind him, relief washed over me for a moment, but anxiety crashed back in. Now I had to deal with Paddy.

Chapter 27

The man who opened the building for Paddy was dark-skinned, thin, and short. He looked Middle Eastern and spoke with a thick accent. "I take care it. Not to worry for you." He looked at Paddy. "Same always?" He held out his hand.

Paddy scoffed at him. "Abdul, are ya kiddin'? Ya fucked up the last deal so bad we had the cops sniffin' so close we had to redirect 'em with a pile o' cash money. You owe me. I'm tryin' to save your business, here. You do this one for free, and we'll see about the rest."

Abdul's face darkened, "Irish! Crooks!" He raised his hand as if to slap Paddy.

Paddy grabbed his arm and spun the smaller man around. "Watch it little man. You're the one who left the body in an incinerator that was out of commission. The stench drew attention. Ya better be smarter this time, or there'll be a feckin' huge price to pay. Do it right, and you're back in. Otherwise..." He let go of the smaller man.

Abdul took a step back. "I do this. One time. Not one more free for you. Understand?"

Paddy laughed. "Oh, Abdul. We own you, don't you know? You'll work when we want, and you'll do what we say."

Abdul clenched his fists at his sides, took a long breath, then nodded his head one time.

Paddy looked at me. "We gotta go. Take Evvie's plates offa the Charger and ride with me. Abdul, you can have the car. At least you'll make a few hundred." He shrugged his shoulders. "See, I ain't without a heart."

We walked out the front of the building where Paddy was parked. He drove a 1970 four-door Chevy Impala, yellow with a black vinyl top. Impalas had always been my favorite car, but this one just seemed boxy and big. I didn't know why he had helped me out and recent experience taught me nothing was for nothing. I wanted Paddy to warm up to me. "So, thanks for helping. An Impala. Impressive."

"Psha. I guess. I wanted a feckin' El Dorado. Show everyone what's what, ya know. But Tommy has an El Dorado. Doesn't think his underlings should show him up."

Paddy's attitude was surprising. These guys were in for life. If he was beefing about his boss to a nobody like me, then I guess things were tense. "What happens to Spider's body?"

Paddy shrugged. "Abdul does what he does. He knows better than to let the body get found. He has a buddy that operates a trash disposal deal. They got incinerators, ya know? Makes fast work of it."

I felt bad that Spider was going to get burned up like so much trash, but what could I do? His body would tie me to enough stuff to ruin my life forever. "How did you get started in this business?"

"Hah. Asked like a guy that doesn't know nothin'." Paddy shifted in his seat. "I was born into it. My old man ran with Tommy's dad. We took vacations with their family, had dinner at each other's houses. My dad tried ta get me ta do sumthin' else, but Tommy and I got to be buddies. He took me ta parties in his fancy cars and got me chicks. You know."

I shrugged.

"Hah. Yeah, you don' know." Paddy drove in silence for a while.

I was trying to figure out if I was safe, or in a car with my executioner. He'd helped me out for sure, but for Norma. I was nobody to this guy. "Where we headed?"

Paddy didn't reply. He looked straight ahead, his left hand atop the steering wheel, the right tucked inside his jacket. The only sounds were the whine of the tires on the street and the purr of the Impala's engine. Light from the streetlamps washed across the hood twice every block.

The relief of getting rid of Spider's body wasn't even a memory. All I saw was Paddy's hand in his jacket, like he was fondling his gun.

The neighborhood changed from a mix of storefronts with apartments above to residential, then commercial again, but this time, nicer places; fancy food shops, furniture stores and fur boutiques. "Where are we?" I asked, not able to contain my anxiety. "Where are we headed?"

Paddy glanced at me and shrugged. "Thought you might like something to eat."

I was hungry, but if Paddy got me dinner, there'd be a price. I didn't answer.

He pulled up in front of a diner. "C'mon, let's eat."

"Sure." What did this guy want from me? *Nothing comes for free.*

We entered Jacob's All Night Diner. The place was half empty. Kitchen sounds reverberated off the tile floor and tin ceiling. It was bright and clean. We took seats at a table in the rear. Paddy sat with his back to the wall, just like I'd heard gangsters and cops were supposed to do.

"What can I get you to drink?" The waitress had flaming red curly hair, her face was a map of wrinkles. The contrast made her look even older than she probably was.

"Coffee. And make sure it's hot, Annie." Paddy winked at the woman then looked at me. "What do you want?"

I looked at the waitress. "Coffee's good."

Paddy scanned the room with half-closed eyes, his face blank.

"You looking for someone?" I asked.

"Why'd you ask that?"

"Because you keep looking around, and you knew the waitress. I figured maybe you were looking for someone you knew."

Paddy's eyebrows rose. "I don't know that waitress. Never been in this place before." He put his elbows on the table. "I always treat people like they want to be treated. So, I read her name tag. Basic respect, see?"

I nodded. I wanted to treat people right, too, but that hadn't always worked out so well for me. Besides, this guy had likely beaten people to within an inch of their lives and beyond. Using the waitress's name seemed trivial. But at that moment, if I knew anything, it was that I didn't know anything at all.

Being with Paddy could go a lot of different ways. I wanted to ask him why he'd helped me, but I was afraid of the answer. Uncertainty gnawed at my gut. At least if I knew what he was thinking I could see about getting away. I had nothing to lose by disappearing. In fact, I felt disappearing was my best shot at survival.

The coffee arrived, and we ordered food. Paddy poured three spoons of sugar and a lot of cream into his coffee. I sipped at mine. It was hot and fresh and somehow made me feel better.

"So, why *did* you help me out?" I asked.

Paddy slurped his coffee, set it down and ignored me.

I hunched over my coffee and took another sip. I was sure he had heard me. "Paddy?"

He scanned the room one more time, back and forth, then looked me in the eye. "I don't know."

The waitress brought our burgers and fries. *He didn't know?* I didn't think these guys did anything without a plan. I thought I was the only one running off into buzz saws, never anticipating consequences. I cut my burger in half, put pepper on my fries, sipped coffee, took a big bite and chewed. I hoped he would keep talking, maybe give me some idea of what he was thinking. My fate hung on Paddy's intentions and his 'I don't know' could lead to a ride out of town, and freedom for me, or some form of enforced labor. Tony's manipulations had almost killed me. I had thought he was on my side, too.

Rather than explain himself, Paddy dug into his food. We ate in silence.

When he was done, Paddy pushed himself away from the table, fished a toothpick out of his pocket and picked at a couple teeth. Then he slipped the toothpick back into his pocket and leaned across the table. "Kid, I done a lotta bad stuff in my life. Some of these things I'm not too proud of." He shrugged. "I don't really give a fuck about what's legal or not so legal. But, I care about right and wrong, see?"

I nodded. At this point, I'd quit caring what was or wasn't legal. I cared about not getting caught. If Tommy's guys used drug money to buy some kid's school lunch, so what? If I ride with Spider to break a guy's finger, why should anyone care? He had it coming. I got that. But, why was Paddy telling me this?

He leaned in even closer and lowered his voice to just above a whisper. "I know a lot more about you than you think. I believe you met our former wholesaler. Guy named Tony." Paddy was looking me right in the eyes.

I felt heat rise in my face and cold sweat on my forehead. I nodded.

"Notice I said 'former'."

I nodded again.

"When Tony eliminated Elwood, I didn't think too much of it. He was a fuck up and a thief. Not a good combination. But, word is that Tony got pissed at you and put you on a fast train to Neverland. I didn't like what I heard, because Tony has offed more than a few guys. I think he liked it. From the story I got, you was just naive, not a thief, so Tony had to go. I'm not ashamed of doing what I had to do, but, I'm tired of it."

Paddy fell silent and sat back in his chair again while the waitress poured more coffee.

Admitting his misgivings to me must have sucked all the pride out of him. I didn't feel sorry for him, but I could see the weight of his past sitting on his shoulders, pushing him into a slouch.

He stood up and stretched. "Let's go." He paid the tab on the way out and ambled to his car. "Let's take a ride."

"Well, why? I mean, thanks for your help and all, but I ought to be going."

Paddy' eyebrows shot up the same time his hands did. "What? You just gonna walk away? I bail your ass out, and you leave?" Paddy shook his head and grabbed my arm. "Naw, you're coming with me."

What could I do? If I ran, he'd just chase me or shoot me on the spot. At least if I went "willingly" I'd still be on Paddy's good side. Once we were on the road, I asked, "Where are we headed?"

"I'm gonna take ya' to our private club. I want ya to meet Tommy."

I almost choked. "What? Are you crazy? He'll kill me!"

Paddy snickered. "Yeah, maybe."

"Stop the car! I got to get out of here." We were going too fast for me to just jump out. "C'mon, Paddy. Don't do this. It'll just add to the list of regrets."

"Shut up." He dragged out the words. "I'm not gonna let him kill ya. Jesus."

"Then why are we going?"

"I've known Tommy a long time. And, like I said at Norma's place, he cares about money and his nephew. So, I wanna take a shot at getting Tommy to see the light about Sean's crappy attitude. That little pecker is makin' us all look bad. Truth be told, I was thrilled when I heard someone busted his finger." Paddy smiled again. "Let me ask ya, why only break one finger? Why not break 'em all. Or, cut 'em off? Makes a lasting impression, believe me."

"What? Cut off his fingers?" The thought made me nauseous. "I could never do that. And we only broke one because we thought maybe going easy might get the message across without starting a war."

"Yeah, whatever. That ain't how things work." Paddy's shoulders slumped. "When Norma called me, all the bad feelins' that had built up over these past few years sorta burst." Paddy rubbed his chin with one hand and steered with the other. I liked that better than when he had kept his right hand inside his jacket. "I'd started questionin' things, mostly because of how Sean treated people. He has no respect. Sure we do illegal things and people get hurt sometimes, but we watched out for the neighborhood. We didn't laugh at people or treat 'em like losers."

I could see how Sean's ridiculous sense of entitlement would have him mocking people and dismissing them as mere pawns in his kingdom. Paddy was showing me a different side of gangsters. He may be ruthless and cruel, but in some weird way, he had values.

"Anyway," Paddy went on, "I've been lookin' for a way to get to Tommy, and you're it."

My heart was beating a mile a minute. "Paddy, he'll kill me."

"I already told you, I won't let him kill ya."

"How, man? How am I going to help you get to Tommy? All I can see is him cutting off my fingers, or worse. Does he know I was with Spider?"

"Doesn't matter. I'm gonna tell him anyway."

"What?"

"Yeah, I'm gonna tell him. And I'm gonna stick up for you right to his face."

This was crazy talk. How could that help him? How could that not get my ass in a wringer? Thoughts of escape flashed through my mind, but I couldn't see a way out.

"But—"

"I'm done talkin' to ya. You're goin' with me. Just keep your mouth shut and don't fuckin' piss in your pants. This is gonna work for you, for me and most importantly for Norma."

What did this have to do with Norma? I started to open my mouth.

"Ah, shut up. We're done talking. Besides we're here. Remember, keep your mouth shut and don't pass out. This is gonna work. You'll be okay."

Paddy pulled the car to the curb in front of the same private club Spider and I had followed Sean to. No one sat outside. Meager light leaked through the blinds in the windows. Paddy got out first. I sat frozen from fear and indecision. Paddy stood waiting until I got out of the car and followed him into the club.

Tobacco smoke filled the air. Men sat in twos and threes around small round tables, many drinking coffee, several with whiskey glasses.

"Paddy!" a voice called from the rear. "Where you been? Come on back."

Paddy sauntered toward the rear, and I followed behind him, trying to hide from whoever it was we were approaching.

"Hi, Tommy. What's up?"

Paddy stepped aside. Oh, shit. It must be Tommy Boyle.

"Been looking for you is all." Tommy pointed to a chair. "Sit."

Paddy stepped toward the chair and pointed me to another.

"Who's your buddy? He doesn't look familiar," Tommy said, then looked at me. "You ain't from here, are you?"

"Uh, no sir," I stammered.

Tommy looked at Paddy. "Who is he?"

Paddy leaned back and crossed his arms, then stretched out his legs to the side. He looked at Tommy, his face relaxed, his eyelids half closed. "Remember I told you that Heroin Tony tried to off another kid?"

Tommy nodded.

"This is the kid."

Tommy shrugged his shoulders. "So? I thought you took care of all that."

"Yeah, yeah, I did. But there's more."

"Get on with it, Paddy, for chrissakes."

"Okay, Tommy, I'll get to the point. You and me grew up together. I been your loyal friend for what, forty years?" Paddy paused.

Tommy shrugged again. "Yeah. That's so."

"So here's the deal. I offed Tony because he was bad for business. He was making us look like we had no honor. You agreed it had to be done, right?"

Tommy nodded.

"So, this kid, Nate, is a friend of a friend of mine. Norma Walsh. You remember her from the neighborhood?"

"Yeah, maybe. You two had something, right?"

Paddy nodded. "Maybe we still do. Anyway, turns out it was Nate and a buddy o' his that busted Sean's finger."

Tommy shot to his feet, his face reddening. "Oh, so this is the son-of-a-bitch that dared to fuck with Sean."

I recoiled in my chair and flung my arm over my face. I didn't think I would get out of there alive.

"Calm down, Tommy. You need someone to tell you the truth, to get you the rest of the story that your nephew never tells. That's why I brought Nate."

"So this kid is your kin or what? Or did you bring him here for me to kill him?"

Paddy was on his feet now, too. "I brought him to explain what happened. You gotta start seein' the shame Sean is bringing on our business, our families."

Tommy balled his fists. "You, too? You're going to malign my family?"

Paddy stood to his full height and took a step toward Tommy. "We're like brothers. I'd not be doin' you any favors lettin' that shit nephew of yours carry on. Those guys broke his finger, one lousy fuckin' finger, because Sean drugged 'em and left in the middle of nowhere. For bennie's, Tommy. For fuckin' bennies. The little shit had it comin'. He beats up women, he rips off anyone he can and laughs about it. He has no honor. If somebody'da ripped us off, we'd a killed 'em. What's wrong with you that you can't see Sean is hurtin' us? These guys didn't want no war with us, so's they just tried to make a point. Now I'm trying to make a point with you. Rein in Sean. Whaddya say?"

Tommy drew deep, loud breaths, but he didn't answer right away. He looked toward me. "What do you have to say?"

Paddy put a hand on Tommy's shoulder. "Sit down. We'll get the whole story." Without turning, he said, "Go ahead, Nate."

If there ever was a time I wished I'd paid more attention in Creative Writing class, it was now. I couldn't figure out where to start, what to omit and where I should stop. So, I started at the beginning. "Spider and I were hitching through New York when we both got picked up by Sean and Brian. We didn't know them. Long story short, they fed us Mickies. We passed out. They stole Spider's drugs and left the car, which was also stolen. We were someplace in Pennsylvania when we came to."

Tommy was staring at me. "So you and this Spider were partners in a deal?"

I told him how Spider and I'd never met before and that all I wanted was to get back home to Milwaukee. That I'd been in Cleveland ever since, but would leave tonight if that would make things better.

Paddy jumped in. "His buddy's dead. I helped him get rid of the body. So, if you want some vengeance, you've got it."

"But he took out one of my guys."

"You're right. But the guy that did that, Spider, is dead, Tommy. Jack, on the other hand, is recovering. Ask him why. Ask Jack who didn't shoot him dead when he had the chance."

"Who?" Tommy asked.

Paddy shifted his gaze from Tommy to me and nodded his head.

"This guy? This guy was in on that whole gun fight?" Tommy turned to me. "Why didn't you take him when you had the chance?"

I'd asked myself that question earlier when I realized I'd put Evvie and Norma in a bad position. Why hadn't I just shot him? "I don't know. Killing just seems wrong."

Tommy scoffed. "Oh brother." He shook his head and looked down. "Yeah, I guess that's a good reason."

The front door opened and the atmosphere in the room changed. Conversations grew quieter. Tension saturated the air.

"What're you lookin' at, loser? Never seen a cast before?"

Chapter 28

Tommy stood up and hollered toward the front, "Sean, shut the fuck up."

The place went silent.

"Uncle Tommy? What's happening?"

"Get your ass back here and stop being a such a dick."

As Sean walked up, Paddy stood and stepped back from the table, pointing at his chair. "Have a seat."

Sean smirked at Paddy before sitting down, then spoke to Tommy. "What's up? Why all these serious scowls?"

No one at the table spoke as the noise level in the front room ramped back up. Sean looked over his shoulder at Paddy. "C"mon, man. What's with this silent treatment?" Sean turned back around and saw me sitting across the table. "You!" He jumped up and lunged for me.

Paddy grabbed him by the collar and pulled him back into the chair.

"You broke my finger. You're dead, man!"

"For the last time, shut up." Tommy's eyes were huge and his face crimson. "Do not threaten this young man or anybody else."

Paddy remained silent behind Sean, who was shaking his head.

Tommy glanced at Paddy, then rubbed his face with both hands before turning to Sean. "You're my kin. I've watched over you since your mother died. But this has gone too far. You need to take responsibility for your actions."

"Me? What the fuck? This little no-count shithead broke my finger. And now, *I'm* in trouble.? How does that work Uncle, huh?"

Tommy's open hand slapped down on the tabletop with a 'whack'.

Sean flinched. "Goddam."

"See? That's what I mean. You can't see nothin' but your own way. What them guys did to you," he jabbed his finger at Sean, "you had comin'."

Sean's mouth hung open as he looked from Tommy to Paddy and back again. "You think I had this coming? Uncle, I'm a Boyle. We don't take shit like this."

Tommy shot to his feet and leaned on the table. "Because we've earned respect!" he shouted.

The front room went silent again.

Tommy walked around the table to where Sean sat. "Because we take care of our own. Because we understand it takes the little people to make sure we were covered. We don't hurt people for fun. We own our actions. And we command respect, Sean. Command, not demand. Know the difference?"

"But, Uncle, this guy is nobody."

Tommy stuck his finger into Sean's chest. "Nobody is nobody. Hear me?"

At first, Sean looked like he was tied to a railroad track with a train fast approaching. But then, he rubbed his jaw and looked at his uncle through narrowed eyes. "Sorry, Uncle. I misspoke." He hunched over in his chair and took several deep breaths. Then he started to shake.

I thought he might be breaking down, seeing how his arrogance stirred people's anger and resentment. But after a few seconds, he sat upright, laughing.

"Did I say he was a *nobody*? I meant *somebody*. Somebody who got in my way!" Sean launched himself across the table at me. "You deserve to die, you worthless piece of shit!"

Paddy pulled Sean back by his shirt tail.

I jumped from my chair and staggered back a step.

Tommy stepped aside and crossed his arms. "Paddy, let him go."

Paddy released his grip.

Sean tried to scramble across the table, but it collapsed. He rolled to his side and stood with fists balled. "We got him, Uncle. Let's show him how we treat our enemies."

"You ain't heard a word I said." Tommy shrugged. "I'm not mad at this kid. You're on your own."

I looked at Paddy. He shrugged, too. It was like I was back on the playground with Nico. Sean didn't pose a great threat, he was just a loudmouth bully, and I wasn't backing down this time. I advanced on Sean, taking a wild swing at his head.

Sean ducked the punch. "C'mon, Paddy. Let's get this guy."

"He's done nothin' ta me. You get 'im, tough guy."

Sean let out a growl and spit at me. "Come on, come and get me."

Anything I did could lead to a bad outcome. If I beat Sean, Tommy might change his mind about Sean fighting his own battles. But Sean wouldn't stop until

I was dead or in the hospital. I rushed head down, smashing into Sean's midsection.

Sean gasped as the wind was knocked out of him. He tripped backward on the broken table.

I leapt onto him, pinning his arms and swinging at his face and head. My knuckles stung, then throbbed as I hit him again and again. Blood flew from his nose.

Sean struggled to throw me off but lacked the strength. "Fuck! Stop! Uncle Tommy! Help me!"

Tommy bent down and looked Sean in the eye. "He's *your* enemy."

I was winded from punching Sean. The adrenaline was fading, and my hands ached in time with every heartbeat. I stopped swinging and drew a ragged breath. I had faced my fears again, but didn't know what to do now. Though I felt Sean deserved a beating, I didn't have it in me to go on. "I'm getting off you. Stay down until I tell you."

Sean nodded.

I rolled to my left to get up. Sean rolled with me and reached behind himself with his left hand.

"Stay down, dammit," I yelled.

But Sean already had his pistol out. I swung at his arm, trying to knock the gun away. A shot discharged toward the ceiling. I grabbed Sean's arm with both hands, wrestling for the gun.

"You're going to die!" Sean shouted.

"Stop!" I screamed.

He swung his cast at me, but I held on until Paddy wrestled his arm away from me, then twisted it until Sean let loose. The gun clattered on the floor.

I stood, hoping to run. I was blocked by the crowd watching the fight.

"What is wrong with you?" Sean wailed between gasps. "Why are you treating me like this?" He sat up, blood dripping from his nose, his eyes black with anger. "I bring you an enemy, and you turn on me. Why?"

"*You* bring me an enemy?" Tommy asked. "No, Paddy brought someone *you* made into an enemy because of your own stupidity. Paddy's been tryin' to tell me to cut you off, and I stuck up for you. But no more. You're on your own." Tommy raised his chin. "I have my honor. I won't let you tarnish it."

Sean pointed at Paddy. "You always were jealous of how Uncle treated me. You've poisoned him against me."

Paddy squinted. His face flushed. "If it was my call, you'd be dead."

"Easy, Paddy. He's still my nephew," Tommy said.

Paddy straightened his shoulders and crossed his arms.

Sean worked his jaw. His eyes darted from his uncle to Paddy like a cornered ferret. He looked down for a moment, then lunged for the pistol laying on the floor, aimed it at Paddy and shot left-handed, sending a bullet past Paddy's head. Then he swung around and fired at me.

The bullet hit my left arm, burning as it passed all the way through. At that moment, I snapped. I didn't care if Sean had a pistol or a machine gun or a fucking cannon. I dove at him, knocking him back to the floor. "You shot me, you little prick!" We rolled around until I wrestled the pistol away. I got on top of him and grabbed the cast on his right hand, cracking it against the hard floor. I grabbed his broken middle finger and pulled it back as far as I could.

Sean screamed, "Stop! You can't! Oh God!"

I pulled harder, trying pull the finger off his hand. "How does it feel, big man?"

Sean kept screaming.

I pulled and twisted. "No one coming to the rescue?" I shoved his hand to the floor and knelt on it.

Sean bawled, "Stop! Stop!"

I smashed the side of his head with the gun.

Sean went silent, unconscious.

I took the gun in both hands and aimed it at his face.

"Nate, don't!" Paddy yelled.

I raised the gun toward Paddy, then back to Sean. "I'm done being a victim."

Tommy stepped toward me. "Son, give Paddy the gun."

"No! This shit has got to stop. My friend is dead because of this prick's fucked-up, nobody-matters-but-me attitude." I slugged Sean again. "I'm done and so are you!" I felt the cold metal as I slipped my finger onto the trigger and started to squeeze.

The gun fired as someone grabbed me from behind and jerked my arms straight up. They kept pulling until I fell backward and looked up into the face of Tommy Boyle.

He held the pistol by the barrel. "It's over, son."

·   ·   ·   ·   ·

The room was black. I was lying on a couch, my body covered with a sheet. For a moment I wondered if I was dead. But when I tried to move, every muscle and joint cried out in pain, assuring me I was still alive. I heard loud snoring.

"Paddy?" I whispered.

The snoring stopped. Then resumed.

"Paddy," I said a little louder.

"Wha... what?"

"What happened? Where are we?"

"Go back to sleep."

Turning my head started a throbbing that matched my pulse. I felt my hands. They were swollen, the skin pulled tight to the point of splitting. I could move everything except my left arm, which was bandaged from the elbow to the shoulder.

My fight with Sean, the bullet burning through my arm, the punching, the wrestling, smashing his face with a gun. And then...I had tried to kill him. I had deliberately, with all intent, tried to kill him. And was sorry I hadn't succeeded. I recalled the blast of the pistol shot. But the pistol wasn't in my hand anymore.

Then, Tommy Boyle was standing over me saying something.

An old guy had pushed his way through the crowd and said, "I can work easier if I just knock him out."

Tommy nodded.

The man had pulled a syringe out of a bag he'd carried.

All I could think of was Tony. "Don't! Don't!"

The guy had grabbed my arm, slid the syringe in, and pushed the plunger.

And now, I was here. Still alive but, once again, in the dark.

·   ·   ·   ·   ·

Paddy had brought me to his place to recover from my wounds. Most of the swelling was gone from my hands. My face escaped almost untouched. The bullet in my arm had passed through, missing bone, blood vessels and arteries. Even after a week, it still hurt when I tried to move it, but I could get around okay.

New clothes and a haircut made me look like a different person. These were Paddy's "suggestions." He fed me and took care of me when I was too sore to move, so I took his suggestions. I was more humble. I'd learned I wasn't who I thought I was. I was just another murderer in the body of a scared boy.

"Let's go, kid," Paddy said, leaning in the doorway. "Bossman wants to see ya."

A shiver sped down my spine. "What's going to happen?"

He shrugged and said, "Tommy's Tommy. He does what he wants."

"But I tried to kill Sean."

Once again, he shrugged. "Don't worry about it. What's done is done."

I got into Paddy's yellow Impala for the ride to the clubhouse. I glanced at my new look in the rear view mirror. I liked the short hair, the clean button-down shirt collar. I liked the gray slacks and shiny black shoes Paddy bought for me. I liked that I didn't feel like a victim anymore. I was uncertain about why I needed to meet with the Boss, but was confident Paddy wouldn't have brought me to Tommy's office if he wasn't sure it would all work out.

When we arrived, a young woman led Paddy and me into a back room and asked us to sit. Tommy's office space was large and bright. Small sculptures and other arty objects covered hardwood shelves. An oriental carpet covered the floor. It was nothing like the club that fronted it. I'd not figured Tommy Boyle for an art collector.

The Boss came in from a side door and sat behind his desk. "Howya feelin' kid?"

I was still sore, but much better and told him so.

"You put a hurt on my nephew."

I couldn't guess what Tommy was feeling by his facial expression. I shrugged. I had learned from watching both Paddy and Tommy shrugging was a universal gesture meaning, among other things, "I have nothing to say."

"You sure did." Tommy stood up. "I'm glad you didn't kill 'im though. Sean's a dick for sure, but he had a tough childhood. I tried with him, but what do I know about raisin' kids, right?"

I shrugged again.

"So, let me get to the point. Sean is going to Ireland for a long-needed visit to his grandmother and his other uncle. We won't be dealin' with any repercussions from the bennies and the broken finger and all that. It's over. See?"

This was good news. "Thanks."

He nodded. "Paddy got me to see the light about Sean. If it hadn't been for Paddy and how fuckin' bizarre this whole scenario was, I'da took you out in a minute."

Again, I was reminded how far in over my head I was. I had passed the place where a ride to the city limits was the solution to my problems. I had to negotiate a place to stand. Tommy's admission that he would have, could have, easily killed me was no longer shocking. Right and wrong as a moral idea was more fluid now. I wanted a stable place. I wanted to be a part of something.

"Okay, Mr. Boyle, where do we go from here?"

Chapter 29

"Come on in, Nate. I'll make coffee." Norma looked even better than the last time I'd seen her. Her face glowed, and she was dressed in a snappy-looking pantsuit. "Evvie's at work, you know."

I timed my visit to make sure Evvie was gone. I was certain she wouldn't want to see me, and I didn't want to hear her lecture about what a mistake it was for me to be working for Tommy Boyle. Norma, it seemed, practiced "live and let live." To her, I was still the nice young boy from Milwaukee.

Norma set a cup of coffee on the end table. "Looks like you're doing all right for yourself. New clothes, haircut, nice car."

"Yeah, Paddy sold it to me on credit. First car I ever owned."

"So, what's Paddy got you doing?"

I looked at my shoes and shrugged. "Ah, you know, a little of this and a little of that."

Norma shook her head. "Well, be careful. You may be a tough guy, but there's always somebody tougher."

I nodded. Hearing someone call me tough was new. But, I *was* tough. I could have pulled the trigger on Sean. That changed something in me. I wasn't afraid anymore, which I liked. But I also didn't care about who got hurt.

"So, how's Evvie?"

Norma drew in a deep breath. "Determined as ever. And, a little brokenhearted. She really fell for you, you know."

"I thought she hated me for running with Spider and the Angels."

"No, she was afraid for you. She was angry because she didn't want to get hurt. And she didn't want you to get hurt either."

"What's she think of me now?"

"I don't know for sure what she thinks. She never mentions your name. I do know as long as you're running with Tommy's gang she'll be angry at you. Are you sure that's the life you want?"

I looked Norma in the eye and said, "I don't know, but I can't go back to how I was."

Norma smiled and said, "No, you can only keep going forward. Maybe one day you'll find what Wendell had."

"What was that?"

"Peace of mind, Nate. Peace of mind."

The End

About the Author

Francis Hicks grew up in a dubious neighborhood in Milwaukee where he got to play drums in a rock and roll band. He took up writing as a way to meet women and ended up writing a novel, *The Long Ride*. Now living in San Antonio, TX, he has been a successful salesman, house flipper and occasional poet.

Thank you so much for reading one of our **Literary Fiction** novels.
If you enjoyed our book, please check out our recommended title for your
next great read!

The Five Wishes by Mr. Murray McBride by Joe Siple

2018 Maxy Award "Book of the Year"

"A sweet...tale of human connection...will feel familiar to fans of Hallmark

movies." *–KIRKUS REVIEWS*

"An emotional story that will leave readers meditating on the life-saving
magic of kindness." *–Indie Reader*

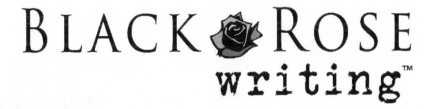

CPSIA information can be obtained
at www.ICGtesting.com
Printed in the USA
JSHW020156110919
1429JS00001B/5